THE DELIBERATION

DONNA BROWN WILKERSON
AND DAWN S. SCRUGGS

WWW.MARTINSISTERSPUBLISHING.COM

Published by

Rainshower Books, a division of Martin Sisters Publishing, LLC

www.martinsisterspublishing.com

Copyright © 2011 by Donna Brown Wilkerson and Dawn S. Scruggs

ISBN: 978-1-937273-02-6
Christian Fiction

Printed in the United States of America

Martin Sisters Publishing, LLC

DEDICATION

~ To our Lord and Savior, Jesus Christ,
who died on the cross,
so that all who believeth in Him
may be forgiven ~

ACKNOWLEDGEMENT

Although words sometimes fail to convey the extent of one's gratitude, we nevertheless offer our sincere appreciation to the following people:

To our families, for your patience and support during the writing process.

To Martin Sisters Publishing for making our dream a reality.

To the Logan Literary Ladies, we are grateful for your inspiration and support; thank you especially to Debby and Patricia for reading the early version of the manuscript and to Bethanie for your rigorous ideals.

To Cindy and Linda for your input into the legal aspects of our book; you helped us keep it real. To Ashley, for your excellent proofreading skills and your kind words of encouragement.

Thanks to each of you for your invaluable contribution to THE DELIBERATION

~ *Donna Brown Wilkerson*
and Dawn S. Scruggs

Christian Fiction

An imprint of Martin Sisters Publishing, LLC

CHAPTER ONE

Sara Anderson paused outside the doorway of Dr. Daniel Parker's office, absentmindedly twirling the small diamond solitaire that had adorned her left hand for less than two weeks. Not wanting to interrupt, she quietly watched her fiancé, who was known simply as Reverend Parker to his congregation, as he spoke to his brother on the telephone.

"Thanks again for driving me to the airport, Andrew." Daniel noticed Sara in the doorway and waved her into the office. "Sara would do it, but she has jury duty in the morning."

It would have been easy for Sara to love Daniel regardless of his looks; that was a bonus. Tall and well built, his dark hair framed his finely chiseled face and set off his piercing blue eyes. If the kind-hearted and easy-mannered Reverend Parker had any flaws, Sara hadn't seen them.

Daniel chuckled and nodded in agreement with whatever Andrew was saying on the other end of the line. "You'd think they'd let a kindergarten teacher relax a little during the summer, wouldn't you? Especially one with a wedding to plan."

Sara's stomach did a nervous flip at the mention of their engagement. She loved Daniel and wanted to be his wife, but something was holding her back from the true joy that she knew

7

she should feel. *I'm just worried about the mission trip, that's all. Everything will be fine when he gets back.*

"I really appreciate you looking after the church while I'm gone. I'll give you the keys in the morning, and Sara will show you around town when she gets out of court." Daniel leaned back in his office chair and smiled broadly as he listened to his brother. "What was that? No, I don't think a home-cooked meal is included in the tour, but she might bring you a take-out menu from the diner if you're really nice to her."

Daniel winked at Sara, "I don't know how she's going to survive being a minister's wife without knowing five ways to make a chicken casserole. At least she has a few months to figure it out. Oh, that reminds me. Be sure to put our wedding date on your calendar, December 15, right here at Maple Springs Community Church. We're counting on you to be the best man."

Daniel wrapped up the call and met Sara in the doorway.

"Hey, you." Daniel leaned down and kissed her hello. "Sorry about the cooking jokes. You know I think you order the best pizza in the world." Daniel tugged playfully at a loose curl dangling from Sara's ponytail.

Sara smiled. "You're forgiven. You know I can't be mad at you when you're leaving for Honduras tomorrow." Her smile disappeared as she said softly, "Do you really have to go?"

Daniel took a deep breath and looked squarely at Sara. "Yes, I do. The guys and I have been planning this mission trip since we were still in seminary. We're being called there to do God's work." Daniel kissed Sara's cheek and whispered into her ear. "We'll be fine. I promise."

"It's just–I've–There's–" Daniel's whisper sent shivers down Sara's spine, and she struggled to maintain her train of thought. "There's been a lot about Honduras in the news lately. They have hurricanes there – corruption, political uprisings. An article on the internet said several Americans have been murdered there."

"That just shows how badly the mission work is needed."

"I suppose you're right, but I'm really worried about you."

"We'll be back before you know it."

"I guess I have to get used to the idea of sharing you. Just promise not to get mad at me for wanting you all to myself every now and then."

"Fair enough," Daniel murmured into her hair as he tightened his embrace.

Sara sighed. "I can't believe we're getting married, Daniel. You're such a good man. You'd be perfect if weren't for the cooking jokes and the desire to scare me to death by traveling to a third world country."

Daniel laughed lightly. "Sounds like I've really got you fooled. Just wait. After we're married, you'll be telling all of your friends how I snore and leave my dirty socks on the floor."

Sara leaned her head on Daniel's shoulder. "I can hardly wait. What am I going to do without you for the next week?"

"I'm sure jury service will keep you occupied for a few days. Maybe God is putting you in that courtroom for a reason. You may be just the voice that the jury will need."

"I suppose it is my civic duty and all, but I can't help but hope I get dismissed. I don't like the idea of sitting in judgment on someone, especially when I already have so much on my mind."

"You'll find it in yourself to do what's right when the time comes."

Sara nodded. "I hope you're right."

"I'm always right," Daniel said with a teasing smile. "Don't forget that."

"Well, you did say it was going to rain today." Sara looked out the office window into the cloudless blue sky. "I guess I should go home soon before I get caught in a downpour. It wouldn't be good for my hair."

Daniel went along with the joke. "Yeah, you wouldn't want that. You never know when you might run into an old flame."

Sara tensed. "I thought you didn't want to hear about my old boyfriends."

"No, *you* didn't want to hear about *my* old girlfriends."

"Oh, was that how it was?"

"That's how I remember it." Daniel laughed lightly and kissed Sara with just enough urgency and promise to make her forget her worry about his trip. "Whatever is in the past is in the past. It's you and me now."

Sara's face clouded. She wanted to believe that Daniel didn't care about her past, but there were things about her that he didn't know; things that might tarnish the image that he had of her. Try as she might, Sara had never found the right words to tell him. She would open her mouth to speak, but nothing ever came out.

"Sara, are you okay?" Daniel asked.

"I'm fine," Sara lied. "I guess I should leave now so you can get back to the parsonage. You need to finish packing and get to bed early. Tomorrow will be a long day."

"Yes, it certainly will."

"Tell me your itinerary again." Sara was eager to change the subject.

"I'm meeting the rest of the mission team in Nashville in the morning. We'll have layovers in Atlanta and Miami and get to Honduras tomorrow night. We'll be in Tegucigalpa – that's the capital city – for a couple of days to get supplies and get organized with the locals. Then, it'll be a long bus ride up into the mountains."

"What did you decide about taking your cell phone?"

"I decided not to take it. The mission board said that American cell phones are unreliable there. Besides, we don't want to take along any expensive gadgets that would attract attention."

"How will I know you're okay?"

"I'll try to call from a pay phone when we reach the airport. After that, the mission board will keep track of us through their contacts in Honduras."

Sara nodded at Daniel and then looked at him for a long moment. "I love you, Daniel Parker. You stay safe and come back to me, okay?"

"I love you, too, Sara Anderson. When I get back from this mission trip, we're going to start planning our wedding."

They shared one last tender kiss, and then Sara walked out into the warm evening air, not bothering to wipe away the tears.

***

Sara's excitement about the wedding, mixed with her fears about Daniel's mission trip and her anxiety about jury duty, made her sleep fitful. In a particularly vivid dream, she imagined Daniel was killed in Honduras and she was on the jury that was trying his murderer. She was wearing a wedding dress, and the other jurors were bridesmaids and groomsmen.

She awoke the next morning to "Seasons in the Sun" playing on the clock radio. *Doesn't that local station have any music from this decade?*

She slapped the clock radio off and tumbled out of bed, accidentally rolling over onto Callie, the large Calico cat she had taken in a few years before. Callie let out a fierce meow and wriggled her way out from under Sara. "Sorry!" Sara yelled to Callie, but the cat was long gone.

Sara quickly pulled on a pair of khaki slacks, a white shirt, and her favorite loafers. Luckily, she had the kind of face that didn't need much makeup. It only took a swipe of eyeliner and a dash of lipstick, and she was ready.

Looking around for Callie, Sara quickly opened a can of cat food. "Here, kitty, kitty, kitty! Callie, breakfast!"

Sara poured the food into Callie's dish and freshened her water. "Please, Callie? Kitty, kitty? I need to make sure you're okay before I leave."

"Meow," Callie finally announced from under the table.

"Looks like you survived," Sara said as she set the bowl onto the floor and stroked the cat's soft fur. "I should have known it would take more than a little squish to hurt someone as tough as you."

Sara picked up her purse and her car keys. "Now you be a good kitty while I'm in court this morning. With any luck, I'll get dismissed and be back in a couple of hours."

CHAPTER TWO

In a small office across town, Assistant District Attorney General Kyle Copeland gave a weary yawn as State Trooper Marcus Thompson sat down in the well-worn chair across the desk from him. "I hope I can stay awake for this case today, Marcus. Chelsea kept us up half the night."

"Is she sick again?" Marcus look surprised. Although their friendship was born out of professional convenience, a genuine camaraderie had grown between the young lawyer and the trooper, and their concerns for one another transcended the courtroom.

"We don't really know yet. Just seems like she's been crying an awful lot lately, especially at night." Kyle stifled another yawn. "Elizabeth is going to try to get her in to the pediatrician this morning."

"Maybe she's just teething. How old is she, six months?"

"Seven. Maybe it is just teething, but I don't remember going through this with Evan."

"You got lucky, then," Marcus laughed. "If you have at least one baby that lets you sleep through the night, you're a lucky man."

"Yeah, I guess you're right." Kyle leaned back in his chair and put his feet up on his desk. "Speaking of lucky, are you ready to try *State vs. Hargis* again?" Kyle asked, pointing to the large file that sat on his desk.

"That was some kind of luck, that Hargis kid getting a new trial." Marcus shifted uncomfortably in his seat, his leather holster squeaking against the vinyl chair. "I'm not looking forward to reliving that particular night, especially when there's no good reason for it. Hargis is as guilty as sin."

"You know it. I know it. Everybody in middle Tennessee knows it except those idiots on the Court of Appeals." Kyle ran a hand over his wavy blond hair. "Apparently, they think we have nothing better to do than spend the next week retrying this case because of a technicality."

"It's glorifying it to even call it a 'technicality.' Who cares if the crime lab sent us Justin Harris's blood test results instead of Justin Hargis's? They'd both been drinking."

"But different amounts, as the appellate court so aptly pointed out."

"There is that," Marcus sighed. "I just wish I'd noticed the mistake during the first trial. To tell you the truth, I barely looked at the report after I confirmed that he was legally intoxicated."

"It's not your fault, Marcus. If I'd been involved in the case the first time, I doubt I'd have caught it either. The defendant's own lawyer didn't catch it. The Court of Appeals labeled that 'ineffective assistance of counsel.' That's what bought Justin Hargis a second bite at the apple."

"What a waste of time. Even before the wreck, that little punk was in a heap of trouble. He'd been in and out of juvenile hall too many times to count – vandalism, theft, you name it. We all knew it was just a matter of time before he killed somebody."

"Just be glad he was eighteen when it happened."

"Yeah, that's the one ray of sunshine to this whole mess. Justin Hargis was eighteen years and six weeks old, to be exact." Marcus tapped his fingers on the arm of his chair. "What I can't understand is why it makes any difference if his blood alcohol content was below the limit by some minuscule amount. We aren't prosecuting him for driving under the influence. This is a vehicular homicide case. He's never denied that he'd been drinking or that he hit that girl."

"As long as we can prove reckless conduct, it won't matter. We'll score another conviction and get him back to the big house by the weekend."

"What can we do to make sure it sticks this time?"

"We'll show the correct blood alcohol report, which does show some intoxication, just not enough for a presumption of DUI. We'll also have that trucker from Texas testify about Hargis speeding past him a mile or two before the wreck."

"Are you sure that'll be enough?"

"I think so. According to the transcript, he testified in the first trial that he and Hargis were headed in the same direction out Winningham Road about 10 or 11 p.m. that night. They were several miles outside of town, out where the road gets narrow and curvy, right before the turn-off to Roaring River. The trucker said Hargis was flat-out flying and blew right past him."

"That kid never had a lick of sense."

"You've got that right. Everybody in the county knows how dangerous that road is out there. I think the trucker's testimony will be enough to prove up the vehicular homicide statute."

"What about sentencing?"

"After credit for the time he's already served on the first conviction, Justin Hargis's dance card should be full for the next three to nine years."

"Not long enough if you ask me. He killed that girl, same as if he shot her in the head."

"I don't make the laws, Marcus. I just try the cases."

"Yeah, well, if it was up to me, he'd get life." Marcus looked out the window. "I don't care who she was or where she came from; nobody deserves what happened to that girl that night."

"Yeah, the pictures were pretty bad."

15

"The pictures don't tell the half of it." Marcus Thompson was a formidable man, broad-shouldered and rock solid, certainly not the kind of guy you'd want to see in a dark alley unless he happened to be on your side of a fight. Still, Kyle knew Marcus had a soft spot, and he could see that his friend was trying to shake the memories of young Marie Flores's twisted and bloody body lying in the ditch that July night three years before.

"Oh, I forgot to tell you about Hargis's new lawyer," Kyle said, turning the conversation to a more pleasant subject.

"What about him?"

"It's a 'her' actually. She's pretty hot, not that a happily married man like me notices such things."

"You mean you aren't the prettiest lawyer in town anymore?" Marcus never tired of ribbing Kyle about the good looks that made him an easy favorite with female jurors.

"Nah, I think Miss Sharese Jackson has me beat now."

"Sharese Jackson? I don't think I know her."

"She's new. A Memphis gal, from what I hear. She's been over at the public defender's office for a few months. From what I can tell, this will be her first real trial."

"They're starting her out with a vehicular homicide case?" Marcus raised an eyebrow. "That's boring with a big auger."

"They're so understaffed over there that they don't have much choice. Besides, it'll be good trial experience for her. Let her learn the ropes in a case where the expectations are low. I'm sure the P.D.'s office isn't expecting a win on this one."

"What you mean is that her boss is setting her up, knowing she'll lose." Marcus laughed. "That's cold, even if it *is* exactly what Hargis deserves."

"It's a rite of passage. Every lawyer loses that first case."

"Did you?" Marcus already knew the answer. Everyone in the Maple Springs legal community knew Kyle Copeland had a flawless trial record.

"Of course not. You know I always play to win." Kyle grinned.

"That you do," Marcus said. "I like that in a prosecutor."

Kyle checked his watch. "It's time to go send this little thug back to prison."

"Let's hope it doesn't take too long. I'd like to get some fishing in this week if the weather holds out."

"I hear that." Kyle grabbed his suit jacket from its hanger on the back of his office door. Checking himself in the small mirror that the jacket had concealed, he straightened his tie and otherwise made sure that he looked presentable for trial. There was no point negating whatever advantage his boyish charm and tall, athletic build bought him by showing up to court with breakfast caught between his teeth.

As the two men passed by the desk of Kyle's secretary, Angela Johnson, Kyle did his best to avoid eye contact with her. She saw him anyway and called out, "Good morning, you two. Don't do anything I wouldn't do. You hear?"

Once outside, Kyle said, "Ugh. Something about that girl makes me feel like I have to watch my back."

"Maybe you've just got a guilty conscience," Marcus said.

Kyle laughed. "I wish. I have to keep my nose clean if I hope to move up around here. You know how it is."

"Yep, sure do. Are you still thinking of running for D.A. next term?"

"Maybe."

"What's the hurry?"

"Elections only come around every eight years. I can't stay an assistant D.A. forever. The next election is my best shot to move up."

"Have you talked to the boss man about an endorsement?"

"He's too busy plotting to be the next criminal court judge to give much thought to who'll take his place as D.A."

"But don't you think he'll endorse you if you ask him?"

17

Kyle drew a long breath, "I don't know, Marcus. The election is still a few years away. It depends on what happens between now and then."

"He likes you. I bet he'll give you the endorsement, if you can stay out of trouble." Marcus winked.

Kyle gave a hearty laugh. "Marcus, my man, when have you ever known me to be in any kind of trouble? I'm a saint; haven't you heard?"

When they got to the courtroom, Kyle and Marcus took their places at the large wooden table nearest the jury box. As Kyle unpacked his briefcase, he nodded to the familiar faces that made up the Maple Springs legal community. The court reporter was getting set up in her usual place just in front of the judge's bench at the front of the room. The bailiff was cracking jokes with the clerk, who was making her way to the bench. "Looks like the gang's all here," Kyle said to no one in particular.

"Good thing you two got here early," the clerk said. "Last week, the judge threatened to hold Jimmy Brown in contempt if he showed up late again."

"Somebody needs to hold ole Jimmy in contempt for something, don't you think?" Kyle shot back.

The clerk laughed loudly. "You got that right, General Copeland."

Marcus had been checking out the prospective jurors seated in the audience behind them in anticipation of the game he and Kyle often played to pass the last nervous minutes before a jury trial began.

"So who do you think will be the first out, *General*?" Marcus loved chiding Kyle about the colloquial shortening of "Assistant District Attorney General."

"Let's see." Kyle ignored Marcus's teasing and took a quick glance at the potential jurors seated behind him. "Who do I think will be the first winner of the 'Oh please, Judge, not me!' contest?"

Kyle spotted a middle-aged man in a cheap suit. He was checking his watch. "That guy in the Stanley Roper outfit." Kyle gestured toward the man with his head. "I think he owns Hill's Hardware. He'll say he's the only one in the store that knows a bolt from a screw."

Marcus laughed. "Yeah. Business will come to a grinding halt without him there. Now, my turn. As our first 'Please pick me!' candidate, I nominate her, the one with the blue hair and the knitting needles."

Kyle snickered when he saw the plump, matronly woman Marcus had indicated. She was fast at work on a chartreuse and plum afghan that would probably never find a permanent home. She would indeed be willing and eager to serve on the jury. "Yep. With this trial to talk about, she'll be the belle of the ball on the next bingo trip to Kentucky."

"Score's tied one to one," Marcus said. "Next up: who will be the first excused for cause?"

Kyle leaned back in his chair, turning his head slightly. "My money's on some dude back there saying he can't be fair and impartial because the Hargis kid beat him up on the playgr–." Kyle froze before finishing his sentence, then quickly turned to face the front of the courtroom, cursing under his breath and slinking down into his chair.

"What's wrong?" Marcus said. "Can't find your guy back there?"

"It's not that." The color had drained from Kyle's face.

Marcus looked around at the crowd behind them. "Then what is it?"

Kyle didn't respond.

Marcus took a closer look at him. "What's the matter with you, Copeland? You look like you've seen a ghost."

"I guess that's one way to put it," Kyle mumbled. He swallowed hard and glanced around again.

Marcus followed Kyle's eyes to the pretty brunette in the back row. "Nice. Is she a friend of yours?"

Kyle couldn't meet Marcus's inquiring eyes. "No. Just somebody I knew a long time ago."

CHAPTER THREE

Across the aisle, Assistant Public Defender Sharese Jackson was studying her client. His dirty-blond hair was cropped short, revealing a youthful, if somewhat troubled, face. Even if Sharese hadn't been privy to his current circumstances, there was something – the thinness of his build or the hardness of his jaw, maybe – that gave away his upbringing on the wrong side of a small, Southern town. Still, except for the iron shackles around his ankles, Justin Hargis could have passed for an average teenager.

The fact was, he was not a teenager anymore, and he wasn't average. He was twenty-one years old and had spent the last three years behind bars for the vehicular homicide of Maria Flores.

"You look nice, Justin. Did your mother bring you those new clothes this morning?" Sharese asked.

"Yeah, she did. She wanted to come to the trial, but I told her not to. It was hard enough on her the first time."

"I see." Even though Justin was entitled to a presumption of innocence in the new trial, Sharese knew the odds were against him. Even so, she couldn't help but have a hopeful feeling. She was inexperienced enough to believe in miracles, and, a true competitor at heart, she really wanted to win her first trial. "I don't want to offer you false hope, Justin, but there is a possibility that we can create some reasonable doubt this time around. After all, your blood alcohol level wasn't actually above the legal limit."

"But there's that truck driver," Justin pointed out.

"In your first trial, your attorney barely cross-examined him."

"He barely did anything except sit in that chair like a lump of coal in June. Considering Mama had to work overtime at the factory for a year to pay him, he was a pretty sorry excuse for a lawyer."

"You do have a way with words, Justin." Sharese tried not to laugh aloud in the courtroom.

Justin smiled. "Maybe I'm being too hard on the guy. I had been in a lot of trouble already that summer, and I know he was gettin' pretty tired of me. To tell you the truth, Miss Jackson, I think everybody in Maple Springs was getting tired of me. Don't think nobody but my mama cared one little bit when they sent me off to the pen."

"At least your mother cared." Sharese said. "Not everyone has that much."

"Yeah. She's a good woman." Justin looked at Sharese. "What about your mama, Miss Jackson? I bet she's real proud of you, making a lawyer and all."

Sharese stiffened. "Actually Justin, my Grandma Eloise raised me. She was a good woman, though, like your mother. She always made sure I kept my grades up." Sharese smiled as she thought about her grandmother. "Because of her, I got into college. I even got a track scholarship. When I was in high school, she came to every meet."

"What happened to your folks? Are they dead?"

Sharese looked away. "No, they're not dead."

"Where are they then?"

"My mother's in Chicago."

"I thought you were from Memphis."

"I am from Memphis, and so was she." Sharese looked at her client. She didn't like to talk about her parents, but she figured she had nothing to lose by telling the young man sitting next to her the truth. "After my father became a guest of the State, she decided she'd rather follow her new boyfriend to Chicago than hang around the projects and raise a baby on her own."

"What do you mean about your daddy? Does he work at the governor's mansion or something?"

Sharese rolled her eyes. "No, Justin. My father is a guest of the state penitentiary, just like you are. I can't believe you've spent three years in prison and never heard that expression before."

"Sorry, Miss Jackson. My bad," Justin said sheepishly. "So, what's his name? What'd he do?"

"I probably shouldn't be telling you all this." Sharese sighed. "His name is Tony Jackson. About two months before I was born, his gang was caught in the middle of an armed robbery. One of them shot a police officer, and they were all charged with felony murder."

"What does that mean, felony murder?"

"Basically, it means that they were all held responsible for the killing, even though it wasn't clear which one of them actually fired the fatal bullet. They had agreed to commit the original crime – the armed robbery, that is – together, so they were equally accountable for the consequences."

"Oh. I guess that makes sense. So, he's a lifer then?"

"No. He took a plea, so he got a lesser sentence. He was at Brushy Mountain until it closed, but he's at Morgan County Correctional now."

"I hear Brushy was real rough."

"I guess so. My grandmother drove up from Memphis and visited him every few months, but I always waited for her in the car with my Aunt Ellen. She's my grandmother's twin sister."

"So you've never even met your father?"

"Nope." Sharese got out her legal pad, carefully shoving her dog-eared copy of *The First Trial: Where Do I Sit, What Do I Say* deeper into her brief case. The two sat quietly for a couple of minutes as Sharese made doodles on her legal pad.

"My old man died in car wreck when I was twelve," Justin broke the silence.

"I'm sorry to hear that, Justin. That must have been hard on you."

"Not really. He was a real jerk. He'd hit me and Mama when he was drunk – spent half his time in jail." Justin looked down at the shackles on his ankles. "Looks like the acorn didn't fall too far from the tree, did it?"

"Looks can be deceiving, Justin. I know you've made a lot of mistakes, but maybe this trial is your chance for a fresh start."

"I don't know about that, but I would like to tell my side of things, at least the little that I remember about that night. I was too scared to testify at the first trial, and my lawyer said I didn't have to if I didn't want to."

"That's right. The Fifth Amendment says that you have the right not to testify. The State can't force you to incriminate yourself." Sharese studied Justin's face. "I have to advise you not to take the stand in this trial either. It's almost never a good idea to testify on your own behalf in a criminal trial."

"I've done a lot of things that are almost never a good idea, Miss Jackson. I don't see as I have much to lose by doing one more."

CHAPTER FOUR

Kyle was relieved when the bailiff called court into session and the Honorable Henry Oaks took his seat on the bench. Although he was not a large man, Henry Oaks had a way of filling up a room with his presence. There was something about his commanding voice and the penetrating, expectant gaze of his dark eyes that held people's attention. The black robe and the gavel didn't hurt, either.

After thumbing through the file for what seemed like fifteen minutes to Kyle but was probably more like three, Judge Oaks asked, "Counsel, will you please approach the bench?"

Kyle and Sharese walked up to the bench as the court reporter scooted her equipment closer to hear the low voices as they spoke out of earshot of the potential jurors.

"General Copeland, why don't I have a sense of déjà vu about this trial?" the judge asked. "Obviously, it's been tried in this court before, but I don't seem to have any recollection of it. Furthermore, why is General Landry not trying this case since he represented the State the first time around? Then at least somebody would know what's going on."

"Your Honor, General Landry's knee-deep in pre-trial motions in that big double murder case that's coming up next

month over in Putnam County, so he asked that I handle this one."
Kyle added, "Also, I believe it was Judge Stephens who heard this
case the first time around. That's why you don't remember it."

"Oh, yes, of course," Judge Oaks grumbled. "This trial must
have come on for trial when I was out on medical leave a few
years back." His bout with prostate cancer was well-known in the
legal community and was the main source of speculation that he
would not seek another term when the next election came around.

Judge Oaks peered at Kyle over the bench, "It should go
without saying that neither the first trial nor the defendant's
conviction is to be mentioned in this courtroom. The last thing I
need is for the Court of Appeals to send this case back down here
again because we tainted the jury."

The judge waited for the court reporter to move back into her
usual place before commencing with his usual jury trial rhetoric.
"Ladies and gentlemen, thank you for coming today. Unlike
myself and the lawyers here, I know you all have somewhere else
you'd probably rather be." Most of the potential jurors chuckled,
and Kyle nodded politely as if it was the first time he'd heard this
line.

"Before we get started, I'd like for counsel to introduce
themselves and their clients and to read the list of witnesses who
will be testifying in the case. Ladies and gentlemen, pay close
attention to these folks because later you'll be asked if you're
personally acquainted with them."

Kyle stood and turned to look at the jury panel. For a moment,
he couldn't focus on anything except the achingly familiar face in
the back of the courtroom. It was the face that still haunted his
dreams, even though the affair had long since ended.

The knot that had been forming in his stomach clenched
tighter, and he was forced to break eye contact with her. He saw
that there were probably forty other potential jurors in the room.
Maybe she'll get dismissed. Yes. Please let her be dismissed.

"You can go ahead now, General," Judge Oaks urged from the bench.

At the sound of the judge's voice, Kyle went into autopilot, relying on the routine that he had honed during his many previous jury trials. "Thank you, Judge Oaks. Ladies and gentlemen, my name is Kyle Copeland. I'm an assistant district attorney general, and my client is the State of Tennessee. Trooper Marcus Thompson of the Tennessee Highway Patrol will be representing the State in this matter. Trooper Thompson, will you stand up, please?"

Marcus did as Kyle asked and then resumed his place at the counsel table. After quickly going over the witness list, Kyle joined him.

"Anything from the defense?" Judge Oaks asked.

"I'm Sharese Jackson. I represent the defendant in this case, Justin Hargis." Sharese had a hint of nervousness in her voice. "Mr. Hargis will you stand up, please?"

Justin stood up carefully, turning around in the small increments that the leg irons on his ankles required. He looked evenly around the courtroom, meeting the eyes of each potential juror. He did not smile, but he nodded slightly towards the potential jurors before edging back around and sitting down.

"The next part of the trial is what the lawyers call *voir dire*, which is just a fancy way of saying 'jury selection.' Some of you are going to be called up to the jury box so that the lawyers can ask you some questions. When that's done, the lawyers will excuse a few of those who were called up from service, and you'll be free to go. If you're excused, don't get mad at the lawyers. It's not personal; they may just not like what color shirt you're wearing today." Judge Oaks laughed at his own joke before continuing.

"The clerk will call more names, and those folks will come up to the jury box to take the place of those who've been excused. There'll be some more questions; some more folks will be excused, and so on until we have our jury. At that time, anyone who is left in the audience will get to go home." The judge looked over at the clerk. "Okay, Madam Clerk, you can begin calling up our potential jurors."

Kyle went through the motions of *voir dire*, but he grew increasingly nervous. He felt very out of his element, angry with himself for allowing her to get to him after all the time that had passed. He fumbled through the list of questions on his legal pad, but he had trouble keeping the potential jurors' answers straight in his head.

When Sharese had her turn, Kyle noted her relative calmness. Although her manner was a bit shaky, she was very thorough in her approach. She asked the jurors about their ages, their occupations, and other pertinent personal information. She told them the name of the victim, the date of the offense giving rise to the trial, and the location where it happened. When a potential juror indicated familiarity with the scene or a relationship with any of participants in the trial, Sharese asked if the juror felt that he or she could put that personal knowledge aside and consider the evidence fairly and impartially.

When it was time for challenges, Kyle conferred with Marcus before scribbling a couple of the potential jurors' names on a slip of paper and handing it to the bailiff.

Judge Oaks read the names, excused those jurors, and thanked them for their service. The clerk then called replacements up to the jury box, and so it went for about two hours.

Just when Kyle thought he was home free, the clerk called, "Sara Anderson and William Gettings, you can come on up now." As Sara walked quietly up to the front of the courtroom and took her place in the jury box, Kyle's stomach began doing back flips. *Sara? I guess 'Josie' was a nickname or something. That explains why I didn't notice her on the roster last week.*

The judge asked the attorneys to approach the bench. "Ms. Jackson, you're down to one peremptory challenge. General, you're all out. We have fourteen potential jurors in the box, and we've agreed to try this case with thirteen, the last one called being an alternate. I don't allow back-striking, so unless we have challenge for cause against Mr. Gettings or Ms. Anderson, we have our jury."

Too beside himself for words, Kyle just looked down at his feet and made his way back to the counsel table. He had intended to save a peremptory challenge in case this very situation arose, but somehow he'd miscounted. Knowing that he couldn't risk having to explain a challenge for cause, Kyle's only hope was that Sharese would excuse Josie or Sara or whoever she was, rather than the other juror, Mr. Gettings.

"Thanks for coming today, Ms. Anderson, Mr. Gettings." Sharese began. "Let me begin with you, Ms. Anderson. For the sake of the court reporter, let me mention that you spell your first name S-A-R-A. There's no 'H', is that correct, ma'am?"

"Yes, that's right. My first name is Sara, S-A-R-A. My middle name is Josephine, J-O-S-E-P-H-I-N-E. My family sometimes uses both names or my nickname, Josie."

"Are you married?"

"No, but I am engaged."

"May I ask to whom?"

"My fiancé is Dr. Daniel Parker. He's a minister here in town."

"And is he originally from Maple Springs?"

"No. His father is an evangelist, so his family moved around quite a bit."

"Thank you, Ms. Anderson. Are you or Mr. Gettings personally acquainted with the defendant or any of the witnesses?"

Sara answered, "No." Mr. Gettings said the same.

"Do either of you have any personal knowledge of the motor vehicle accident in which Maria Flores was killed?"

Again, Sara answered, "No."

"What about you, Mr. Gettings?"

"I don't know anything about the wreck, but I do live on that end of the county. I drive Winningham Road every day."

29

"What about you, Ms. Anderson? Are you familiar with the highway where the accident occurred?" Sharese asked.

"I'm somewhat familiar with it," Sara said nervously.

"Can you explain, please?" asked Sharese.

"I'm not from Maple Springs originally, but I visited my grandparents in the summers when I was growing up. They have a little place at the river. So, I've been on the highway a few times with them. And, um–"

Sharese noticed Sara's hesitation. "And what, Ms. Anderson?"

"I, uh, stayed at the cabin one summer when I was working on my thesis for graduate school. I was getting my masters in elementary education, and I needed a quiet place to write."

"You're a teacher?"

"Yes. I'm a kindergarten teacher at Maples Springs Elementary School. I just finished my first year there."

"Thank you, Ms. Anderson. That's all the questions that I have."

Sharese sat down, scribbled a name onto a slip of paper, and passed it to the bailiff. Kyle did likewise, except that his slip of paper was blank. The rule in Judge Oaks' courtroom was that both attorneys were to turn in a paper – even if there wasn't a challenge – so that the jury would not know who had excused whom.

Marcus whispered to Kyle, "They'll excuse Gettings. He knows how crazy it is to speed on that curvy road."

Kyle nodded his agreement, although he was still hopeful that Sharese would find some reason to excuse Sara.

"Okay, Mr. Gettings, you can leave. We have our jury," Judge Oaks announced after he looked at the slips the attorneys had passed up. Looking out at the remaining potential jurors still seated in the audience section of the courtroom, the judge continued, "The rest of you are dismissed. Thank you for coming in today. Be sure to call the clerk's office on Friday to see if you need to report back next week for another trial."

After waiting a few minutes for the dismissed panel members to file out of the courtroom, the judge addressed the jury. "Ladies and gentlemen, you may have noticed that there are thirteen of you and be thinking that we've miscounted somehow. In cases where a trial will last more than one day, it's the court's practice to seat thirteen jurors instead of the usual twelve.'

"Ms. Anderson here, as the last seated juror, will be our alternate. Ms. Anderson, you'll need to listen carefully to the evidence and do everything as if you'll be part of the deliberation process once the case goes to the jury. If we're lucky enough that the other twelve jurors are still with us at that time, I will dismiss you."

Judge Oaks looked back at the attorneys. "Let's break for lunch before we move forward with opening arguments." Kyle and Sharese nodded their approval. Judge Oaks then faced the jury, "I need to admonish you folks not to discuss the case with anyone, not even with each other, until it comes time for the deliberation.'

"Normally, I prefer that the jury stay together during lunch and other breaks. However, since we haven't started with the evidence yet, I don't see any harm in letting you all separate during the next hour so that you can make whatever arrangements you need to with your employers, babysitters, or whomever. Let them know that this trial will likely last a few days."

As the jurors began to make their way out of the courtroom, Judge Oaks called out, "Please be back here at 1 p.m. sharp. I like to stay on schedule."

***

Sara hurried past the other jurors, who had gathered in front of the elevator. She could barely breathe, much less engage in meaningless banter with strangers.

She quickly located the stairs and ran down them as quickly as her wobbly legs would carry her. She was almost to the first floor when she saw a familiar form ahead of her and realized that she was not the only one who had plotted the quickest route of escape.

"Kyle," Sara whispered. The taste of his name on her tongue brought all the feelings she once had for him flooding back – the attraction, the infatuation, the love, and the hurt that had formed the chapters of their affair.

Kyle stopped in his tracks but didn't turn around.

"This should never have happened, Kyle. I shouldn't be on this jury," Sara said to Kyle's back. "You should have said something to the judge."

Kyle drew a long breath, and then turned to face Sara. "Josie – or is it Sara now? I don't even know who you are anymore."

"You don't know who *I* am? You never even told me you were from Maple Springs. I thought you were from Knoxville," Sara wiped the tears from her eyes.

"I went to law school in Knoxville. I had planned to go back there after the bar exam, but–," Kyle tried to explain. Drawing a deep breath, he continued, "Anyway, I had no idea you were in Maple Springs, Josie. When did you come back?"

"About a year ago, after my grandfather died. I wanted to be close by, for my grandmother's sake."

"I guess things didn't exactly work out the way either of us planned."

"No, they certainly didn't." Sara eyes, brimming with bitterness and hurt, pierced through Kyle. "I can't handle an entire week in that courtroom with you, not after what happened between us. You have to fix this."

"I'm sorry, Josie, but there's nothing I can do about it now. I couldn't think straight in there when I first saw you, and I can't exactly ask Judge Oaks to excuse you for cause at this stage of the game."

"Why not?"

"Because I would have had to tell him and the other attorney how I know you. I doubt that my wife or your fiancé would be too thrilled if that particular story got back to them. Word travels fast in a small town, you know."

"Isn't there some other way for me to be excused?" Sara's voice was weak.

"I thought I had saved a peremptory challenge in case you were called, but I miscounted."

"So that's what I am to you now, a 'peremptory challenge'? I don't even know what that means."

"It's when a potential juror is dismissed without the attorney having to give specific reasons to the judge for letting the person go."

Sara's eyes narrowed as she glared at Kyle. "I guess that fits then. I certainly understand what it feels like to be dismissed by you with no explanation."

"It wasn't like that, Josie. I told you I was going back to my wife."

"But she had already filed for divorce."

"It was complicated."

"It took me two years to get over you, Kyle," Sara's voice cracked.

"I'm not sure if I ever got over you, Josie. That summer was the best time of my life. Or maybe it was the worst. I've never known which."

With that, Kyle was gone, leaving Sara standing in the stairwell alone.

CHAPTER FIVE

Kyle hurried to his office, hoping to have a few minutes of peace and quiet to collect his thoughts. Angela looked up as he passed her desk. "Oh my goodness! What in the world happened to you? You look just awful."

Kyle ignored her curious eyes. "I'm fine, Angela. Just a long morning in court, that's all. I just need a few minutes to clear my head." Thinking fast, Kyle added, "Oh, and maybe a bite to eat. Will you call down to Eddie's and have them deliver me a ham sandwich and some fries?"

Kyle wasn't really hungry, but he thought it best to distract Angela with something to do before she asked too many questions. The last thing he needed was to rouse her suspicions that something out of the ordinary had transpired in court that morning.

He closed the door to his office and took off his suit jacket. As he was about to hang up the jacket, he saw his haggard reflection in the mirror on the back of the door and shuttered. He sat down at his desk, crossed his arms in front of him, and banged his head on the desk. *This cannot be happening.*

Angela burst into the room, ignoring as usual Kyle's oft-repeated instructions to knock before entering. "Kyle, I forgot to give you your messages. Your wife called."

Kyle tried to look as normal as possible. "You can just put the messages on the desk, Angela."

Thumbing through the messages before laying them down, Angela went on, "Yeah, she called like four times this morning. First, she was at home and wanted to ask you whether you still thought she should take the baby to the doctor."

Remembering his beautiful daughter, Kyle smiled for the first time that morning. "She was really fussy last night. Probably nothing, but you know how Elizabeth gets where the kids are concerned."

"Well, the second time she called, she wanted to let you know she had made an appointment for 11 a.m. She thought Judge Oaks might break for lunch early enough for you to meet her over at Dr. Bradshaw's office. Then, she called again at about 11:15 a.m., while they were waiting at the doctor's office. Then, just before you got here, she called to say that Dr. Bradshaw said the baby's just teething, that's all."

Kyle was relieved that the pediatrician had pronounced his baby girl okay. "I'll call Elizabeth as soon as I can." Kyle motioned his head toward the door. "I think I heard someone come in. Maybe it's my sandwich. Here's some money." He handed Angela a few bills. "Tell the delivery guy to keep the change."

As Angela disappeared into the lobby, Kyle quickly dialed Elizabeth at home. "Hey hon. I got your messages. I'm glad Chelsea's okay."

There was a slight edge in Elizabeth's tone. "I was really hoping you would meet us the doctor's office this morning."

"Sorry I couldn't make it. I was stuck in court all morning."

"What kind of case is it?" A law school graduate herself, Elizabeth often asked Kyle about his work. "I'm sure you told me, but I've forgotten."

"It's a new trial in an old vehicular homicide case from a few years back. The defendant hit a young Mexican girl on that curvy road going out toward Roaring River. The girl was a runaway, probably didn't speak much English. She must have gotten lost, or she would never have been walking alone out there after dark. The defendant had been drinking and was driving too fast. He hit her so hard it propelled her body a good fifty feet. Poor girl probably never knew what hit her."

"Let's hope not."

"Crazy appellate court granted a new trial because of the supposed incompetency of the defendant's lawyer in the first trial."

"Why would they do that?"

"They said he should have noticed that the crime lab had sent the wrong blood tests. They sent the results for some guy named Harris instead of Hargis."

"What was the difference in the blood alcohol levels?"

"Unfortunately, Harris was above the legal limit for driving under the influence, but Hargis was just below it."

"That's too bad. Can you still win?"

"Yeah. We just have to prove reckless conduct. Got a truck driver coming in from Texas that'll say the defendant blew past him just a few miles before he hit the girl."

"Oh, you should be okay then. I'd better go now. The kids are yelling for me."

Kyle could hear both of the kids in the background, clamoring for their mother's attention. "Okay. Love you. Bye." Kyle glanced down at his wedding band as a familiar guilt settled itself onto his shoulders.

Angela came in with the food, but Kyle avoided further conversation with her. "Thanks, Angela. Close the door behind you, okay?" Kyle dismissed her without looking up. She eyed him suspiciously but put the bag on the desk and left the room as instructed.

When she was safely on the other side of the door, Kyle threw the sandwich in the trash, yawned loudly, and hung his head in his hands, wondering how in the world he was going to make it through the rest of the day, much less the rest of the week.

***

After her inadvertent run-in with Kyle in the stairwell, Sara walked out of the courthouse in a daze. She got into her car and sat in silence, stunned at the freshness of the ache in her heart. *How can it still hurt so much to see him? It's as if no time has passed at all.*

The stifling July heat soon brought her to her senses, and she started the car. As she drove through town, everything looked different than a few hours before, as if she were seeing things through the eyes of the girl who had been in love with Kyle those years before. *No. I can't think like that. It's over. It's been over for a long time.*

A few minutes later, she sat at the small kitchen table in her apartment staring at a cup of yogurt and an apple. She willed herself to eat, knowing that a growling stomach would call unwanted attention to her in the courtroom later that afternoon. Out of the corner of her eye, she noticed a picture on the front of the refrigerator. *Daniel! How could I have gone all morning without giving you so much as single thought?* Sara felt ashamed of herself for forgetting Daniel, even for a few hours.

She thought about Daniel's mission trip, the danger that he could soon face in a foreign and maybe even hostile country. As fear washed over her, she tried to concentrate on the silly picture of Daniel on the refrigerator and remember the happy day that it represented. They had taken the church youth group on a trip to Six Flags, and Daniel had just gotten off Georgia Cyclone with some of the kids. "Show me your happy face!" she had said to them, and Daniel had grinned at her like a crazy man. With his windblown hair and slightly sunburned nose, it was a picture that always made her smile.

Oh, Daniel, I wish you were here right now. Thinking about that for a moment, Sara reconsidered. *I meant to tell you about Kyle, but I thought I was over him. Now I'm not so sure.*

Callie pounced into Sara's lap, causing her to jump several inches into the air. She had been too distracted by the events of the morning to have thought about the cat when she came into the apartment. "Oh Callie, you scared me half to death!" Sara stroked Callie's fur, making her purr loudly.

Sara looked quickly at her watch and began talking to the cat. "I saw an old friend of yours this morning. I wish I had time to tell you about it, but I have to get back to court. The judge said opening arguments, whatever they are, start at 1 p.m. sharp."

***

Sharese and Justin ate lunch together in the small room where prisoners were kept when court was not in session. The guard gave Sharese an odd look when she asked if it was okay; apparently most defense attorneys chose to leave the courthouse during lunch rather than spend time with their clients. Sharese, however, saw it as an opportunity to get to know Justin a little better and maybe talk him out of testifying on his own behalf. Because of his incarceration, their pre-trial contact had been very limited, and his request to testify had come as a surprise.

"So, Justin, which is better: prison food or jail food?" Sharese asked.

"Not that there's much of a difference, Miss Jackson, but I think Maple Springs jail food is a little better. Winona makes a pretty good pot of soup. You should try it sometime."

"Let's hope I don't have that opportunity any time soon."

"Yeah, let's hope not. Hey, what do you think of the jury so far?" Justin asked.

"I think they'll do their best to be fair. It's a good mix, eight women and four men. Oh, and the alternate is also a woman. I think women will make better jurors for you. Hopefully, they'll see you sort of like a son."

"You think so?"

"Well, maybe a juvenile delinquent son, but redeemable nonetheless," she teased.

39

Justin giggled and nodded in agreement. "Maybe so. Do you really think it'll make much difference though?"

Sharese sighed. "The good news is that you only had 0.07 percent blood alcohol, which is not enough for a presumption of driving under the influence. The bad news is that the trucker will say you were speeding, which the State will argue created reckless conduct under the vehicular homicide statute. The bottom line is that you could still be found guilty, but it'll be a closer call than in the first trial. We just have to hope the jury finds enough reasonable doubt for an acquittal."

Justin looked Sharese directly in the eye. "I know there's not much chance of that. I'm pretty much expecting another guilty verdict. It's just–" His voice trailed off, and Sharese had to ask him to go on with what he was saying.

"Can I ask you a personal question, Miss Jackson?" Justin was cautious.

Sharese nodded. After all, she had already told him that her father was in prison. There was not much Justin Hargis could ask her that would be any more embarrassing than that. "Sure. What do you want to know?"

"Do you go to church?" Justin asked.

Sharese looked up from her lunch and gave her client full attention. "Yes, Justin, I do. I gave my life to Christ when I was eleven years old."

Justin looked relieved. "Well, maybe you can understand it, then. Just let me think about how to say it."

"How to say what, Justin?" Sharese urged. "Whatever you want to talk about, I'll do my best to understand."

"I just don't know if it was my fault, Ms. Jackson," Justin blurted. "I know that sounds crazy. I mean, during the first trial, I didn't even question but that I killed that girl. But, well, there was a preacher man that come to the prison every Sunday night when they had me at Riverbend down in Nashville. At first, I just went and listened to him because I didn't have nothing else to do. I figured it was better than looking at my cell walls.'

"After awhile I started listening to him. I even started reading that Gideon Bible in my cell late at night after my roommate went to sleep. One night, I don't know what came over me, but I started praying. I'd never talked to God before, but, that night, I just felt like He could hear me, you know?"

Sharese nodded. "Yes, I understand."

"So, then, over the next few weeks, I kept thinking about all the stuff I'd done wrong in my life – the lying, the stealing. I'd just be laying there in my bunk, and I'd remember something crazy that I hadn't thought about in years. Something like calling Freddy Wilson "fatso" in grade school. Little stuff like that, but also big stuff like buying that crank the night of the wreck. I thought about my mama's face when the cops told her they'd found it in my truck."

"I've been meaning to ask you about that. If you were a meth user, why didn't the blood test show methamphetamine in your system?"

"Believe it or not, it was the first time I'd bought any. I had the wreck before I got out to the river to party, so I hadn't smoked it yet."

"Hmm, interesting," Sharese said between bites of her sandwich.

"I think the meth worried Mama more than anything else did. When the jury come back in the first trial, Mama didn't cry like I thought she would. She said, 'At least you have a chance to live now. On that stuff, you would have been dead in a year or two.' In prison, I dreamed a lot about her saying that."

Sharese looked at Justin, thinking how young he looked. How young he still was. She understood about him still needing his mother, even in prison. Sometimes she dreamed about her father. She could never see his face, but, in her dreams, she could hear his

41

voice telling her he loved her. "Are you sure you don't want your mother to be in the courtroom during your trial?" Sharese asked.

"I'm sure. It was so hard on her the first time, Miss Jackson. I just can't put her through it again," Justin replied.

"I guess I can understand that."

Justin drew a deep breath. "Like I was saying about the wreck, I tried real hard to think about it – about that girl dying that night. But, nothing would come to me. Even after I started feeling all guilty over all the other stuff I'd done wrong, the part about the wreck never would come. I never even dreamt about it or nothing."

"Hmm," Sharese said. "That is a bit odd, I suppose."

Justin shrugged his shoulders. "When I would try to remember that night, I would just feel, well, nothing. After awhile, it made me wonder what really happened. So, one night, I talked to the preacher man about all of it. He called it 'being under conviction,' the way that I had started taking responsibility with the Lord for all the stuff I'd done. He prayed with me. He told me that I should ask God to forgive me for the wreck. Said maybe I could write an apology letter to the girl's family and start to put it all behind me."

"And did you?" Sharese asked.

Justin shook his head and tapped his fingers on the table. "I tried to, Miss Jackson, I really did, but I just couldn't remember anything about the wreck. No guilty feeling ever would come over me about it. Finally, I told the preacher that I just couldn't ask for forgiveness for something I couldn't remember doing. That's when he offered to go over my case with me."

Justin let out a small laugh. "I think he figured there'd be enough evidence in my file to make me accept my part in what happened and then some. I guess the good Lord must have sent that preacher man my way because, when we started looking at them papers, he helped me figure out about the messed up blood test results. You know, Harris instead of Hargis. That's how I got my new trial."

"That's quite a compelling story, Justin."

"The way I see it, this new trial is a sign for me to get up there on the stand and face the music, good or bad. Maybe – and I've been talking to the Lord about it a lot – some of what happened that night will come back to me this week."

Sharese leaned her arms on the table and studied her client carefully. "I know you want to testify on your own behalf, Justin, but I'll have to go on the record as advising you against it. Right now, you at least have a chance of walking out of that courtroom a free man. You've been in either the county jail or the state prison for three years. Don't you want your freedom back?"

"It ain't that I don't want to be free, Miss Jackson; I do. It's just that getting out of prison won't make me that-a-way by itself, not 'til I can understand in own mind what happened that night. The only way I know to do that is to testify."

"It's such a huge risk, Justin." Sharese shook her head.

"All I want out of this is peace. What I'm looking for won't be coming from Judge Oaks or anybody else in Maple Springs." Justin looked up. "It'll come from the good Lord, if and when He's ready for me to have it."

"What if you get sent back to prison?"

"I'm not worried about that. Since I turned my life over to the Lord, He's been taking care of me in there. I'll be alright. I just can't go on without knowing for sure if I killed that girl."

Sharese sighed. "I hear what you're saying, Justin, but there's nothing in the facts to suggest that anyone except you was responsible for the death of Maria Flores. If there had been another car or something like that, we might have something to argue before the jury. There's just no evidence of that."

"I didn't mean somebody else done it. I don't know how to explain it, Miss Jackson." Justin thought for a minute. "Conviction is what the preacher called it. I just don't feel convicted about it like I should – convicted by the Holy Spirit, I mean – and I have to know why."

"Justin, if you testify, the State's attorney will rip you to shreds. His job is to make sure that girl's family gets some sense of justice through the legal system. You won't have to worry about feeling guilty after he gets finished with you, I can assure you."

"Maybe that's what needs to happen, then," Justin said.

There was a knock at the door, and the bailiff came in. "Judge Oaks is back from lunch. Court will resume in five minutes."

Sharese tried one last time to reason with her client. "Justin, the burden is on the State to prove that you're guilty beyond a reasonable doubt. Even though you've been found guilty in an earlier case, the State has to prove it all over again. The Court of Appeals decided that your first attorney did not render you the effective assistance of counsel that you're guaranteed under the Constitution. The man let somebody else's blood test be used against you in court, for crying out loud! That means that this trial is a total do-over. You really don't want to blow that by putting yourself up there on the stand, especially when you, yourself, can't remember anything about the wreck."

"I'll think about it, Miss Jackson. I'll pray real hard on it tonight. I'll have a day or two to decide for sure, won't I?" Justin asked.

Sharese stood up and walked toward the door. "Yes. The State has several witnesses, so I can't see you testifying for a least a couple of days. Tell you what, I'll pray about it tonight, too, and we'll talk about it again tomorrow."

"That sounds good," Justin said. "Thanks for having lunch with me, Miss Jackson. It's the first time I've had a meal with a lady since they sent me off."

CHAPTER SIX

Inside the courtroom, Kyle and Marcus sat elbow to elbow at the defense table, Kyle's gray wool suit lightly touching the starched tan shirt of Marcus's uniform. Kyle was drumming a pen on his yellow legal pad, and Marcus was looking at the clock on the courtroom wall.

Marcus sighed. "Two minutes to go 'til ole Hang 'em Henry takes the bench."

"Yep. Give or take thirty seconds," Kyle replied, not looking up from his legal pad.

"Just time enough time for you to tell me about that chick on the jury. Sara, was it?"

Kyle's tapping stopped. "Let's just forget it."

"What's the deal, Copeland? Is she Jimmy Hoffa's ex-wife or something?"

"I wish." Kyle's eyes remained fixed on the legal pad. "Let's just drop it, okay?"

To Kyle's relief, Judge Oaks came on the bench precisely at 1 p.m. "Is the State ready for opening arguments, General Copeland?"

"Yes, Your Honor, the State is ready."

"What about the defense?"

"Yes, Your Honor, the defense is ready," Sharese said.

"Go ahead then, General."

A queasy feeling came over Kyle as Judge Oaks peered down at him expectantly. He had long since conquered the butterflies that had plagued him during his first few trials and usually had a friendly, easy manner in front of a jury. This was not an ordinary day, however.

Usually, if he started getting nervous, he simply reminded himself that the jury was made up of regular people, nothing to get excited about. Somehow, he knew that little pep talk wasn't going to keep his knees from buckling as he faced this jury – or, more accurately, one juror in particular. His well-crafted opening statement suddenly flew out of head as surely as a bird in flight.

Forced to improvise, Kyle totally forgot his usual routine of thanking the jury and giving lip service to the State's burden to prove the defendant guilty beyond a reasonable doubt. Instead, he launched into the first thing that he remembered from his notes. "On a warm summer night three years ago, the defendant, Justin Hargis, decided to go for a drive. Nothing wrong with that, of course, but Justin Hargis made two mistakes that night. The first was he got behind the wheel after drinking several alcoholic beverages. Second, he was speeding. You'll hear testimony by a truck driver who saw the defendant driving at a high rate of speed just minutes before the accident."

Suddenly going blank, Kyle stammered, "And that, ladies and gentlemen of the jury, is why Maria Flores is dead and why the State will be asking you to convict the defendant of the crime of vehicular homicide." Unable to think of anything else to say, Kyle slunk back to his seat and hung his head, avoiding Marcus's incredulous stare. *That's the worst opening argument I've made since my debut on the law school moot court team.*

Kyle glanced at the defense table, expecting Sharese to begin her opening argument. She sat in her seat with a confused look on her face, looking at Kyle for some assurance that his opening statement had not been some kind of cruel joke. He gave her a nod to indicate that it was her turn.

Sharese nodded back and stood to address the jury. "Ladies and gentlemen of the jury, on behalf of my client, Mr. Justin Hargis, I want to thank you for your service here today. We understand that, with civic responsibility, comes inevitable inconveniences. We appreciate your willingness to participate in this most important of judicial processes. First, I'd like to talk to you about the State's burden of proof in this case. It's a heavy burden. To be successful, the State must prove to you, beyond a reasonable doubt, that Justin Hargis is guilty of the crime of vehicular homicide."

Kyle drifted off in thought as Sharese continued with her opening argument. *How long has it been since I saw Josie? Not Josie. Sara. Sara Anderson, about to be Mrs. Sara Parker. Other than the name, she hasn't changed much. Still so beautiful. And a teacher now. I wonder if Evan will get her for kindergarten in a few years.* With that thought, Kyle began a coughing fit of such proportions that Sharese had to stop her opening statement.

Kyle saw her glaring at him. "I'm okay, go ahead." As he cleared his throat, he saw Marcus in his peripheral vision, looking at him as if he had lost his mind. *We'll just have to move out of the state if my son gets her as a teacher. I hear North Dakota is nice.*

Finally, Sharese concluded her statement, which, for a first time performance, was not bad. In fact, compared to Kyle's meager opening, Sharese spoke with the relative eloquence of a Supreme Court Justice, albeit a wordy one. Kyle knew he'd have some serious ground to make up with his first witness, and he began to scribble furiously on his legal pad.

Judge Oaks, who had been staring at the ceiling and visiting whatever mental playground trial court judges venture to when the opening statements of counsel drag on a bit too long, suddenly came alive. "General, you can go ahead with your first witness."

Luckily for Kyle, Marcus was as strong and ready to present his case as Kyle was weak in the knees every time he looked towards the jury box. "Raise your right hand to be sworn, please," the clerk told him before administering the standard oath.

"State your name and occupation for the record, please," Kyle began.

"I'm Marcus Thompson. I'm a trooper with the Tennessee Highway Patrol." As Marcus testified to the routine preliminary information concerning his employment, education, and so forth, Kyle began to breathe a little easier. *Just keep looking at Marcus, and everything will be fine.*

"How long have you been a state trooper here in Maple Springs?"

"About four years. I started my career in another part of the state, but I was transferred here after a couple of years of service."

After a few minutes, Kyle fell into an easy rhythm in his questioning of Marcus. It was not unlike one of the pickup basketball games they played from time to time at the local gym. *Pass the ball; let your teammate take the shot. Score!*

"So, were you the first officer at the scene?" Kyle asked Marcus.

"Yes. A truck driver had called 911 on his cell phone, and I was dispatched in response to the call."

"Can you describe the scene of the accident as you found it, Trooper?"

"When I arrived, I saw that an older model, brown Chevrolet Blazer had crashed into a tree and was blocking part of the roadway. As I approached the driver's side window, I saw the defendant, Justin Hargis, inside of the vehicle. He was leaning forward with his head on the steering wheel. He appeared to be unconscious. I attempted to wake him, but he was out cold. I noticed that the windshield was broken where the defendant's head had apparently made impact with it."

Kyle continued questioning Marcus. "Did you see any other vehicles at the scene?"

"Yes, I saw a semi-truck that had pulled off into a clearing near the accident scene. The driver of the truck was one Larry Turner. Mr. Turner told me that he had been the one to dial 911."

"Your Honor, the defense moves to strike the Trooper's last remark on the grounds that it's hearsay," Sharese interjected.

Kyle quickly retorted, "It's an excited utterance, Your Honor, an exception to the hearsay rule."

Judge Oaks looked at the jury. "Ladies and gentlemen, when the attorneys argue over the admissibility of a particular bit of evidence, it sometimes becomes necessary for the jury to be sent out of the courtroom until the issue is resolved. That way, I don't have to tell you later to disregard something that maybe you shouldn't have heard in the first place."

A few of the jurors looked confused when the judge declared, "You can take a ten-minute break while we get this settled."

Once the jury left, Sharese renewed her motion. "Your Honor, anything that the truck driver, Larry Turner, said to Trooper Thompson is blatant hearsay. If the State wants to admit Mr. Turner's testimony, it should be done through Mr. Turner himself, not through Trooper Thompson."

Kyle replied, "Mr. Turner's statement falls under Tennessee Rule of Evidence 803(2) in that it's an excited utterance." Flipping through the rules to the passage in question, Kyle continued, "Excited utterance – a statement relating to a startling event or condition made while the declarant was under the stress of excitement caused by the event or condition."

Sharese argued, "The State has failed to establish that Mr. Turner was under any supposed 'stress of excitement' at the time of his statement to the trooper."

Judge Oaks addressed Kyle. "General, since you've got the trucker here, can't you just get this in through him? Let's not risk

DONNA BROWN WILKERSON AND DAWN S. SCRUGGS

this case getting sent back down by the Court of Appeals on an evidentiary ruling."

"With all due respect, Your Honor, we're only on the first witness," Sharese said. "My client isn't quite ready for an appeal yet."

Kyle shot Sharese a look. It was a gutsy statement for attorney trying her first case. Even though his nerves had calmed down a bit since he'd first seen Sara that morning, he still didn't have the presence of mind for a lengthy battle over an evidentiary matter, especially when his opponent was so much more on her game that he was. "I'll withdraw the question, judge. No reason to make this case more complicated that it has to be."

"Very well, then," Judge Oaks said. "Let's get the jury back in here and get on with it."

***

During the break, it dawned on Sara that she had not checked her cell phone for messages during lunch. Per the sign outside the courtroom, she had switched it to "silent" mode first thing that morning. The run-in with Kyle in the stairwell had upset her too much to give the phone much thought until then.

There were two voicemails. The first was from Daniel. "Hey. I guess you're still in court. We're in Nashville, waiting on the plane to Miami. I'll call you again when we get there. Love you." Hearing Daniel's voice made Sara's heart melt. Could it only have been a day since she had seen him? Something about seeing Kyle again had made it seem so much longer.

She wondered what she would say to Daniel when he called her again. She had never told him about Kyle. She told herself that the timing had never been right; that she had just hadn't found the right words. Deep down, though, she knew the truth: she had never told Daniel about Kyle because she didn't want him to know how damaged that summer with him had left her.

She didn't want Daniel to know how much she had longed for another man. A married man, as it had turned out. She didn't want him to know how destroyed she had felt when Kyle left her or that somewhere there was a stack of un-mailed letters she had written begging him to come back to her. *How would it look to a minister that his fiancé had dreamed of a married man every night for months, even after he had made it clear that he was going back to his wife?*

Time had healed many of her wounds. By the time she met Daniel, Kyle was already fading into a bittersweet memory. As her relationship with Daniel had blossomed and grown, Sara had bundled up what was left in her heart for Kyle and placed it neatly into a dark closet in her soul. Daniel's love had pushed the ever-shrinking box so far back on the shelf that Sara had been quite certain it no longer held any power over her.

Seeing Kyle that morning had expanded the package so exponentially that it had tumbled from its familiar spot and landed squarely in her lap. With it had come the realization that, try as she might to forget that summer, her feelings for Kyle would never completely go away. It was an unfortunate but unavoidable truth: love, once born, does not die.

Putting those thoughts aside before they threatened to consume her, Sara retrieved the second message. She felt guilty at her relief when she heard Grams' voice instead of Daniel's. "Honey, will you please stop by the store and get me some cheese? I hope you're having fun in court, dear," Sara heard her grandmother say.

Cheese? What kind of cheese? Pondering whether Grams wanted shredded cheddar, sliced Swiss, or one of those boxes of processed cheese so seemingly necessary to the rural Southern kitchen, Sara mused at Grams suggestion that she was "having fun" in court. Nothing could have been further from the truth.

***

After the break, Kyle resumed his questioning of Marcus. "Can you tell me, Trooper Thompson, without repeating anyone else's words, what you observed at the scene?"

DONNA BROWN WILKERSON AND DAWN S. SCRUGGS

"Yes. I observed a red semi-truck – a Freightliner, I believe it was – pulled off in a clearing beside the road near where the Blazer had struck the tree. The driver of the truck approached me as I was going to my cruiser to radio for an ambulance to come and transport the defendant to the hospital."

"At what point did you realize that Maria Flores had been killed?" Kyle asked.

"The truck driver, Larry Turner, pointed out her body to me. She was lying in a ditch about twenty or thirty yards away from the defendant's car," Trooper Thompson explained in a way that skirted the hearsay rules. "I didn't know her identity at the time. I found out a few days later that she was a teenage runaway."

"Objection to the hearsay, Your Honor," Sharese interjected again.

Kyle quickly withdrew the question and moved on, not wanting to break the easy rhythm that he and Marcus had established. He knew he could get in plenty of information about Maria Flores later when he called her brother to testify. Angela had managed to track down the brother, who was still doing migrant farm work, in a nearby town.

The rest of the afternoon was consumed with Kyle questioning Marcus about the finer details of the accident, going over measurements and photos of the scene and so forth.

Finally, Judge Oaks interrupted Kyle to ask him when he would be at a good stopping point.

"I guess now's as good of a time as any, Your Honor. We can pick it back up here tomorrow."

"Alright then. Remember folks, be back here at 9 a.m. sharp."

Kyle took his time picking up papers and packing them into his briefcase. "Nice job up there, Marcus," he said as the trooper rejoined him at the State's table. "I can always count on you to save the day."

***

Sharese, who had been sitting silently at the defense table since her last objection had been overruled, noticed that the judge did not acknowledge her or her client before launching into the boilerplate instructions to the jury about not discussing the case with each other or listening to any media reports about the case that night. It didn't bother her much.

When she made the decision to leave Memphis fresh out of law school, she knew the tiny town of Maple Springs would be another place she would have to conquer, just like the track fields she had mastered as a high school and college athlete. *This may still be new turf for me, but it won't be long until I'm running circles around these good ole boys. Just watch me.*

Once the jury left, Sharese remained by Justin's side until the deputy came over to escort him out of the courtroom and back to the county jail.

"Justin, remember what we talked about at lunch. Please think long and hard about whether you want to risk your case by testifying on your own behalf," Sharese reminded her client as she was leaving.

"Yes, Miss Jackson. I will. I'll pray real hard on it tonight," Justin said as he was handcuffed and led away in leg irons.

CHAPTER SEVEN

Sara walked out of the courthouse into the hot summer sun. It was a confusing feeling, and her body needed a few minutes to adjust from the icy cold and the florescent lighting of the sterile courtroom. Taking in a breath of fresh air, she willed herself to think about anything except Kyle.

Her mind settled on the defendant, Justin Hargis. *How much fresh air will that young man get if he is convicted and sent to prison?* Having not been privy to Justin's first trial and conviction, she had no way of knowing that he'd been incarcerated since the day after the accident.

Sara also thought about Maria Flores, the girl who had been killed in the accident. Not much had been said about her so far. Sara thought of a little girl named Maria in her kindergarten class. Little Maria's birthday had fallen during the last week of school and had been duly celebrated despite there being a long list of other things that needed to be done before school let out for the summer.

In Sara's classroom, birthdays were the subject of much attention. Most of the children were five when they started school in the fall. As a child reached his or her sixth birthday, Sara would make that child "Star of the Day." To be a "Star" meant a brightly colored crown for the birthday child, treats for the entire class, and, of course, a loud chorus of the "Happy Birthday" song.

Most of the children's mothers brought cupcakes for the occasion. Knowing that sometimes a mother might forget or might be unable to afford the cupcakes, Sara kept a few boxes of packaged snack cakes in a cabinet by her desk. While not as exciting as a brightly colored cupcake with a favorite cartoon character on top, the children never complained.

Cupcakes, snack cakes, GROCERY STORE! Sara suddenly remembered Grams' message earlier requesting cheese. *I'll have to call and ask her what kind of cheese she needs.* When Sara got her cell phone out of her purse, she saw two messages. *Daniel.*

Sara listened to the first message. "I just wanted to let you know that we're in Miami on a one-hour layover. We should be in Honduras by late afternoon. I'll try to call you from Tegucigalpa, but I don't know what kind of phone service I'll have after that. I love you."

A feeling of guilt passed over Sara, as certain yet intangible as the clouds now casting shadows over the clusters of white lilies lining the court square. *I have to tell him. When he comes home, I have to tell Daniel about Kyle.*

Checking the time of the second message, she realized that she had missed Daniel's call letting her know that he had made it to Honduras. "Guess I missed you again," she heard him say, disappointment evident in his voice. "We've made it to Honduras. We'll be heading for the mountains in a day or two, so it may be awhile before I can call you again. Anyway, I love you. I miss you already."

Sara held the phone close to her heart for a minute and thought about how much had happened since she kissed Daniel goodbye the evening before. The phone vibrated against her chest, and she hoped that it was him. Answering quickly, she found that it was her grandmother.

"Hey Grams. Glad you called. I needed to ask you what kind of cheese it is that you need."

"Oh honey, that's alright, I don't need it anymore," Grams answered. "That's what I was calling to tell you. When you didn't call me back, I figured you'd be tied up in court all day."

"Yes, I just got out. It's been a really long day." Sara was glad she wouldn't have to go to the grocery store. Now she could go directly home and bury her head in her pillow for the rest of the night.

Sara's relief soon faded when she heard Grams say, "So, I planned something else for our supper tonight. I have some green beans and new potatoes from the garden, and I'm going to fry us a chicken. I figured Brother Andrew might like to have some meat instead of just a casserole. If you can get here a little early, you can help me make the biscuits. You're going to be a married woman soon, so you need to start learning these things."

"Andrew?" Sara drew a complete blank.

"Yes, honey, Andrew Parker, your brother-in-law to be. He is still standing in for Reverend Parker while he's on the missionary trip this week, isn't he?"

"Oh, of course! I almost forgot. I'll go over to the parish house right now and check on him." Sara silently chastised herself for forgetting not only her fiancé earlier in the day, but now his brother as well.

"That'll be fine, dear. I'll go ahead with the biscuits by myself. Maybe I can show you how to make them another time," Grams said, let down that Sara's cooking lesson would have to wait for another day.

Sara knew this was no time to express her opinion that the frozen biscuits readily available at the supermarket were quite tasty and didn't have the unfortunate side effect of coating her clothes with an annoying layer of Martha White flour. "Okay, Grams. We'll be there in an hour or so." *Okay, maybe this is a good thing.*

I need a distraction or else I am going to go crazy tonight thinking about Daniel. Or even worse, Kyle.

Sara ended the call and got into her car gingerly, trying not to burn herself on the hot seat. When she started the car, the radio was blaring. *I don't even remember having the radio on when I went home for lunch. It's no wonder; I was so shaken up from talking to Kyle.* Sara quickly switched off "Bridge Over Troubled Water" and drove the short drive to the parish house that was located beside the church where Daniel served as pastor.

She thought about her fiancé and what an interesting contrast the young pastor made with the old church. The building had been erected when Grams' mother was just a girl. Covered in white wooden siding and sporting a beautiful steeple that reached towards the heavens, Maple Springs Community Church was a local landmark.

The parish house beside the church was less impressive. Small in size and dated in décor, it left a lot to be desired as a residence. Still, Sara was sure that she and Daniel could make a home of it. As she knocked on the door, she said a quick prayer asking God to help her put aside the worries of the day and show proper hospitality to her future brother-in-law.

"Hey, Sis!" Andrew opened the door. "I'd better start calling you that, even though it won't be official until December. Are you sure you want to marry my rascal of a brother?"

"More than anything." Sara smiled. The mention of Daniel and their upcoming marriage warmed her heart and gave her the focus she so desperately needed. "He's the best thing that ever happened to me. And the best thing that ever happened to *you* is that my Grams is cooking dinner for us tonight!"

"Amen to that!" Andrew replied. "I hear Mrs. Viola's cooking is legendary around here. I can't wait to see what all the fuss is about."

"I promise you won't be disappointed," Sara said easily. "Oh, by the way, I got a message from Daniel this afternoon. He made it to Honduras safely."

"Yes, he called here, too. Uneventful flight, he said. That's always good."

"Absolutely," Sara said. "How about I show you around Maple Springs on the way over to Grams'? Daniel asked me to give you a tour, show you all the big sights like the hardware store, the Piggly Wiggly, and the Co-op."

"Sounds great." Andrew followed Sara to her car. "Oh, what happened with your jury service today? Anything exciting?"

Sara stopped in her tracks, grateful that Andrew couldn't see her face. The last thing she wanted to talk about was her day in court. Then, she remembered with gratitude Judge Oaks' stern instructions not to discuss the case with anyone until all of the evidence was in. "Actually, the judge told us not to discuss the case until the deliberation."

"Well, then, mum's the word." Andrew got into Sara's car. "We can still talk about the weather, right?"

"Yes, as far as I know that's still a safe subject," Sara chuckled.

"So, is it hot enough for you?"

"Oh yeah, it's definitely hot enough."

"I don't think it can get much hotter, at least not for those of us who are living right."

"Sounds like good inspiration for a sermon," Sara replied. "Maybe you can speak on that Wednesday night."

"That is a good idea. Unless a cool front blows in," Andrew joked.

Sara laughed easily. "It's always something, isn't it?"

"Yes, it surely is," Andrew replied. "As the saying goes, 'If it ain't one thing, it's another.'"

***

Kyle stopped by his office to check messages and return a few calls before heading home. As he drove the familiar route through town, his thoughts kept turning to Sara. *Put her out of your mind. You made your choice; now live with it.*

It was a quick drive, and he was home before he realized it. He looked up at the two-story Colonial, shaking his head at the mixed blessing that it had become. On his salary, it would have been years before he and Elizabeth would have been able to afford a house in Fox Creek. Her parents had given them a generous down payment, for which Kyle had been grateful. Over time, however, the house had come to symbolize the basic differences between his working class background and his wife's more affluent upbringing.

As Kyle turned his key in the lock, his son Evan ran to greet him. Kyle reached down and patted the boy on the head, "Hey little man! Did you have a good day? Where's your Mommy?"

"Kitchen!" Evan pointed, hugging Kyle's leg.

Kyle walked to the kitchen, dragging Evan – who would not let go of his leg – along with him. "Hey hon, I seem to have something wrong with my leg. Will you take a look at?"

Elizabeth smiled as she turned around. "I'm not falling for that one again." She shushed Evan, who had started to shriek as he tightened his grip on his father's leg. "Don't be so loud! Chelsea's still asleep."

"So the doc said she's just teething, huh? That's good." Kyle couldn't help but notice but how tired his wife looked. Even though the baby was almost a year old, she still hadn't mastered the art of sleeping through the night. It was beginning to take its toll on all of them.

Evan had been an entirely different story. An angelic baby, he had easily settled into a routine in his first few weeks. The couple had agreed that Elizabeth would stay home with him for awhile before going back to work. Less than two years later, they were expecting Chelsea.

"What's for supper?" Kyle asked.

"I'm making some mac n' cheese for Evan," Elizabeth answered. "I didn't get to the store today. By the time we got out of the doctor's office, the kids were going wild. Want me to make you a sandwich or heat up a can of soup?"

"I'll find something later. I'm gonna go look at this Hargis file in the den," Kyle said. Just then, Chelsea woke up from her nap, and Elizabeth went to her.

When Kyle finally emerged from the den hours later, he found Elizabeth in a rocking chair in the nursery. She was holding Chelsea, and they were both asleep. He peeked in on Evan. The usually rambunctious little boy was sleeping sweetly in his toddler bed, a Pottery Barn exclusive that had been a gift from his mother-in-law shortly before Chelsea's birth. Evan was holding his basketball print blanket tightly in his hand.

Kyle's stomach rumbled, and he realized that he had not eaten since breakfast. Checking the fridge, he found some leftover macaroni. He heated it in the microwave and ate it standing up at the kitchen counter.

His mind returned to Sara. Sara in the back of the courtroom. Sara in the jury box. Sara in his arms after he told her that he was going back to Elizabeth. '*Sara.*' *I didn't even know her real name.* Shaking his head in an attempt to get her out of his thoughts, Kyle finished the macaroni and started up to bed.

As he climbed the stairs, he looked at the family pictures that lined the wall. Evan on his first birthday. Chelsea at Easter. He and Elizabeth on their wedding day. What a beautiful bride she had been with her soft blond hair and sky-blue eyes. When he got to his bedroom, Kyle collapsed onto the bed without changing his clothes. He slept soundly and recalled no dreams when he awoke in the morning.

CHAPTER EIGHT

The next morning, Sara awoke in a much better frame of mind. She had slept better, satiated by Grams' delicious dinner. It had been comfort food at its finest – fresh vegetables right out of the garden, steaming hot biscuits with local clover honey, and fried chicken that only a woman of a certain age was capable of putting on the table.

The evening of fellowship with Grams and Andrew had raised her spirits, too. Her future brother-in-law's tall tales about his and Daniel's boyhood had kept Sara and Grams entertained for hours.

When the evening was over, Sara had relaxed in bed with the Bible in her hands and Callie curled warmly beside her. As she drifted off to sleep, she had prayed, *Father, I have confessed my wrongs to you and sought your forgiveness, but I know that I still must face the earthly consequences of my sins. Please give me the strength and wisdom to get through this week. Please watch over Daniel and bring him home to me safely. Amen.*

As she walked into the courthouse Tuesday morning, she said another prayer asking that all of the other jurors remain on the jury until time for the deliberation. *Forgive me Lord for wanting to shirk my civic duty, but I have too much on my mind to be a fair juror to that young man. He deserves someone who can think about his guilt or innocence instead of wallowing around in her own troubles.*

***

Sharese and Justin had both arrived early to court, Justin in the same shirt and tie as the day before and Sharese in a new suit that flattered both her figure and her face. She almost convinced herself that her choice had nothing to do with the handsome state trooper she would be examining that morning.

Judge Oaks promptly took the bench, called court to order, and reminded the jurors that they were still under oath. "General Copeland, are you ready to continue your examination of Trooper Thompson?"

"I am, Your Honor," Kyle said.

"Is the defense ready, Ms. Jackson?" the judge asked Sharese.

"The defense is ready, Your Honor."

"All right, then, Trooper Thompson, you can take your place on the witness stand," the judge said.

As Marcus walked by the defense table, Sharese noted that his left hand was ring-free.

Kyle began his questioning. "Trooper, I believe that you told us yesterday how you found the scene of the accident. Would you refresh our recollections on that, please?"

Marcus cleared his throat before beginning. "As I said yesterday, I arrived at the scene to find that the defendant's Chevrolet Blazer had crashed into a tree."

"What kind of damage did you observe, Trooper Thompson?" Kyle asked.

"The windshield was broken, as was the left headlight. The left fender was badly dented, and the hood was sticking up several inches. It appeared that the Blazer had struck the tree at a high rate of–"

Sharese quickly interjected, "Objection, Your Honor. This witness has not been qualified as an expert in accident reconstruction, and therefore any testimony that he purports to offer on the subject of vehicle speed prior to the accident is inadmissible." *Take that, Mr. Marcus Thompson.*

"Counsel, approach the bench please." Judge Oaks was clearly annoyed. Sharese, Kyle, and the court reporter all gathered in front of the bench and spoke in whispered tones. "Folks, I was really hoping we'd make it at least five minutes before our first round of objections."

"Me, too, Judge." Kyle shot a mischievous grin at Sharese.

Sharese's knees were knocking, but she was intent on holding her ground. "Then you shouldn't be directing expert witness questions at someone who clearly isn't qualified to answer them," she said to Kyle.

Judge Oaks let out a long sigh. Looking at the jury, he said, "All right folks. We're going to take a short recess here. Bailiff, give us about ten minutes."

***

As Sara waited in the jury room with the other jurors during the break, she overheard two of the older women talking.

"What do you think so far? Is he guilty, or is he innocent?"

"I don't know about the defendant, but I think we should find that handsome young prosecutor guilty of impersonating Matthew McConaughey!"

"Or Brad Pitt," the other juror retorted, and they both laughed loudly. "Too bad he's married. He would have been perfect for my niece."

Sara felt the shame creep over her like an unwelcome wool blanket on a summer day. *Yeah, too bad he's married. He would have been perfect.* Sara escaped into the restroom to avoid explaining the hot tears that the women's remarks had incited in her.

When the jury was called back into the courtroom, Sara hoped no one noticed that her eyes were red and swollen. She tried her best never to lie, but she would have to make an exception if any one asked about her eyes. She would suddenly become a victim of seasonal allergies, or perhaps pinkeye.

The humiliating truth was that hearing those two words – "Kyle" and "married" – used aloud in the same sentence had brought bitter tears to her eyes. The words had gone through her thoughts and her prayers too many times to count, but somehow they were more real when they were spoken by someone else.

After the jury returned to the courtroom, Kyle continued questioning Marcus about the accident scene. No mention was made as to the judge's ruling on Sharese's objection, but Kyle's line of questioning seemed to have shifted ever so slightly. *So easy for him to just change his tune and go right on without skipping a beat.*

When Kyle finally moved on to another line of questioning, Sara was left only with the general impression that the Blazer had hit the tree hard enough to render it undrivable. A photograph the trooper took at the scene confirmed this. *Why did Kyle make something so simple seem so complicated?* Sara wondered. She remembered his words the day before in the stairwell. *The man truly has a gift for complications.*

"Trooper, did you speak with the defendant at the scene?" Kyle asked.

"No. When I approached the defendant's vehicle, I saw that he was unconscious. I radioed for an ambulance. It arrived within a few minutes. Paramedics removed the defendant from the vehicle and carried him to the hospital. I didn't actually speak to him until the following morning."

"Can you tell me about the conversation the next morning?" Kyle asked.

"The defendant was in the hospital, lying in bed. He was awake and seemed to be fine except for a bruise and cut on his forehead. I introduced myself, told him that he was being charged with the vehicular homicide of Maria Flores, and then read him his *Miranda* rights."

"What are *Miranda* rights?" Kyle asked.

"Among other things, the right to remain silent and the right to an attorney. They're based on a Supreme Court case, *Miranda v. Arizona.* Basically, it's just reminding someone of their Fifth Amendment right not to incriminate themselves."

Sara frowned. *Kyle's an expert on a person's right not to incriminate himself.*

Kyle went on with the questioning. "And did you verbally advise the defendant of those rights, Trooper?"

"Yes, I did. I have a small card that I keep with me that lists all the *Miranda* rights. I read it directly to the defendant before proceeding further."

"Did the defendant waive those rights and talk to you about the accident?"

"He claimed to have no recollection of the night before, so it was a very short conversation," Marcus stated.

"Okay," Kyle said in a slightly self-righteous tone that Sara knew was supposed to convey his disgust that the defendant had killed someone and didn't even have the decency to remember it the next morning. "Moving backward just a bit, did you ask the hospital to do a blood alcohol test on the defendant on the night of the accident?" Kyle asked.

"Yes, I did. I instructed the paramedics to see to it that a blood sample was drawn the night of the accident. It's standard procedure in a motor vehicle accident involving a fatality."

"When did you know for sure that there was a fatality?"

"By the time that the ambulance arrived at the scene, it was clear that Miss Flores was dead. I had already checked her for a pulse and not found one. She was lying in a ditch, covered in dirt and blood. Her legs were mangled. The paramedics worked with her for a few minutes, but it was useless. She was already gone."

Sara noticed a couple of the other jurors wipe their eyes as the trooper's voice cracked ever so slightly.

"I'm sorry, Trooper Thompson. I know these cases are hard to talk about," Kyle said. "Can you tell us what happened next?"

Marcus nodded. "Yes. After the defendant was taken to the hospital for medical treatment and the girl's body was taken away, I attempted to determine her identity. It took a couple of days, but I eventually linked her to a family of migrant farm workers in the area. They had contacted the sheriff's department the day after the accident and reported their daughter missing."

"Did it turn out to be the same girl?"

"Yes, it did. The father came to the morgue to identify the body, and it was clearly his daughter. I tried to talk to him about the accident, but he was very upset and spoke very little English. He indicated that he wanted to get the girl's body home to Mexico for burial, so I gave him the telephone number of the local funeral home in hopes that they could help him arrange that. I also gave him my card and asked him to call me in a few days."

"Did he call you?" Kyle asked.

"No, he did not. I never saw him again."

"Going back to your conversation with the defendant, Trooper, what happened after you advised him of his *Miranda* rights?"

"As I said earlier, he didn't remember the accident. He told me that his head hurt, and I explained to him about the broken windshield. He said that he wanted to go home and sleep in his own bed."

"Objection, Your Honor. Hearsay." Sharese rose to her feet.

"Overruled." Judge Oaks barely looked up from the notepad he had been scribbling on.

"Was the defendant able tell you anything at all about the night of the accident, Trooper?" Kyle continued with his questioning.

"Not really. I also told him that I had searched his vehicle following the arrest and had found a small amount of methamphetamine. He neither admitted nor denied that it was his. When the doctor released him later that day, I took him into custody."

"The State has no further questions, Your Honor," Kyle said.

As Kyle took his seat at the counsel table, Sara saw him steal a glance at the jury box. She put a shaking hand in front of her face, willing herself not to return the look. Her diamond engagement ring caught the morning sunlight, causing a fleeting prism to cross Kyle's guilty face.

**

Sharese went to the podium. Noticing how handsome the trooper was, she suddenly felt a wave of nervousness come over her. Looking at her notes, she tried to put it aside. "Trooper, you're not an accident reconstruction expert, are you?"

"No, ma'am, I'm not," Marcus replied.

"And you didn't actually see the accident, is that correct?" Sharese continued. *Stay in your lane, girl. Just stick to the facts.*

"That's correct."

"And neither the truck driver nor the victim's family actually witnessed the accident, is that correct?"

"Yes, ma'am. That's right."

"The defendant, Mr. Hargis, had no memory of the accident, true?"

"That's what he said, ma'am."

Sharese looked squarely at Trooper Thompson. "So, there were apparently no eye witnesses to the accident and you are not an expert at reconstructing accident scenes, is that right, Trooper?"

The trooper lowered his head slightly. "That's right."

"No further questions, Your Honor," Sharese said confidently before sitting down. Even if Marcus Thompson looked amazingly sharp in that uniform, he hadn't really said much to damage her client. She had done a good job of showing the jury just how little the trooper actually knew about the accident.

Judge Oaks looked at Kyle, who stood and said, "No more questions from the State. Trooper, you can come down from the stand."

69

The judge looked at his watch. "Let's go ahead and break for lunch."

***

The members of the jury left the courtroom together, and the bailiff escorted them to a restaurant on the court square. Hoping none of the jurors would feel compelled to discuss Kyle's marital status or compare him to movie stars, Sara stared at the menu.

Despite her rolling stomach, she knew she needed to eat something. For a distraction, she challenged herself to find something healthful on the menu to atone for her grandmother's fried chicken and biscuits the night before. "The garden salad, please, with light ranch dressing on the side," Sara told the waitress. "Oh, and a bottle of water."

As they waited for their lunches to arrive, the jurors made small talk. The male jurors seemed to know each other and talked mostly about the high school football team's chances of making the playoffs.

The younger women talked about their children, bringing out their wallets and proudly showing off pictures. The older women talked about their gardens, bemoaning the fact that jury duty was keeping them from canning their tomatoes. Not having any particular expertise in football, parenting, or tomato canning, Sara kept mostly to herself.

After the food arrived and everyone began eating, Sara noticed that one of the older women was looking at her quizzically.

As Sara met her gaze, the woman asked if she was Viola Anderson's granddaughter.

"Yes, I am. How do you know Grams?"

"Child, I have known your grandmother most all my life. Well, my life and her life; we're the same age. You are the spitting image of her when she was a girl. My name is Fredonia Miller. You be sure and tell her I said, 'Hello,' alrighty?"

"I will. I'm sure she'll be glad to hear from you, Mrs. Miller." Sara was glad to have something neutral to talk about.

"Oh, you can call me 'Fredonia.' Your Grams and I are practically family," Fredonia spoke easily. "I saw Viola not too long ago. She said you're gonna get married, is that right?"

Sara smiled at the mention of her engagement. "Yes. Our wedding is set for December."

"You must be very excited."

"Yes, but not as much as Grams. She's glad I have something else to think about besides whether she's taking her arthritis medicine on time."

"Ah, yes, that sounds like Viola," Fredonia agreed. "Not wantin' anybody up in her business. Frank understood that about her. Those two were quite a pair."

"I know she misses him a lot, but she doesn't talk about it much."

"Nothing prepares you for being a widow." Fredonia sniffed and dabbed at her eyes with her napkin. "She's lucky to have you close by."

As the others finished their meals, Fredonia broke out a pair of knitting needles. "Guess I'll get in a few stitches on my afghan. I'm making this for my niece's birthday."

Sara nodded politely as she got out her cell phone to check for messages. *Nothing.* She thought about Daniel, wondering where he was and what he was doing. *Please Lord, keep him safe. I don't know what I would do without him.*

***

"Yeah, hon, I think it's going pretty good," Kyle spoke into his cell phone as he walked from his office back to the courthouse. "Marcus did a nice job, despite some objections. Sharese Jackson from the P.D.'s office is doing better than I expected, especially considering that the sales tag's still attached to her law degree and her client has already been convicted of this crime once."

"What do you know about her, Ms. Jackson that is?" Elizabeth asked.

"She went to law school in Memphis. I think she's from there. She just started working for the P.D. a few weeks ago. She must have taken the bar in February. Nice enough gal, just still green. You know how it is," Kyle said.

"No, actually, I don't know." Elizabeth's reply was icy.

"Oh, yeah, right." Kyle instantly recognized one of the hot spots of their marriage.

An awkward moment of silence filled the phone.

Kyle looked at his watch. "I gotta go, hon. Judge Oaks will hold me in contempt if I'm half a heartbeat late to court." Kyle spit out the words quickly and snapped the phone shut as he walked through the courthouse doors. He knew Elizabeth had mixed feelings about her stay-at-home status, although she rarely voiced them.

Most days, she seemed content to be a wife and mother. She generally took the long hours of young motherhood in stride, although she always seemed happiest on days when she had been able to drop the kids off at Mothers' Day Out for a few hours. Kyle certainly saw nothing wrong with that. He was glad when the kids finally went to sleep at night and couldn't imagine what it was like to deal with their constant needs and demands all day, every day.

Kyle wasn't sure what had set Elizabeth off during their brief phone call, but it obviously had something to do with the new public defender. Elizabeth sounded jealous, but why? Because Sharese Jackson was using her law degree for something other than decorating the wall of the guest bedroom or because she was a woman – and a very attractive one, although Elizabeth didn't know that – who was spending long hours in court with her husband? *How ironic would that be?*

Kyle resolved himself to talk less about the trial in the few hours that he would be able to spend with his family that week. As he walked into the courtroom, he saw that Sharese and Justin were already at the defense table. He sat down at the State's table, and Marcus soon joined him.

"I'm glad this morning is over." Trooper Thompson sighed heavily. "I hate being on the stand."

"She didn't rip you up too bad." Kyle grinned. "I think she likes you."

"Give it a break, Copeland."

Kyle shrugged his shoulders and changed the subject. "Played any b-ball lately?"

"Actually, I was thinking of shooting some hoops tonight. Want to join me and try to win back your self-respect? I seem to remember wiping the floor with you last time."

Judge Oaks returned to the bench before Kyle could answer Marcus's invitation. As the jury came back in, Kyle wondered if he would technically be lying to Elizabeth if he told her that he had to work late when he was really playing basketball with Marcus. *We could talk about the trial between shots.*

Kyle didn't like to lie to Elizabeth. There were two reasons for that. First, he knew that she deserved better than to be lied to. Everybody did, of course. Secondly, he was afraid of the consequences of being caught in a not-so-innocent fib. So, whenever things came up that he didn't want to tell her, he just didn't tell her.

It wasn't too hard to convince himself that an omission was not as egregious as an outright lie. There was really no reason to tell his otherwise beautiful wife that she had baby food in her hair. It would just worry her to know that he sometimes had to make a choice between paying the electric bill on time and making the car payment. And she certainly didn't need to know that he had once fallen in love with another woman.

***

After waiting for the jury to be seated and the court reporter to get situated in her chair, Judge Oaks was ready to begin. "General, who do we have next?"

"The State will now present its witnesses pertaining to the chain of custody of the defendant's blood sample on the night of the accident. The testimony of most of these witnesses will be short, but there are several of them, as is usually the case."

"Approach the bench, counsel," the judge said, looking mildly annoyed. Once Kyle, Sharese, and the court reporter had made their way to the bench, the judge looked pointedly at Sharese. "Counsel, can you not stipulate to the chain of custody so that we can save some time?"

Sharese shook her head in the negative. "No, Your Honor, my client is not willing to make any stipulations here. After all, he was unconscious when his blood was drawn." Sharese looked pointedly at Kyle. "While I understand that it would be easier on the State to just call the toxicologist that actually analyzed the defendant's blood sample, it is the State's burden to prove its entire case beyond a reasonable doubt. That includes the chain of custody of the defendant's blood."

The judge looked perturbed but simply said, "Very well. Proceed, General."

Kyle first called the nurse who drew Justin's blood, followed by several other witnesses who were involved in the blood being physically transported to the crime laboratory of the Tennessee Bureau of Investigation. Sharese objected a couple of times, but Judge Oaks overruled her objections. The witnesses testified in rapid succession, and no single testimony lasted more than fifteen minutes.

"Next, Your Honor, the State will call Sharon White," Kyle said. "Her testimony will be much more involved, so this might be a good place to take a recess, if the Court is so inclined."

"Yes, General, I'm sure the jury could use a little break. I know I could. Let court stand in recess for ten minutes."

***

During the break, Sharese again tried to dissuade Justin from testifying. "Please tell me that you've changed your mind about taking the stand."

"I was awake most of night thinking about it, Miss Jackson. I prayed a lot, and the only answer I got was that I have to do it. I have to see if getting up there on the witness stand will help me remember anything about the wreck," Justin said with a quiet resolve.

"You'll make yourself vulnerable to a nasty attack from the prosecutor," Sharese said. "You have a constitutional right to remain silent, even in the courtroom. The State can't make you testify against yourself, Justin. Why do you insist on doing it when you know it could backfire?"

"Because I have to know. I can live with whatever happens. Like I told you before, I'm okay with going back to prison, although it would be nice if I didn't have to," Justin said. "It's real nice being back home again."

"What would you do if you were acquitted?"

"I don't know, Miss Jackson. I haven't thought that far ahead."

"You could look into going to community college. I hear Vol State has a good program."

Justin shook his head. "I never was one of the smart ones back in school. Don't think I'd do too good in college."

"Maybe trade school then."

"Yeah, vocational school might be nice. I took a couple of auto body classes in high school."

"That sounds good. But first we have to win this case. Are you absolutely sure that you have to testify?"

"Yes, ma'am. I'm certain of it."

Sharese breathed a deep sigh. "You'd better not make me lose my first case, Justin Hargis. I might have to do something to you that'll get me sent to prison, too."

Justin laughed. "You mean I can't say 'Miss Jackson told me to say I was drunk as a skunk and driving faster than a NASCAR driver that night?'"

Sharese shook her head at Justin but laughed along with him.

***

After the break, Judge Oaks called court back to order. "Who's your next witness, General?"

"The State calls Sharon White to the witness stand," Kyle said. The witness was an older woman, short and heavyset. Her gray hair was permed, and her glasses kept sliding down her nose. She had an expression that made it clear she didn't tolerate much flack. After she was sworn, Kyle began his questioning. "Give us your name, address, and occupation, please."

"My name is Sharon White. I live and work in Nashville, Tennessee. I work for the Tennessee Bureau of Investigation as a toxicologist."

After asking Ms. White several more questions pertaining to her background, education, training, and work experience, Kyle moved on to more pertinent questions. "What exactly do you do for the TBI?"

Pushing her glasses back up on her nose, the witness began, "About half of my job is analyzing blood samples of drivers who are suspected of violating the driving under the influence laws. I check their blood for alcohol and drug content." In a monotone voice, she continued, "The other half of my job is to testify about those results in court." It was clear from the look of disgust on her face which half of her job she preferred.

"Did you have an occasion to analyze a blood sample of one Justin Hargis? H-A-R-G-I-S?" Kyle asked, ever so slightly emphasizing the "G."

"Yes, I did."

"Could you tell us about that, please?" Kyle urged.

"A blood sample was taken from Justin Hargis at a local hospital here in Maple Springs. It was sent to the TBI via standard procedure. When I analyzed Mr. Hargis's blood sample, I found that it showed a BAC of 0.07 percent."

"What is a 'BAC'? Can you explain that term for the jury, please, ma'am?" Kyle asked, nodding toward the jury members but not actually looking at them. *Don't look at her; don't look at her. Don't even think about her.*

"'BAC' means blood alcohol content. It's the level of concentration of alcohol in a person's blood," Ms. White explained.

Kyle and Ms. White continued to discuss the technical nuances of blood testing and gas chromatography for well over an hour, long past the time that anyone else in the courtroom was able to feign attention. *I'm about to even put myself to sleep.*

"What type of impairment might a person experience at 0.07 percent BAC?" Kyle asked, not really expecting to get an answer to the question. He assumed Sharese would voice an objection to the witness's qualification to testify to this subject matter, but a look in her direction explained that she had her hands full trying to keep her client awake through the tedious testimony. *Let's just hope the jury's still awake. No, no, no, don't look over there!*

Too late, Kyle's eyes met Sara's. His heart sped up, even though she immediately looked away. Fortunately, Ms. White didn't miss a beat, droning on and on in the absence of an objection by the defense.

"From what I've read in the medical literature, somewhere between 0.06 percent BAC and 0.10 percent BAC, a person begins to lose their sense of inhibition and reasoning. There would also begin to be a loss in a person's depth perception, distance acuity, and glare recovery. Maybe even a loss of peripheral vision," Ms. White said. After she said it, she gave the jury a little proud look and pushed her glasses up just a bit.

Figuring that it was best to quit while he was ahead, Kyle quickly made his way back to the counsel table. "That's all the questions that I have, Judge."

Not bothering to suppress a yawn, Judge Oaks said, "I think this would be a good time to stop. I've had a motion come up in another case that I need to take care of before leaving today. Let's meet back here at 9 a.m. in the morning."

CHAPTER NINE

Sara couldn't get out of the courthouse fast enough. After the bailiff told the jurors they could go, she walked as quickly as she could without calling attention to herself. Once she reached the stairwell, she skipped down the stairs at an impressive pace, making sure that she got out of the courthouse before the attorneys made their way out of the courtroom. *No way am I chancing another reunion on the stairwell.*

She got into her car, quickly opening the windows to let out the stifling hot air until the air conditioning could kick in. "And now, folks, we have a little number coming to you straight from 1954," the disc jockey announced as the Chordettes came on the radio singing "Mr. Sandman." *This station does grow on you after awhile.* Sara relaxed a bit as the music carried her away.

She drove by the church to check on Andrew. His car was not there, nor was it at the parish house. *Hmm. Guess he's found his way to Eddie's for a sandwich.* She quickly scribbled a note and left it on the door. *Stopped by after court but missed you. Call me if you need anything. –Sara.*

She then went to her grandmother's house, parking under one of the large shade trees lining the street. "Hey, Grams. I'm out of court. Thought I'd check in on you," Sara said loudly as she let herself into the screen door.

"I'm in the kitchen, honey. Come on in."

"What? You're not cooking another meal fit for a king this afternoon?" Sara teased as she went into the kitchen and saw her grandmother making herself a bologna sandwich.

"I thought I'd just make myself a little sandwich for supper tonight. It's so hot, and I didn't want to heat up the kitchen to cook for just one," Grams said. "There's some fried chicken leftover from last night in the fridge. Help yourself."

"Thanks. The salad that I had for lunch wore off in the middle of the last witness."

"How was court today? We didn't get to talk much about it last night."

"To tell you the truth, Grams, I'll be glad when the whole thing is over." Sara helped herself to a piece of cold chicken and a glass of milk.

"It's hard having someone's fate in your hands." Grams gave an understanding smile. "So, what's the case about?"

"The judge told us not to talk about it until all of the evidence is in," Sara replied. "We're not even allowed to talk about it with the other jurors." *Can I even tell her that I'm only an alternate juror? Let's hope that's all I have to be and this whole thing is behind me in a day or two.*

"Well, that's too bad. Humph," Grams snorted, obviously displeased. "Who are the lawyers? Can you at least talk about that?"

I'd rather not. Sara tried to think of a way to avoid the subject but couldn't remember any specific admonition from Judge Oaks concerning the attorneys. *Let's start with the easy one, and maybe she'll lose interest.* "The, um, defense attorney, I think her name is Sharon – no, Sharese Jackson. Yes, that's it, Sharese Jackson."

"I wonder if she's Delores Johnson's granddaughter. I think she has a granddaughter that went to law school."

"No, Grams. Her last name is 'Jackson' not 'Johnson.'"

"Oh. I guess I don't know her then. What's the other lawyer's name?" Grams asked.

"Is there any more chicken?" Sara stalled, swallowing hard and trying not to choke on the food in her mouth.

"Sure, honey, in the same orange Tupperware bowl where you found that piece." Grams eyed Sara with concern. "Is something wrong?"

"I'm fine," Sara lied. She took a large sip of the milk and went to the refrigerator to get another piece of chicken. Her appetite was gone, but she knew that she had to keep up appearances for Grams' sake.

Grams finished making her bologna sandwich and sat down at the kitchen table across from Sara. "You were telling me about the other lawyer."

I was trying not to, actually. Have to love her persistence. "Kyle Copeland. That's the prosecutor's name." Sara felt her face flush slightly at having actually said his name aloud.

"Oh, of course. What a pleasant young man."

Sara froze. *Oh no! I guess Maple Springs is even smaller than I realized.* "You know Kyle? Uh-Kyle Copeland, the prosecutor?"

"Yes, I know him through his grandfather, Ernest Copeland. Back when your Grandpa Frank was still alive, he and Ernest would often fish together out at the river. The Copeland family's cabin is just two doors down from ours."

Of course – the cabin. Just because I didn't grow up around here doesn't mean our families aren't connected in some way.

"I can remember Kyle and his parents coming out to the river with Ernest sometimes when Kyle was just a little boy. He was a cute little thing. He's grown up to be a handsome man, don't you think?" Grams looked questioningly at Sara.

Sara felt her face growing hot. "He's okay, I guess," Sara said, not meeting Grams' gaze.

"Oh, honey. You don't have to be embarrassed. Even an engaged young lady can't help but notice a handsome young man like Kyle Copeland." Grams smiled. "It's funny to think of him all grown up with kids of his own now. I tell you, time sure does fly."

Still married then. And they have children already? "How old are his kids?" Sara asked, feeling the blush disappear along with the rest of the blood in her face.

"The oldest is probably around two or three, and the youngest is still just a baby," Grams answered.

Sara wavered in her seat just a bit, suddenly feeling dizzy. *Kyle certainly didn't waste any time after he went back to his wife.* She felt another blush pass across her face.

"I think this July heat is getting to me, Grams. I need to go home and rest a bit and check on Callie, too – make sure she has plenty of water. I may have forgotten to check it this morning."

"That red-headed weatherwoman on Channel 4 said we might break some records this week," Grams replied.

Getting up and making her way to the door, Sara called behind her, "Thanks for the chicken, Grams. I'll see you tomorrow!"

When Sara got to the car, she was glad she had left the windows rolled down. Between that and the fact that she had parked in the shade, the car was much cooler. Otherwise, she would have just melted into the upholstery. She started the engine, turning the radio off as she dialed the parish house on her cell phone.

"Hello?" Sara heard Andrew say.

"Hi, Andrew. It's Sara. I just wanted to make sure that you were doing okay. I stopped by there, but I missed you."

"I was out grabbing a bite to eat. A fast food burger doesn't hold a candle to your Grams' home cooking, but I knew I couldn't expect a feast like that two days in a row," Andrew joked.

"Okay, then, good. It's been a long day, and I'm heading home. You have my number; just call me if you need anything," Sara told Andrew.

"Thanks, Sis. Will do!" Andrew replied.

"Oh, and Andrew? Have you heard anything from Daniel today? The last I heard was yesterday when they'd made it to the capital city in Honduras."

"Nope. Haven't heard from him today. It'll take awhile for them to get up into the mountains, you know."

"Yeah. I'd just feel better if I could talk to him."

"If he calls in, I'll relay the message."

"Okay. Have a good night, Andrew."

"You, too."

When Sara got home, Callie met her at the door. "Meow, meow," the cat sang loudly, rubbing herself against Sara's legs and walking around her in a figure eight pattern.

"Hey there, girl!" Sara scooped her up for an overdue scratch behind the ears. "I missed you, too. Let's check your food dish, shall we?" Seeing that there was water but no food, Sara put down Callie and picked up the dish. She opened a can of Callie's favorite cat food and filled the dish with fresh water. Callie ran to her dinner, suddenly losing interest in Sara.

Sara sat down at the table and looked at Daniel's picture staring back at her from its place on the fridge. *Don't look at me like that, all handsome and perfect. I feel bad enough already.*

***

Kyle picked up and put down the phone several times before finally phoning Elizabeth from his office. "Hey hon. How's the baby? I hear crying," Kyle said.

"She's fussy, but she's okay. She just missed her nap this afternoon. That's probably Evan that you hear crying. He just fell down and hit his knee," Elizabeth replied. "It's okay, sweetie. It's okay," Kyle heard her whisper to Evan.

"I just wanted to let you know I'll be late tonight," Kyle said. "I need to go over a few things with Marcus." *No need to tell a woman stuck at home with two fussing kids that you're planning to go play a little b-ball.*

"Okay," Elizabeth sighed. "Thanks for letting me know."

Kyle's next call was to Marcus. "Hey, dude. You still up for some ball?"

"Sure," Marcus said. "See you at the gym in a few?"

"Sounds good," Kyle answered.

"Bring your jumping' shoes, Mr. Prosecutor!"

"Will do, Trooper T!"

Kyle changed into the shorts and t-shirt that he kept in his desk drawer for such occasions and walked the short distance to the gym. When he arrived, he saw that Marcus was already warming up. "Yo! Don't hog that ball!"

Marcus tossed the ball to Kyle, and the two played a long game of one-on-one, working out the frustrations of a long day in court. When they finally tired, Marcus said, "Good game, man. Let the record reflect that the attorney for the State has finally one-upped the lawman. Whoo-hoo!"

Kyle patted Marcus on the back. "I'll enjoy the victory while it lasts, my friend. It may be the only one I get this week."

"You think we might lose the Hargis case?" Marcus turned serious.

"I hope not, but 0.07 percent BAC versus 0.11 percent BAC does make a difference. Let's just hope we can prove 'conduct creating a substantial risk' through that trucker tomorrow." Kyle made little quotation marks in the air with his fingers.

"I sure hope so. Hargis had a juvie record a mile long before the wreck even happened. He needs to stay locked up for a long time."

Kyle nodded in agreement. "A very long time."

Not knowing what else to say, the two men simply stood up after a few minutes and walked to the door. They exchanged quiet goodbyes and walked out into the warm night air to go their separate ways.

CHAPTER 10

Sharese arrived at the courthouse earlier than usual Wednesday morning, not for any particular reason other than that she had been up since dawn and had nowhere else to go.

Although she had gone to bed early, she had woken up frequently thinking about the trial. An early morning phone call from her grandmother, Eloise Jackson, had just given her another thing to worry about.

Now, in addition to feeling personally responsible for whether Justin Hargis went back to prison – and she increasingly hoped that he did not – she also had to worry about whether her own father would be denied a chance to get out of prison – and she hoped that he was. According to the phone call from Memphis, one Tony Darnell Jackson was up for parole in a few months. *And it might help if you wrote a letter on his behalf, don't you think, Sharese, baby? Since you're a lawyer and all now.*

It wasn't that Sharese hated her father; she just simply didn't know the man. Tony Jackson had been incarcerated longer than Sharese had been alive. Being a normally logical person, she told herself that her parents had been victims of their circumstances – poverty, prejudice, lack of education. A lot of folks ended up the same way, either in prison (in her father's case) or leaving a child behind and running off at the first hope of something better (in her mother's case). That's what she told herself in the light of day. On one level, of course, it was certainly true.

Many people back in the old neighborhood had gone down that same road. Boys joined gangs in order to have a "family" who had their back, and the money wasn't bad, either. Girls got pregnant at fourteen or fifteen because they thought they'd finally found someone who loved them. The lies revealed themselves quickly, and those who believed them paid a heavy price. *Problem is, it's not just the ones who had the luxury of making a decision in the first place who have to suffer the consequences of poor judgment.*

It was in the dark of night that Sharese considered herself as the human carnage of her parents' bad choices. It affected her entire self-concept, whether she admitted it to herself or not.

First, there was the feeling that she was damaged goods, the child that was thrown away to be raised by an aged grandmother. She loved her grandmother, of course, and was grateful that Eloise had stepped in and done right by her. Still, not having the tangible love of her parents or even just the benefit of their company hurt more than she could describe.

Worse than the self-esteem issue was the bitterness and resentment that swelled in Sharese when she thought too long about her parents. Her mother's sin was the most unforgivable, because – at least as far as Sharese saw it – she had acted intentionally. Found something more appealing than raising a baby whose daddy was in prison and moved on. *No grass grew under her feet, that's for sure.*

With her father, Sharese struggled more. He had made a conscious choice to participate in a crime. That much was for sure. A man had died as a result of that choice, a veteran Memphis police officer with a wife and three kids.

The question that bothered Sharese was, did her father really have the level of thought necessary to foresee *all* of the consequences of his decision that night so many years before? In law school, Sharese had learned about the concept of "proximate cause." Both criminal and civil responsibility often hinge upon whether the result of a wrongful act was the natural, direct and uninterrupted consequence of the act. There's also a "but for" test; would the injury have occurred but for the wrongful act?

Clearly, her father failed the "but for" test, but the other part of the test was more troublesome. *Could he have been stupid enough to think that he wouldn't be caught, that he'd somehow manage to live a life of crime and be a father at the same time? Doubtful, but, if so, does that make him more forgivable than a sixteen-year-old girl who just couldn't muster the motherly self-sacrifice required to raise a child on her own?*

Sharese nodded a greeting to a young couple coming out of the courthouse as she went in. *All I need to think about today is Justin Hargis. Justin Hargis. Justin HarGis.* Sharese mentally prepared for the morning of cross-examination as she rode the elevator up to the courtroom.

When she walked into the courtroom, she saw that Justin was already seated. "How long have you been in here?"

"Just a few minutes," Justin said.

Sharese noticed that he was smiling. "You seem awfully happy for someone in your current situation. What gives?" Sharese looked at him expectantly.

"My mama come to see me again last night. It's always nice to see her." Justin smiled.

Sharese nodded.

"And," Justin continued, "I finally remembered something about the wreck. I think there was an Elvis song on the radio that night. Maybe not Elvis, but something from the 1950s, I'm pretty sure."

"Well, that's nice, Justin," Sharese laughed. "Being from Memphis, I'm all for the King, but I don't really think the fact that you were listening to one of his songs that night is going to sway the jury one way or the other."

Justin looked sorely disappointed, and Sharese offered an apology. "Really, Justin, it's great that you remembered that much. Maybe you'll think of something else, too, something that might be a bit more helpful to your case." She patted his arm lightly.

"Did you ever go see his house, Miss Jackson – Elvis Presley's house there in Memphis?" Justin asked.

Sharese shook her head. "No, I'm afraid not."

"Humph. That's a shame. I bet it's something to see."

Kyle and Trooper Thompson strode into the courtroom, giving Sharese an excuse to avoid explaining to Justin that people from Memphis don't hold the same fascination with Graceland as the rest of the world. *I can't believe I'm actually glad to see Starsky and Hutch this morning.*

The two men had been talking as they walked up the center aisle of the courtroom but stopped abruptly when they got within earshot of Sharese.

"Good morning," she said. *Don't mind little ole me.*

Marcus gave her a blank nod, and Kyle politely said, "Morning." They then went to their seats and continued talking lowly.

It was enough to make Sharese nervous, wondering what tricks they had up their sleeves for the day.

***

Sara also had an early morning, going for a long walk at sunrise. She had even stopped by to check on Andrew, finding him sitting on an old deacons' bench on the front porch of the parish house reading his Bible and praying. He had seemed both surprised and a bit embarrassed to have been caught publicly in what he had apparently intended to be a private time of worship.

"I'm in the habit of doing Bible study on the balcony at my apartment. There's no balcony here, so this was the next best thing."

"I wanted to make sure you were finding everything in the house and at the church. Have a good day," Sara had said hurriedly, even more uncomfortable than Andrew at her untimely interruption.

She didn't know what to make of Andrew. At Grams' house on Monday, he had been all jokes and revelry, but this was clearly a glimpse into his more serious side. An only child herself, Sara was fascinated by the similarities and differences between siblings. Physically, Andrew looked somewhat like Daniel – slightly shorter and with lighter hair, but with the same azure eyes – but she was only starting to appreciate how much the two brothers were alike on the inside. They had the same studied quietness, the same reverence, and the same seriousness when the topic of ministry came up. Both had followed their father's footsteps into the ministry, and both had considered it an obvious and natural choice. *If Daniel and I have sons, I wonder if they, too, will become ministers.*

The sudden realization that she was about to become not only a minister's wife but also a minister's daughter-in-law, a future minister's sister-in-law, and a not-yet-conceived possible minister's mother made Sara stop in her tracks. *I don't know if I can do this. How will I ever be worthy of Daniel's love?*

Sara wasn't sure if it was the exercise, the heat, or her runaway thoughts, but she had to work very hard to keep from hyperventilating as she made herself walk the rest of the way home and prepare herself for another day in court. *Please give me strength, Lord. Help me make it through this week.*

***

"Did you get a good look at her?" Kyle asked Marcus, as the two leaned toward each other from their respective chairs.

"Yeah. She's all right I guess. Not that it matters," Marcus replied.

"Well, maybe not right now, but you could ask her out when this case is over," Kyle urged. "Not many women with looks like that *and* brains around here."

"I know that's right," Marcus laughed, keeping his voice inaudible to Sharese. "She'd probably just say 'no' anyway. That's always my luck."

"Never hurts to try, my man. Never hurts to try," Kyle said. "I hear she's from Memphis, a West Tennessee gal. Be nice to have a home girl, huh?"

"I'm from Brownsville, man. That's a long way from Memphis." Marcus was insulted.

"Not from this side of the Tennessee River, it's not," Kyle said. "You know how it is. Around here, everything on the other side of Nashville is pretty much the same: Memphis, Brownsville, Jackson... whatever else is over there," Kyle said, trailing off.

"Yeah, I know what you mean. I used to think everything on *this* side of the state was the same: Knoxville, Chattanooga... Never even knew there was such a place as Maple Springs, Tennessee. It's not all that different from Brownsville in some ways, though – nice enough little town. Of course, Tina Turner's not from here," he laughed.

"Can't have everything, I guess." As the jurors filed in and Sara took her place among them, Kyle repeated his last sentence under his breath. *Nope, you can't have everything.*

CHAPTER 11

"Where are we, folks?" Judge Oaks asked.

"We left off with the State tendering Ms. Sharon White to the defense, Your Honor," Kyle said smoothly.

"Is the defense ready?" Judge Oaks looked down at his desk and scribbled something on his notepad.

"Ready, Your Honor," Sharese answered, even though the judge made no eye contact with her. *Don't tax yourself too much there, Judge. Wouldn't want you to get a neck strain from acknowledging that my client and I actually exist.*

"Proceed." The judge was still looking at his notes.

Sharese let out a small sigh but began her cross-examination. "Ms. White, do you specifically recall analyzing the blood of my client, Mr. Justin Hargis?"

"No, of course not. I've done thousands of these tests over the years. I don't remember them individually." Ms. White gave a little smirk to the jury as she finished.

"Yesterday, you gave us a lengthy description of the testing procedure used by your office. Is that procedure one hundred percent accurate?" Sharese asked.

"It's as close as we can get it!" Ms. White said, taking offense and giving her glasses an angry shove back up to their proper place on her wide nose.

"But," Sharese said and then looked at the jury knowingly, "there is no way that the test can be one hundred percent accurate, is there?"

"Not one hundred percent, no," the witness said begrudgingly.

"Occasionally, errors are made, aren't they?"

"I don't make mistakes." Ms. White gave Sharese a dirty look.

"Ever?" Sharese inquired pointedly.

"Not that I'm aware of," the witness replied.

"But isn't it possible that even you," Sharese said with a tilt of her head towards Ms. White on the witness stand, "might occasionally be wrong about something?"

"Possible. Not likely." Ms. White drew in an annoyed little breath.

"So, it is possible that you could have made a mistake in the analysis of Justin Hargis's blood, although you wouldn't be able to say for sure because you've done so many of these tests over the years that they all just run together in your mind?" Sharese asked with a satisfied look. She knew that she had discredited the witness's testimony as much as she possibly could under the circumstances. *It isn't much, but "reasonable doubt" is sometimes cumulative.*

Ms. White just shook her head, unable to put her highly agitated thoughts into words. When she finally spoke, she said, "You twisted what I said." With that, she took off her unruly glasses and rubbed her nose.

Realizing that she had the witness in exactly the maximum state of annoyance, Sharese ignored the witness's answer but added one last question. "Oh, and by the way, Ms. White, 0.07 percent blood alcohol content is within the legal limits in Tennessee, correct?"

"Well, yes it is, but—"

Sharese quickly cut her off. "You've answered the question. Thank you. That's all, Your Honor." Sharese said the last sentence without looking at the judge, just spoke the words directly to her shoes. *Two can play that game.*

"Any redirect, General?" the judge asked.

Sharese looked across the aisle at Kyle as he leaned his head back and scratched his neck. He then rubbed his face and contorted it slightly. "No. The State has no redirect."

"The witness is excused," Judge Oaks said. "Let's take a break."

***

When Sara made her way into the jury room, Fredonia Miller, the older juror with whom she'd made acquaintance during lunch the day before, gave her a broad smile. "I hope you said 'Hello' to Viola for me, child!"

Suddenly realizing that she had not given the matter another minute's thought, Sara froze for a few seconds. "Actually, Mrs. Miller, I forgot to tell her. I stopped by to check on her after court yesterday, but I didn't think about it." Improvising quickly, Sara said, "I guess I was just too busy eating Grams' fried chicken to remember much." Both women laughed easily then, and Mrs. Miller seemed to take no offense.

"Well, you can just tell her the next time that you see her," Mrs. Miller said, "If you don't get too busy eating Viola's biscuits. They're mighty good, too!"

"Yes, ma'am, that they are." Sara was ready to move on to a new topic of conversation. She just smiled politely, hoping Mrs. Miller would think of something else to talk about.

"What do you think of these lawyers? That young lady seemed to be on a roll this morning, don't you think? Did you notice that state trooper eyeing her? It was like he didn't know whether to jump up and kiss her or go running out the back door! Whoo-whee! It was about to get hot in there!" Mrs. Miller let out a huge laugh at her own joke.

Sara smiled and made herself chuckle. "I guess I'm scared of Judge Oaks. I've tried not to think about the lawyers, just listen to evidence." *Yeah, right, who do you think you're kidding?*

"Well, good for you, honey. Some of these women in here can't seem to keep their eyes off that prosecutor. He sure is a sight for sore eyes."

Feeling herself start to blush at the mention of Kyle, Sara quickly excused herself to the restroom. She splashed some cold water on her face and then reapplied her lipstick. *And why exactly are you doing that? It's not as if it's going to matter to him. He's married. He was married, he is married, and he's even a father.* Sara felt sick to her stomach.

I hope his wife and kids don't ever have to know about what happened between us that summer. Just because I was stupid enough to fall in love with a married man doesn't mean his family should have to suffer.

Sara blotted her lipstick, dried her face, and tried to pull herself back together before going back into the courtroom.

***

As the jury was called back into the courtroom, Sara made an effort to notice the supposed chemistry between Trooper Thompson and Sharese. It wasn't that Sara particularly cared whether the young defense attorney and the handsome state trooper had eyes for each other; it was just something to think about other than Kyle. *Anything for a distraction. If I can just get through the rest of the trial and – God willing – be released before the deliberation, everything will be okay. Daniel will be home in a few days, and this will all just be a distant memory.*

Sara focused on Sharese. Sara hadn't noticed anything between her and the trooper, and she suspected that Mrs. Miller was just trying to entertain herself with her talk of a courtroom romance – something to take the place on *The Young and the Restless*, perhaps.

Still, both Sharese and the trooper were young and attractive. Maybe Mrs. Miller's suspicions might come to fruition after all. Sara thought she saw the trooper steal a glance towards the defense table. Sharese seemed oblivious, but then she seemed to lean forward slightly so that she could look across Kyle at the trooper.

From the jury box, Sara could see that neither wore a wedding ring. *In their case, I hope that actually means what it's supposed to mean. There are enough secrets in this courtroom already.*

CHAPTER 12

"Call your next witness, General," Judge Oaks said.

"The State calls Larry Turner to the stand, Your Honor," Kyle said.

The bailiff opened the door at the back of the courtroom, and a heavyset, middle-aged man walked up the aisle and took his place on the witness stand. He was wearing blue jeans with stains on the knees, a plaid cotton shirt that snapped up the front, and a large white belt buckle that said "COWBOYS" in royal blue. His reddish hair was thinning, and what was left of it was slicked back on the sides. There was a deep scar across his left cheek.

"Tell us your name, please," Kyle said to the man.

"Larry Alvin Turner."

"Where are you from, Mr. Turner?"

"Calvert, Texas."

"And what part of Texas is that, Mr. Turner?"

"Twix Dallas and Houston," Mr. Turner replied in an accent that would have told the world that he was from East Texas even if his words had not.

"How old are you, sir?"

"Forty-three."

"What do you do for a living, sir?"

"Long-haul truck driver."

"What type of truck do you drive?"

"A Freightliner FLD120."

"Do you have a regular route?" Kyle asked.

"Nope."

Kyle waited for a further explanation, but Mr. Turner just bowed his head and squirmed nervously in the witness chair. *What happened to that mile-a-minute talker when we spoke about this case on the phone?* Not wanting to break his stride, Kyle continued. "Have you ever had an occasion to drive through Maple Springs, Tennessee, in your profession as a trucker?"

"Once."

"When was that, sir?"

"'Bout three years ago, I reckon."

"Were you delivering a load here?"

"Nope."

"Why were you here?"

"Dropped off a load over towards Knoxville and was dead-headin' back home." Mr. Turner averted his eyes and shifted uncomfortably in his seat.

Seeing the confused looks on the jurors' faces, Kyle felt the need to delve deeper into the Texas trucker's reason for being in the neighborhood. "What is 'dead-heading,' sir?"

"No load. No freight."

Kyle nodded. "Okay, so you'd dropped off your load and were pulling an empty trailer back to Texas, is that right?"

"Yep."

On the phone, Mr. Turner had gone into a lengthy explanation of the practice of dead-heading, including how it sometimes meant leaving the trailer behind and how annoying it was to a trucker because it meant he made no money for the return trip. *Guess he's not feeling so chatty today.*

There was really no reason to continue questioning the suddenly sullen trucker about the specifics of his occupation, seeing as how it was not relevant to the case, so Kyle moved on to the more important question of what a Texas truck driver with no freight was doing in the small town of Maple Springs, Tennessee.

"Maple Springs is a little off the beaten path, sir." Several members of the jury laughed. "Was there a particular reason that you chose to come through our town or were you just taking a short-cut?"

Mr. Turner gave Kyle a piercing look and pinched up his mouth. After a minute, he let out a heavy breath and said, "Okay, I was lost, alright? Got me one them GPS thangs and hadn't figured it out yet. Musta hit the 'scenic route' button on it or something." With that, he let out another sigh and started tapping his fingers on the arm of the witness chair.

Kyle was confused. *GPS? I don't remember anything about that.* Mr. Turner was very talkative and friendly when he was discussing the case over his cell phone from the confines of his truck. He'd easily told Kyle the whole story and then some. Sensing a need to move ahead before angering the witness further, Kyle asked, "Do you remember the date that you were here in Maple Springs?"

"Sometime in July, 'bout three years back."

"Does July 20th sound about right?"

"Guess so."

"What do you remember about that day?"

Mr. Turner squinted his eyes tight and then rolled his eyes directly upward. "Hmm. It was real hot."

Kyle, who was growing increasingly agitated with his cat-got-your-tongue witness, struggled not to give a flip reply. *Tennessee hot in July. Well, duh.* "It was a hot day. Do you remember about what time you came through town?"

"Not exactly."

Looking at the accident report, Kyle said, "Does 10:30 p.m. sound about right?"

"Nope. Got here 'fore dark. Eat dinner at some little roadside place."

This was the first that Kyle had heard about this. "Roadside place? In Maple Springs?"

"Out on the highway."

Kyle struggled to think of a roadside restaurant anywhere near Maple Springs but could not think of any such establishment either now or three years earlier.

"Do you remember the name of it?"

"Uh. Um." Mr. Turner cleared his throat. "Cotton something?"

Cotton's wasn't a restaurant. It was roadhouse, and a sleazy one to boot. Everyone in town knew that, including the jury. Kyle knew that he had to think quick before his witness lost all credibility. Kyle vaguely remembered that he had seen eighteen-wheelers parked behind Cotton's in the past, although he himself had never actually been in the place. It wasn't exactly the kind of establishment where a man with political ambition would want to be seen.

Maybe they serve food there, too? "Did you say you had dinner there?" Kyle asked. *Please say 'yes.'*

"Yep. Burger and onion rings. Greasy."

Kyle thought it best not to ask Mr. Turner what he had washed his greasy onion rings down with. "What time did you leave the restaurant?" Kyle stressed the last word just a bit in case there was anyone in the courtroom who didn't know the real nature of Cotton's.

"Don't remember. It was dark, though."

"Which direction were you headed when you left?"

"Don't remember."

You remember what you ate for dinner three years ago but not which direction you were headed? "Were you headed toward the river?"

Mr. Turner looked out the window and thought for a moment before answering. "Don't know exactly. Just trying to get back to a main road and get headed home before daylight."

"All right, Mr. Turner. Let's just get to the reason that you're here in court today. What happened after you got back out on the road?"

"I got a few miles under me, and then I come up on a wreck."

"What did you do?"

"I called 911 on my cell phone."

"Do you remember what type of vehicle was involved in the accident?"

"Yeah. It was a Bronco or Blazer. Something like that."

"Did you get out of your truck and talk to anyone at the scene of the accident?"

"I got out, but I didn't talk to nobody. The boy was out cold. The Mexican girl was dead."

"You're talking about Maria Flores?"

"Yep."

"Do you see the driver of the Blazer here in the courtroom?"

"Him," Mr. Turner said, pointing at the defendant. "It was that little punk over there."

"Motion to strike, Your Honor," Sharese said. "There's no reason for Mr. Turner to characterize Mr. Hargis in such a derogatory manner."

"Sustained," Judge Oaks grumbled.

"Let the record reflect that the witness has identified the defendant, Justin Hargis, as the driver of the Chevrolet Blazer on the night in question," Kyle said. "So, Mr. Turner, how long was it before the highway patrol got there?"

"Not too long. Maybe 15 or 20 minutes?" Mr. Turner said, turning his answer into more of a question.

"Did you talk to the trooper?"

"Yeah. Told him that boy had passed me a mile or two back and then I'd come up on the wreck."

"Are you sure it was the same driver?"

"Yeah."

"How can you be sure?"

"Same color car, same rebel flag in the back window. Wouldn't but the one boy in the car, so it had to be the same driver. It hadn't been but a minute since he'd passed me."

"How fast were you going when the defendant passed you?"

"Posted speed limit."

"Which is?"

"Don't remember."

"What's the road like through there?"

"I don't remember that either."

"Let me rephrase that question. Can you describe the road near the scene of the accident, whether it was curvy or straight, wide or narrow, that kind of thing?"

Sharese stood up with an objection. "The defense objects, Your Honor. Asked and answered."

The judge let out yet another annoyed sigh. "Overruled."

The witness glanced down at his watch but didn't answer the question until the judge instructed him to do so.

"I just can't remember much 'bout that road. Been awhile back, you know," Mr. Turner finally said, crossing his arms.

"Okay." *Well, let's just cut to the chase then.* "Mr. Turner, can you tell me the approximate speed that the defendant was traveling when he passed you?"

"Objection, Your Honor. The witness has not been qualified as an expert on determining vehicle speed," Sharese said.

Before the judge could respond to Sharese's objection, Mr. Turner said, "Well, the little punk left me in the dust!" With that, Mr. Turner let out a big laugh.

No one else laughed, though, and Sharese was quick to her feet. "The defense moves to strike Mr. Turner's last statement, Your Honor."

"Approach." Judge Oaks motioned the attorneys to come up to the bench and covered the microphone with his hand.

"As long as we're up here, Your Honor, can I please get a ruling on my objection?" Sharese said. "It seemed to have slipped the court's mind just now."

Kyle winced, knowing what was coming. Judge Oaks didn't like to be cornered, especially by an attorney who was young enough to be his granddaughter.

"Ms. Jackson, both your objection and your motion to strike are overruled," the judge hissed. "In the court's opinion, a lay witness is qualified to testify to his own speed and to the fact that the defendant 'left him in the dust,' whatever that means."

"Thank you, Your Honor," Kyle said, unsure of what else to say when Judge Oaks looked at him from across the bench after overruling Sharese's objection.

"We're going to break for lunch here in a minute. General, it looks like you'll be finished with this witness in another hour or two. How long will your cross take, Ms. Jackson? Any chance we can send this case to the jury today?" Judge Oaks asked.

Sharese was obviously shocked at the judge's impatience. She and Kyle had made it very clear to the court that the case was likely to take a full week to try. "No, Your Honor, I don't think so. I'm sure that the defense's cross-examination of Mr. Turner will be quite lengthy, and then I believe that the State has a couple more witnesses after Mr. Turner. Also, Your Honor, my client has indicated that he wishes to testify on his own behalf."

"He what?" the judge asked, looking directly at Sharese with a look of both contempt and disbelief. "Didn't you advise him against that, Counsel?"

"I did, Your Honor, but he has a right to testify if he insists. I'll go on the record against it, but he's pretty set on telling his side of things," Sharese said.

Kyle, who was thinking to himself that Mr. Turner's testimony had done very little to advance the State's case, knew

103

that he had to think of something quick. He had a vague recollection of something from his evidence class the first year of law school. Something very unusual, but it was worth a shot. "Actually, Judge, I don't think we'll wrap it up today either. I'd like to make a motion for a view in this case. The jury needs to be taken out to the accident scene so that they can see for themselves where this happened."

"A view? And you're just now making this motion, Counsel? You know my local rules require evidentiary motions to be filed in advance of trial if at all possible." Judge Oaks was clearly growing more annoyed by the second and leaning further across the bench. "You'd better have a good argument, General."

Kyle wasn't too sure how good his argument was, but he began anyway, "Well, Your Honor, we have testimony that the defendant was intoxicated and was speeding. Mr. Turner apparently can't remember enough about the accident scene to explain how narrow and curvy that road is out towards the river. For the State to meet its burden of proof of guilt beyond a reasonable doubt, the jury needs to see the scene so that they can determine whether that combination amounted to 'conduct creating a substantial risk of death or serious bodily injury to a person' under Tennessee Code Annotated § 39-13-213 (a)(1)."

"Can't you get that in through this witness?" the judge asked.

"Based on my prior communications with Mr. Turner, I believed that he could give the jury an adequate description of the road, but he seems to be having a temporary memory gap."

"So you want to use a view to refresh his recollection, is that what you're saying?" the judge asked.

"Something like that, Your Honor," Kyle replied. *I'm glad one of us knows what I'm talking about.*

"And what do you say to that, Ms. Jackson?" Judge Oaks looked at Sharese expectantly.

"The defense will need a few hours to research this matter and prepare a response, Your Honor."

The Honorable Henry Oaks could not have looked more perturbed if someone had run over his favorite hunting dog and toilet-papered his front yard all in the same night. He was just barely able to contain himself and only made the effort for the jury's benefit.

"General," the judge growled, "we're going to give the jury a two-hour break for lunch today, but I want you two back here thirty minutes early to argue the State's motion. You'd better make it good." The judge glared at Kyle.

"But, Judge, that doesn't give the defense enough time to —" Sharese started to say, but the judge was already dismissing the jury.

"We're going to take a two-hour break here, folks. Mr. Turner, you can step down from the witness stand, but you'll need to be back here when we resume. We'll give the jury some time to eat lunch, check in with your employers and babysitters and whatnot while the Court takes care of a little business. See you back in a couple of hours," the judge said as he smiled at the jury.

As soon as they were out of sight, he scowled at Kyle and Sharese and walked out of the courtroom so fast that his robe went flying out behind him and got caught in the door. Not one soul left in the courtroom dared to laugh as he opened the door to free the robe and then slammed it shut it so hard that the clock fell off the wall.

CHAPTER 13

"What was that all about, Ms. Jackson?" Justin asked Sharese.

"The State just asked for a view," Sharese answered, looking a bit confused herself.

"What does that mean?" Justin asked. "The judge looked real mad."

"The State's attorney wants the jury to be taken out to the scene of the accident so they can see what the road looks like. The judge was hoping to get this case wrapped up today, but that's not going to happen."

"What do we do now?"

"I need to get back to the office and do some research. This kind of motion doesn't come up very often, and I need to be prepared to argue against it."

"Okay. I'll see you later then," Justin said, as the deputy came to escort him back into the holding area.

Sharese was busy picking up her things when Kyle and Marcus stopped by her desk on their way out of the courtroom.

"Hey, I didn't mean to blindside you with that motion," Kyle said. "I don't know what happened to that trucker since I talked to him on the phone a few days ago. It was like somebody zipped his lips shut."

Sharese looked up from her briefcase, surprised that Kyle and the trooper were actually talking to her. "I can't say as I was expecting a motion for a view this early in my career."

"It's my first one, too. They don't come up much," Kyle said. "My man Marcus here thinks I'm nuts."

Marcus smiled politely and shook his head. "Never know what you lawyers are going to come up with."

Sharese felt her face flush slightly as she noticed that the trooper was even more handsome when he was smiling. "I guess not." She couldn't think of anything witty to say, and the impromptu conversation stalled.

"Okay, then, I just thought I'd offer an apology for making you miss your lunch today," Kyle said.

"It's okay. You're just doing what you have to do." Sharese offered a smile as she snapped her briefcase shut. The three walked to the elevator together.

"Guess we can share a ride," Kyle said.

"I'm taking the stairs. Thanks anyway," Sharese said.

"Guess we're feeling lazy today. See you in a couple of hours then."

***

Kyle and Marcus waited for the elevator while the stairwell door closed behind Sharese. As soon as Sharese was out of sight, Kyle punched Marcus lightly on the arm. "What's wrong with you, man? Couldn't you at least say a few words to the woman? I gave you the perfect opening, and you totally missed the shot!"

Marcus just shook his head, saying nothing.

"Am I the only guy in the courthouse that has the ability to make a complete sentence today?" Kyle said to the elevator door. "Really, Marcus. I've never seen you at a loss for words."

"I spoke to the woman," Marcus said. "What else do you want from me?"

"Whatever," Kyle said as the doors opened. "On another note, now that I've made this crazy motion, I guess I'd better go hit the books. Need to at least sound like I know what I'm talking about."

"Yeah, good luck with that," Marcus said as the two parted ways on the courthouse steps, and they both laughed.

***

Sara sat in Eddie's Sandwich Shop surrounded by the other jurors but feeling very alone. Ever since she had heard Kyle ask the truck driver about his whereabouts on the night that Justin struck Maria, her head had been spinning with the realization that the accident occurred during the same summer that she had fallen in love with Kyle.

How did I not realize that before now? Surely Trooper Thompson testified about the date; how did I miss it?

As she sat quietly at the lunch table listening to the other jurors make idle chitchat, she realized that she was feeling somewhat lightheaded and was breathing very rapidly. Knowing she needed to calm herself down before reaching full panic mode, she began to take slow, deep breaths. She also attempted to rationalize her rising anxiety.

It was easier to see Kyle in the courtroom this morning than it was yesterday. The shock of seeing him again after all this time is finally wearing off. It must just be the thing about Maria's death happening that same summer that has gotten me so upset. One thing has nothing to do with the other, so I just need to calm down.

Even when she disassociated her feeling about Kyle from the facts of Justin's criminal trial, Sara still couldn't shake the uneasy feeling that had come over her during the truck driver's testimony. *There was just something odd about all that.*

She wondered whether any of the other jurors had noticed the increasingly uncomfortable vibe that had developed between Kyle and the witness, but she was determined to keep her thoughts to herself. For at least the hundredth time since the trial began, she

109

hoped that she would be excused and not have to participate in the deliberation at the end of the trial.

Sara thought about what Daniel had said about God putting her on the jury for a reason. She mused that her placement as an alternate would have had even Daniel scratching his head and wondering what His plan was. *But if Daniel knew the whole story with Kyle, he might not be wondering. Maybe I'm here to deal with MY past, not Justin Hargis's.*

Shortly, the bailiff excused himself to go to the restroom, and it became clear that Sara was not alone in her impression that something strange had transpired in the courtroom between Kyle and Larry Turner. Fredonia asked to anyone who was willing to listen, "Just what in the world was going on in there with that trucker? That handsome young prosecutor's got a mess on his hands, don't y'all think?"

Sara thought it best to speak up before the entire jury went off on a forbidden tangent. She was also worried about losing control of the emotions over which she had only the barest of control since the trial had began. "Oh, let's try not to get ourselves in trouble by talking about things we aren't supposed to talk about yet." *Or, in my case, hopefully ever.*

"But, it's just that—" Fredonia started, but one of the male jurors followed Sara's lead and changed the subject.

"Hey, how 'bout them Vols? I don't know if the Big Orange has much hope this year. Of course, that new tight end from Oak Ridge could make some difference. I hear he was something to see in high school."

Sara smiled a relieved smile at the man, glad that the conversation had been steered to a subject that was sure to keep the jurors busy for an hour or two. "I don't want to be a naysayer, but I'm thinking Tennessee's a dark horse this year," she replied. "They have some coaching problems that no tight end can fix, even if he was All State."

College football talk, while somewhat mindless to Sara, was at least safe territory. As the other jurors chimed in their opinions on the Vols' chance of a Southeastern Conference victory given the difficulties of the previous season, Sara did her best to ignore the wounded look on Fredonia's face. Instead, she concentrated hard on the menu, pretending that it somehow mattered whether she ordered a tuna melt or pimento cheese.

When the waitress came back, Sara ordered a pimento cheese sandwich and water. *It won't be as good as Grams', but whose is?*

Sara then noticed that a couple of the other jurors were looking intently at the wall behind her. When she turned her head, she saw a map of Central America on a television screen. The sound on the television was muted, and she couldn't tell what the news story was about. Some sort of civil unrest, apparently. She thought of Daniel and said a quick prayer for his safety. *Lord, just let this trial end, and bring Daniel home safely so we can get on with our lives.*

After an agonizing hour and a half of random small talk about football, gas prices, and the general plight of small town America, Sara was greatly relieved when the bailiff finally signaled that it was time for the jury to head back to the courthouse. She had long since eaten what she could stomach of her sandwich (not much, given its lack of flavor and her rising level of anxiety concerning all things Daniel and many things Kyle). She had also drank at least three glasses of off-tasting tap water and come to the conclusion that she could fake her way into being a Big Orange fan even though she had attended Big Ten schools for both college and graduate schools.

As the jury walked back to the courthouse in the blistering summer sun, Sara couldn't help but remember a sermon that Daniel had preached recently on the issue of temptation. He had said that the enemy has a way of knowing a Christian's weaknesses and that he concentrates his efforts on areas of vulnerability. Sara knew that the weakness of any juror had to be the desire to talk with others about the case that was being tried. The judge's instructions against doing so were the legal equivalent of God telling Eve to leave the apple alone.

Sara had resisted the temptation to talk about the trial thus far, but she didn't dare pat herself on the back for her efforts. She knew that she wanted to talk about the case just as much as the others did. It was just that, in her mind, the trial involved not only the guilt or innocence of Justin Hargis, but also her own culpability in events that took place that very same July. It was only out of an intense sense of self-preservation that she resisted the urge to discuss the trial or even think about it too much, fearing the floodgate of emotions that were becoming increasingly interwoven with the outcome.

***

As the jurors passed another thirty minutes with small talk and turns in the small restroom in the jury room, Kyle and Sharese readied themselves to argue their respective positions on Kyle's motion back in the courtroom. Luckily for the attorneys, Judge Oaks returned from lunch in a much better mood.

"General, correct me if I'm wrong, but I see your motion for the jury to view the crime scene in this case as a Rule 401 issue under the Tennessee Rules of Evidence," Judge Oaks said.

Kyle answered, "Yes, Your Honor, that's correct. It's the State's position that the jury will be better able to understand the facts of this case if they are allowed to personally view the location where the defendant's vehicle struck and killed the victim, Maria Flores."

"What makes this scene different from the crime scenes in the legions of other cases on my docket?"

"Well, Judge, this is a unique case. In the first trial, everyone was operating under the presumption that Mr. Hargis's blood alcohol level met the threshold for DUI, thus triggering section (a)(2) of the vehicular homicide statute."

"Yes, I believe that was the situation," Judge Oaks agreed.

"We now know that the defendant's BAC was 0.07 percent, which is just below the statutory limit of 0.08 percent. But, and this is the crux of the issue, the State's position is that the defendant is still guilty of the crime because his excessive speed on that pig trail leading out to the river created a 'substantial risk of death or serious bodily injury' under section (a)(1) of the statute. The last witness testified that the defendant passed him going in excess of the posted speed limit. The only way for the jury to understand how reckless the defendant was in driving too fast on that road is for the jury to go out there and see Winningham Road for themselves."

"As a practical matter, how do you propose we go about arranging a view, General?"

Kyle hadn't thought that far ahead and stuttered several um-uh-er's before the bailiff spoke up. "The county has a bus to transport convicts out to the edge of town to pick up trash. It'll hold about 30 people."

"That would work." Kyle was relieved that someone other than him had thought of a solution to the transportation problem.

Judge Oaks nodded. "All right, so it is logistically possible then. Ms. Jackson, what does the defense have to say about this motion?"

Sharese, who had apparently spent every minute of the recess reviewing the applicable law, presented the judge with a stack of cases that she had printed from Lexis-Nexis. "The defense objects to the State's motion, Your Honor. While we acknowledge that there are a few cases where a view might be appropriate, we don't believe that this is such a case."

"And why is that?" the judge asked.

"Among other things, this alleged crime took place three years ago. We have no way of knowing whether the scene is the same as it was that many years back. A lot can change in that amount of time. The highway could have been repaved; the trees could have grown. All sorts of things could have changed."

Kyle interjected, "Judge, this is Maple Springs. Not much has changed around here in the last thirty years, much less the last three."

"Be that as it may, General, I'm still having some trouble with this motion."

From past experience, Kyle knew that when Judge Oaks was "having trouble" with a motion, it was a bad sign. Scrambling for something else to say, Kyle continued, "We believe that the view will serve to refresh Mr. Turner's memory and that he'll be able to verify that the scene has not changed in a meaningful way since the accident."

Sharese responded to what even a newcomer could recognize as the last grasp at straws by Kyle. "Your Honor, the State has not pointed to any statutory authority for its motion, nor has it obtained the defendant's consent for a view. In absence of one or both of those things, it would be reversible error for the court to grant the State's motion."

Judge Oaks flipped through the stack of papers that Sharese had passed up to him. "I'm going to have to read these cases and do some research of my own. I really hate to do this, but I think we're going to have to let the jury go home for the day."

Kyle groaned inwardly at the delay – he wanted the case over as bad as the judge did, but for very different reasons – but he just said, "Sounds like a good idea, Judge."

"Bailiff, let's get the jury back in here. Oh, and bring your witness back in, too, General," Judge Oaks said,

"Okay, Your Honor. I'll go get him," Kyle said.

When Kyle went out into the hallway, however, the troublesome Larry Turner was nowhere to be found. Kyle reluctantly dialed Angela on his cell phone. "Do you know where Larry Turner is? I need him back at the courthouse."

Angela replied, "No, I haven't seen him. I wouldn't even know him if I saw him. What does he look like?"

114

"Oh, that's right; I guess you've never actually seen him. He has red hair, what's left of it anyway. Kind of heavy-set – scar on his face – plaid shirt, big belt buckle. Call around to the restaurants and see if you can find him." *Just what I need, a witness that can't answer a direct question OR listen to a judge's instructions about getting back to court on time. This is the trial no one warned me about in law school.*

Kyle went back into the courtroom and steeled himself for the wrath that he knew was imminent. "Judge, Mr. Turner must have misunderstood the court's instructions. He hasn't made it back from lunch yet."

"You mean he's not out there? I told him to be back here thirty minutes ago!" Judge Oaks thundered. He took punctuality very seriously and considered tardiness as a personal offense.

"I've got my secretary looking for him, Your Honor. I'm sure we'll find him any minute." Kyle was growing more annoyed with the elusive Larry Turner by the minute.

"I'll deal with him later. I'll issue a bench warrant if I have to," the judge growled. "Get the jury back in here, Bailiff."

Once the jury was seated, the judge said, "I hate to do this to you folks, but I'm going to have to give you a little vacation this afternoon. We've had some legal matters come up that we need to settle before we go further with this case, so you all are free to go home early this afternoon. Maybe you can work in the garden or get a little fishing in," he added with a wink. "We'll see you back here at 9 a.m. sharp tomorrow morning."

After the jury was safely out of the room, the judge looked squarely at Kyle. "You'd better find that trucker and straighten him out, General. Now!"

***

The bailiff escorted Justin back to the holding room in the courthouse as soon as the judge left the bench. The next hour passed slower than molasses dripping off a wooden spoon in February.

Sharese wasn't completely sure whether she was obliged to remain in the courtroom until Kyle located his witness, but she thought it best to stay put. Besides a fear that the judge's next threat of a warrant would be for her if she dared move from her seat, she was also motivated by the entertainment value of what she perceived as a rare moment of animosity between the salty old trial judge and the enthusiastic young attorney for the State.

She pretended to look at her file, making scribbles on her legal pad and checking her cell phone for messages. *No, Grandma, I'm not calling you back until I'm sure you're over that business about me writing a letter to the parole board on behalf of my so-called "daddy."* When she couldn't stand the silence a minute longer, she stole a sideways glance at the handsome state trooper seated on the other side of Kyle. "Tough luck about your witness."

Kyle was punctuating the silence with calls to his secretary for progress updates and whispered remarks to Marcus. "Yeah. I'm not believing this. What a day, huh?"

"Yeah. Crazy," she replied. "Where do you think that guy went?"

"No clue. Just hope he gets back here before the judge decides to throw us all in jail," Kyle joked. "Bet you didn't count on this much drama your first time out, huh?"

"No, I didn't." Sharese was barely able to keep her amusement to herself. *I knew Siegfried and Roy were up to something this morning, but I didn't know they were going to make their own witness disappear.*

"Not the kind of thing they teach in law school, that's for sure," Kyle said. "At least not at UT. You went to Memphis, right?"

"Yeah. That's where I'm from."

"Thought so. You know, Marcus here is from Brownsville."

"Oh. Brownsville. I think I may have some cousins there," Sharese said.

"I've been gone for a few years now. I don't know everybody like I used to," Marcus said.

Sharese and Marcus spent the next half hour talking about various people and places in Memphis and Brownsville. There was only a vague connection between them in their pre-Maple Springs worlds, but it didn't seem to matter much. There was an easy flow in the words they exchanged, and the conversation kept rolling along despite the apparent lack of common ground.

Judge Oaks returned to the courtroom exactly one hour after he had dismissed the jury for the day. "Well, General, did you find him?"

"No, Your Honor. I've had my secretary calling everywhere we can think of, but no one has seen him."

A look of disgust and aggravation flashed across Judge Oaks' face. Then he looked out the window and raised an eyebrow, apparently realizing that there was just enough time left to get in a round of golf. "Tell you what, General, we've already sent the jury home for the day, so I'll give you til morning to find your witness. Maybe he had car trouble, or truck trouble, or whatever those big rigs have."

"Thank you, Your Honor. I'll do my best to find him and get him back here in the morning."

"In the meantime, I'm going to go ahead and overrule your motion for a view. I don't see any reason to waste another half a day of trial time when we're behind enough as it is. Court's dismissed until tomorrow at 9 a.m."

When the judge left, Sharese gathered her things. "Til tomorrow, then," she said to Kyle and Marcus.

"Yeah, til tomorrow," Kyle replied.

"When you go back to headquarters, see what you can do to track this guy down. This case is falling apart quick," Kyle told Marcus when he was sure Sharese was out of earshot.

"I'll do what I can," Marcus replied. "Any idea where to start looking?"

"No. I already had Angela call every restaurant and gas station in town, even Cotton's. Nobody's seen him."

"You think he took off?"

"Don't know of any reason that he would have, but he sure was acting different up there on the stand than he was when I talked to him on the telephone a few days ago."

"Did you do a background check on him?"

"Yeah. He's clean except a few traffic citations. Stuff you'd expect from a trucker."

"Do you know where he was staying?"

"No. I know it wasn't in Maple Springs, though. Angela already checked the bed and breakfast on Main Street and the Motel 8 on the highway."

"I'll get back to headquarters and make some calls. He couldn't have gone too far, right?"

"Yeah, I'm sure he's around here somewhere," Kyle said, trying to convince himself.

CHAPTER 14

Tired from all the sitting around at the courthouse and vaguely worried about Daniel, Sara drove straight home from the courthouse when the jury was dismissed in the early afternoon. "Hey, girl!" she said when Callie met her at the door. "Do you think we could trade places tomorrow? You go curl up in my seat in the jury box, and I'll lie around here and sleep all day?"

Callie rubbed her head against Sara's leg and purred. She was a fickle animal, capable of vacillating between craving physical attention and wanting to be left alone at a moment's notice.

Sara was grateful that Callie was in a loving mood and took the rare opportunity to pick her up. "What a big kitty you've grown into!" Sara thought about the tiny kitten that Callie had been the first time that she had seen her. *Don't go there.*

Sara tried to stop the sudden barrage of memories associated with Callie as a kitten, but it was too late. She closed her eyes and was back in her grandparents' cabin at the river three summers ago. Books, papers, and her laptop covered the small wooden dining table. There was a knock at the door and then a friendly, if unfamiliar, face on the front porch holding up a little ball of fur.

"Hi, there. Would this happen to be your kitten?"

"No, she's not mine." Sara squinted at the kitten through the late afternoon sun.

"She just showed up on my porch," the man gestured to a cabin two doors down. *"I checked with the guy next door, but she isn't his."*

"She's a cutie."

"Yeah, and hungry, too. All I had to feed her was some burnt gumbo left over from my feeble attempt at supper last night. You wouldn't happen to have any cat food, would you?"

"No, but I have some milk."

"That would be great. I'm Kyle, by the way. Kyle Copeland."

"Josie Anderson." Sara opened the door. *"Excuse the mess. I'm working on my thesis."*

Kyle looked around. *"We have the same decorator. Except my style is 'early bar exam.'"*

"It's a great place to study. It's very quiet out here by the river." Sara set a bowl of milk on the floor for the kitten and offered Kyle a soft drink.

"Thanks. It's so hot out today. I was hoping this little girl had a home, but I guess she's just a stray."

Sara scratched the kitten behind the ears. *"I think you can stop looking now. She seems to have found a home right here."*

Kyle smiled. *"She's a lucky kitten, then. What can I do to thank you?"*

"You can start by helping me name her."

"How about 'Callie,' for her pretty calico coat?"

"Perfect."

Sara had been alone for days – all of her life, in some ways – and appreciated the company of Kyle and Callie. Kyle returned the next afternoon and the next and the next. They would grab some sandwiches and head for the front porch, talking about everything and nothing until the fireflies danced in the heavy evening air.

Sara opened her eyes before her memories consumed her. She needed a change of scenery, and quick. Gently setting Callie down, she grabbed her car keys from her pocket and headed back out the door. "Sorry Callie, no offense. You know I love my kitty-girl!" Sara stroked Callie's fur gently behind the ears, "I'll bring you back a treat, I promise."

As she left her apartment, Sara wasn't sure whether to go for a walk or for a drive. The sweltering heat of a July afternoon soon made it an easy choice. As she got into her car, Sara paused long enough to adjust the radio. She needed something to occupy her mind and was happy to find one of her favorite old songs, "Put Your Head on My Shoulder," playing on the local station.

When Hank Williams started belting out "Your Cheatin' Heart," Sara switched the radio off abruptly and began to drive aimlessly around town. *If I ever meet the programmer at that station, I'm going to have a few choice words for him.* She drove past the funeral home and the feed store, the pawnshop and the parsonage. *No sign of Andrew's car.*

Sara reminded herself that it was Wednesday night and that she would need to be at the church by 6 p.m. for the weekly fellowship meal and Bible study. She checked the dashboard clock and saw that it was only 3:30 p.m. Taking a left turn onto Main Street, it occurred to Sara to keep driving until she hit the interstate and drive as far as she could before she changed her mind. She wanted to run away from Maple Springs, from the quagmire that her life had suddenly become now that she knew Kyle was living in the same town.

Sara was amazed that their paths had not crossed before now. After all, she had been in Maple Springs for over a year and Kyle had apparently moved back to town after finishing law school. *Where does he live? Where is his office? Does he go to church here in town?*

Sara knew who would know the answers to all of her questions. She picked up her cell phone. "Hey, Grams. Do you need anything from the store? I'm going run in and get Callie a treat."

"As a matter of fact, honey, I just ran out of sweet milk. Could you get me a half gallon, please?"

"Sure. I'll have it there in a few minutes."

Having talked herself out of an immediate escape by her plan to quiz her grandmother more thoroughly about Kyle, Sara made a U-turn and headed for the grocery store on the other side of town. Ten minutes later, she was standing in the checkout line holding a can of tuna for Callie in her left hand and a carton of whole milk for Grams in her right hand.

As she waited, Sara noticed a petite blond woman in front of her. Most folks around Maple Springs had a similar look about them, not surprising since they shared bloodlines, hairdressers, and general life experiences. Somehow, the striking woman in line ahead of Sara at the grocery store looked out of place.

She had shining honey blond hair and flawless skin, but it was something in the way that she carried herself that made her stand out. There was a gracefulness that Sara couldn't name but recognized as special. Even the woman's children – a baby girl and a young boy – were more beautiful than the kids that Sara was used to seeing around school and in her classroom.

Just as Sara was starting to daydream about what it would be like when she and Daniel had children some day, the beautiful baby girl started to wail. The cashier said, "Oh, sweetie, what's the matter? I'm trying to get your mama out of here as fast as I can. I've got little ones, too, so I know how much you want to get home."

"She's just teething. She's been keeping us up for a week now with all this crying. Well, me, anyway. My husband can usually sleep through it," the blond woman replied.

"How's Kyle doing?" the cashier asked. "I went to school with him, you know."

Kyle? Did she just say Kyle? Grams said he had two children – a baby and a little boy. Surely this can't be – Sara froze as she listened to the woman ahead of her.

122

"Oh, he's fine. Working hard, as usual. He's in a big trial this week. A retrial of that vehicular homicide from a few years ago." *Retrial? What does that mean?*

"I thought that boy was in prison," the cashier said.

"Yeah, he was. *Is*. He got a new trial on a technicality," Elizabeth said.

"Well, Kyle will take care of him, I'm sure," the cashier said with a smug look.

I don't need to hear this, especially not from Kyle's wife. Lord, please make them shut up and talk about something else.

Just as Sara was wishing that the floor of the Piggly Wiggly would open up and swallow her whole, the cashier noticed her waiting behind Elizabeth. "Hey, Ms. Anderson! You havin' a good summer vacation? My little Jack really enjoyed being in your kindergarten class, you know!"

Sara, who had not even realized that the cashier was the mother of one of her former students, stood open-mouthed and mortified. Elizabeth turned around. "Oh, are you a kindergarten teacher? Maybe Evan here will be in your room when he gets old enough."

Sara tried to open her mouth to speak, but only a squeak came out.

Elizabeth gave her a strange look, but turned her attention back to the cashier as she announced the total.

"He looks just like you," the cashier said. "How old is he?"

"He turned two this past January," Elizabeth said as the baby's screaming intensified. "And Chelsea here is seven months," she said above the screaming.

Sara hung her head as Elizabeth handed the cashier a check and left the store. *If that little boy turned two in January, could that mean–*

"Nice girl, that Elizabeth Copeland," the cashier interrupted. "I heard she and Kyle had some trouble a few years back, but it sounds like everything's okay now."

123

"Yes, it sure does," Sara mumbled as she grabbed her grocery bags and walked out of the store as quickly as her shaking legs would carry her.

***

After court, Sharese walked over to the jail to talk to Justin about Judge Oaks' denial of the State's motion for a view. She was surprised when the head jailor told her she would have to come back later if she wanted to talk to Justin. "How about if I just have a seat and wait?" she asked the jailor, wondering what could so pressing that a young man who had spent the last three years behind bars didn't have time to see his attorney.

"That's fine. He may be awhile though. He's talking to his mama."

"Ah," Sharese nodded her head. "Now I understand."

The jailor smiled politely and went back to the paperwork on her desk. After about twenty minutes, a thin woman with dirty-blond hair came out of the large metal door that led into the main part of the jail. Sharese knew who she was right away, even though they had never been introduced. "Mrs. Hargis, I'd like to introduce myself. I'm your son's attorney, Sharese Jackson."

The woman immediately threw her arms around Sharese and hugged her. "Bless you, honey. You don't know how much it means to us for you to be Justin's lawyer." Breaking away from the embrace to wipe her eyes, she continued, "I know you'll do all you can for him."

"Yes, ma'am. I'll do my best," Sharese managed to say before Mrs. Hargis's emotions got the best of her and she was overcome with tears.

"I done the best I could by him. It was hard after his daddy died. Well, to tell the truth, it was hard even before he died. Anyway, it just kills me to see him in here."

"I'm sure it must be very difficult for you," Sharese replied.

"I know he's done a lot of wrong, but I feel like the good Lord might give him a second chance with this new trial. You don't know how long I've prayed for this."

Sharese wasn't sure what to say. Something deep inside of her wanted Justin to walk out of the courtroom a free man, but she knew the odds weren't good. "I'll do all I can do help him. You just pray for both of us, okay?"

"I will. I guess you need to get on back there and talk to him now, don't you?"

"Yes, ma'am. Nice meeting you."

With that, Sharese nodded to the jailor that she was ready to go back and talk to Justin. When she got to the holding room, she saw that Justin was in tears. "I just met your mom," she said.

Justin wiped his eyes. "She's a good woman." He looked up at the ceiling, trying to keep the tears from coming again. "Too good to have got me for a son, that's for sure."

"Oh, I'm sure she doesn't see it that way. She loves you very much."

"You really think so?"

"Of course I do," Sharese said. Changing the subject of the natural bond between parent and child before it hit too close to home, she gave Justin a big smile. "So, that was good news back at the courthouse, huh?"

"What do you mean?" Justin asked.

"Judge Oaks denied the State's motion to take the jury out to view the scene of the accident," Sharese explained.

"I didn't really understand what was going on too much, but that does sound good."

Sharese tapped her pen on the table. "I just wonder why that truck driver didn't come came back to court this afternoon."

"Yeah, that was kind of weird. At the first trial, he like to never shut up talking trash about me, but, today, it was like the cat had his tongue."

"I've read the transcript. He certainly did seem to have a different attitude back then."

"What happens if he doesn't come back tomorrow either?"

"It means that we won't have the chance to cross-examine him."

"Oh," Justin said, with a confused look on his face.

"The State could ask for a continuance while they keep looking for him. If they opt to go forward without him, we can ask for a mistrial because we didn't get the chance to cross-examine him. The Constitution guarantees a defendant the right to confront the State's witnesses, which can't happen if they don't find him soon," Sharese continued. "That could drag this out for awhile, I'm afraid."

"I hope that don't happen. I was really hoping for some – what's the word I'm looking for?"

"Closure?" Sharese guessed, pretty sure that was the word Justin sought.

"Yeah, closure. I want to get this behind me."

"We'll just have to see what happens between now and tomorrow morning. In the meantime, I'm going to get out of here and get my mind off this case for a little while." Sharese rubbed her hands through her hair. "This has been a crazy day."

"Have enough fun for both of us." Justin winked.

"Please. I'm probably going to go over to the high school track and go for a run. Clear my head."

"I remember you saying something about running track in college."

"Yep. I still hold the school record in the 500-Meter Run."

"Wow. Smart and fast, huh? Some people get all the breaks," Justin said playfully.

"I saw a way out, and I took it," Sharese said without her usual smile. She wasn't sure why, but something about Justin's implication that anything about her life had been easy irritated her.

"Nothing wrong with that," Justin replied.

Sharese managed a pleasant nod towards Justin as they led him away. When he was gone, she felt a true smile growing on her face, knowing that – for at least an hour or two – she would be free of the burden and responsibility that had taken on the personification of Justin Hargis.

CHAPTER 15

Thirty minutes after her chance meeting with Elizabeth Copeland at the Piggly Wiggly, Sara found herself driving in circles around Maple Springs as if waiting for someone to tell her which way to go. If she turned left on Main and headed out toward the high school, would she stop seeing Kyle's face on every corner? If she turned right and headed toward Grams' house, would the rhythmic pulsing in her ears that began with Chelsea's cries begin to fade, maybe just a little?

Not sure which way to turn, Sara slowed her car to a stop in the middle of the street. The pickup truck behind her let out an annoyed honk, and the driver swerved around her, just missing an oncoming motorcycle. The screeching of the truck's brakes brought Sara back to her senses, and she pulled the car over into the nearest parking lot, hung her head, and let the tears come.

Normally, she would have been careful to avoid the curious eyes of passers-by, but she lacked the presence of mind to breathe normally, much less worry about her reputation. With the air conditioning blasting her in the face and her tears streaming with hot shame, it didn't take long before Sara was a total mess.

After awhile, it occurred to her that Grams was waiting across town for the milk that she had thrown carelessly into the floorboard as she slunk out of the store praying that she made it to the car without breaking down in the parking lot.

As if on cue, Sara's cell phone rang, and Grams' number showed prominently as the incoming caller. Knowing that she would probably sound quite strange from all the crying, Sara ignored the call long enough to fish through the glove box for some tissues. She wiped her face, checked herself in the rearview mirror, and gave her nose a good blow. With as much normalcy as she could muster under the circumstances, she picked up the phone. "Hi, Grams, I'm running a little late, but I'll be there in a minute."

From the tone of Gram's voice, Sara knew immediately that something was wrong. "Have you talked to anybody yet, honey?" Grams asked carefully.

"No. What's wrong?" Sara asked, hoping with all of her might that Elizabeth had not somehow recognized the guilt on her face and confronted Kyle when she got home. Normally, Sara would have been smart enough to realize that, even if that had been the case, there was no way that her Grams could have known about it so soon, even in Maple Springs.

"I don't want to worry you, but there's been, um..." Gram trailed off before finishing.

Panic set in, and Sara quickly demanded, "There's been what, Grams?"

"There's been an earthquake in Honduras," Grams said.

"An earthquake? In Honduras? Are you sure?" Sara asked.

"Yes, honey. It's all over the news."

"Please, God, let Daniel be okay," Sara prayed aloud, as a completely new level of terror struck her.

Sara's cell phone gave a quick beep. "Hang on, Grams. I've got another call." Sara saw Andrew's number on the screen and immediately shifted the call over to him.

"Sara, have you seen the news? There's been an earthquake in Honduras."

"Grams just called me a minute ago. Have you heard anything from Daniel?"

"No. I'm sure the phone lines are down though," Andrew said. Sara could hear a television playing on the other end of the phone. "The news reports are just coming in. Quite a bit of damage, especially in the Tegucigalpa area."

"Do you think Daniel is still there in the city? How long does it take to get up into the mountains where he was going?" she asked as a fresh wave of fear swept over her.

"I don't know, but let's just pray that he's okay," Andrew said. "Why don't you pick up Miss Viola and come to church? I think we'll have a prayer meeting tonight instead of the usual services."

"That's a good idea. We need to pray," Sara said. "I'll be there as soon as I can." Forgetting about Grams on the other line, Sara clicked the phone shut, put the car into drive, and pulled out of the parking lot so quickly that she left tire marks on the pavement in front of the Farmers' Co-op.

A few minutes later, Sara and Grams met Andrew in front of the church. Several of the female church members walked quickly towards them, hugging them and telling Sara that they were praying for Daniel's safety. Noticing Sara's tear-streaked face, the women exchanged sympathetic looks.

As they proceeded into the sanctuary, Sara caught a glimpse of herself in the mirror hanging in the vestibule. It dawned on her that she was still a horrific mess from her breakdown after the incident with Elizabeth at the grocery store. She was humiliated to think that the women had assumed she had been crying out of concern for Daniel.

"I need to use the restroom." Sara lowered her head and ducked into the ladies' room at the back of the church. Grams and the other women nodded their understanding, wiping their own eyes and exchanging muffled sniffs.

Sara proceeded slowly into the restroom, checking that she was alone. She went into the back stall and hit her knees, weeping uncontrollably and fearing that she was going to be sick to her stomach. Though her sobs were racking, her prayers were quiet.

Father God, you are the only one that I can turn to. You are the only one who can understand and who can forgive me for my sins. So many times, I have prayed to you for your forgiveness for what happened with Kyle. I've confessed that I was in love with a married man, but in my heart, I've excused my own behavior and put the blame on him.

Knowing that there was no stopping now, Sara continued.

Father, the truth is that I knew it was wrong to be with Kyle. Your Holy Spirit was convicting me, telling me not to fall in love with him. I ignored all the signs and gave in to the temptation. The worst part was that I went right on loving him after he left me and went back to his wife.

With that, Sara hung her head so low that it almost touched the floor.

I know now why he left me. It was that little boy. Evan. Kyle's wife was pregnant; that's why he went back to her. He did the right thing. I didn't understand it at the time, but now I do.

After a few minutes, Sara's breathing returned to normal. Silent tears continued to stream down her face as a feeling of peace came over her. Whether it was the closure that came from finally understanding and acknowledging why Kyle had left her or the sense that she had finally received full forgiveness for her sin, Sara could not be sure. She only recognized a calmness that she had not felt since before the affair. Before standing up, she prayed one last prayer, this one for Daniel.

Please, Father, bring him home safely. I promise that I will never keep a secret from him again. Just bring him home to me. Amen.

Sara washed her face in the bathroom sink and patted it dry with a coarse paper towel from the dispenser. The abrasive paper felt scratchy against her blotchy and swollen cheeks, but she didn't mind the pain. Blowing her nose one last time, she headed out of the bathroom, leaving the final remnants of her love for Kyle behind her and moving toward her future with Daniel, whatever that future had in store.

***

As she walked out of the jail after meeting with Justin, Sharese felt the weight of the world on her small shoulders. She couldn't even remember the last time that she had taken a few hours off from work. Since being assigned to Justin's case, she had been at her desk well past the time that the secretaries and receptionist turned off the office lights and went home to their families.

She had told Justin that she was going to go for a run, but once she was outside she started having second thoughts. She worried that her time might be better spent looking through Justin's file or doing additional research on the State's motion for a view in case Judge Oaks decided to reverse himself the next day. *You never know what the good ole boy network might cook up. It would be about like the Green Hornet and Kato to talk Judge Roy Bean into changing his mind.*

As she contemplated her options, the voice of one of her law school professors began to rumble through her head. *"When it all gets to be too much, and it will, step back and let it all go for a couple of hours. You need to clear your head from time to time so that you can properly focus on your work."* The professor had spoken those words during orientation, and she had found it to be an excellent bit of advice during exams.

Just as in her law school days, she knew exactly what she needed to do to break away from the worry and stress that was threatening to suffocate her. She needed to run – to feel her heart pounding in rhythm with her feet, to feel the wind rushing in her face, and to feel the sweat tingling down her back.

She didn't even take time to go by her office and check messages. She had just spoken to the only person to whom she had any inkling to speak with at the moment anyway, so she went directly to her car and drove home. Minutes later, she emerged in a tank top, shorts, and running shoes.

In the sweltering July heat, she broke a sweat before she even got to the end of the first block. She quickly sprinted the short distance to the track at Maple Springs High School. As she ran, she thought about the days' events, relishing the fact that she had won the motion hearing. *A view? Seriously? What was he thinking, anyway?*

Outside the pressure cooker of the courtroom, Sharese began to see Kyle's motion for what it really was: a sign of desperation. Her confidence began to grow as flashes of the trial kept popping randomly into her mind – things like Kyle's confused look when the judge told him he was out of challenges during *voir dire*, his bumbling opening statement, the increasing hostility of Larry Turner towards Kyle during what Kyle had surely counted on to be a very damaging bit of testimony against Justin.

He's scared that he's going to lose this case!

The thought hit Sharese so hard that she stopped running and stood for a moment catching her breath. Seeing a water fountain and a bench in the distance, she decided to take a break. Not seeing anyone else around, Sharese lay down on her back and stared up at the vibrant blue sky. *Okay, he's probably right to be scared now with his missing witness and all, but what was the deal during voir dire and opening statements?*

Thinking back on that first day of trial, Sharese realized that she had been so weak in the knees that she hadn't fully appreciated how nervous Kyle seemed to be as well. But, he had considerably more experience than she did, and he had to have thought the case was a sure win. Or did he? *Is there something that he knows that I don't?*

Sharese knew the State was legally obligated to pass on any exculpatory evidence against her client, but she wasn't foolish enough to believe that always happened. *Is he really hiding something, or am I just being paranoid?*

With an unsettled feeling in her stomach, Sharese got up off the bench, stretched briefly, and continued her run. There was definitely something strange going on, but she couldn't put her finger on what it was exactly. She resolved to stop dwelling on it and to do what she had come to do: clear her head. Only once or twice during the next hour did thoughts about the trial creep into her consciousness. She shook it off and continued to listen to her feet slapping the pavement in pace with her breathing.

When she had totally spent herself, she slowed to a walk and headed home. As she made her way back to her apartment, she decided that, surely, she had gained some advantage in the trial that day, even if the advantage had come more in the form of the State's difficulty with the witness rather than anything of her own design.

Sharese was okay with that. Sure, it would have been nice if Judge Oaks had found anything that she said to be remotely convincing or even interesting, but she would take any advantage that she could. It was like when she was in college running track. She certainly wouldn't wish a sprained ankle or a nasty bout of the flu on an opponent, but she didn't back down when it happened. Sharese was in the game to win, whatever the game happened to be.

CHAPTER 16

Unlike the night before, when Kyle was more inclined to shoot hoops than to face his wife and children with the guilt of Sara written all over his face, he truly longed to go home on Wednesday afternoon. The day had started innocently enough – Sharon White's testimony on cross had not done the State much harm. But then, that crazy truck driver. *What was up with that?*

As he made his way back to his office after Judge Oaks dismissed court, he kept going over his previous conversations with Larry Turner in his mind. He'd always seemed to be a pleasant man, very eager to help the State. When Kyle had offered to send him a copy of his testimony in the first trial, Mr. Turner had refused, saying that he would not have any problem remembering exactly what had happened on the night of Maria Flores's death.

In fact, Mr. Turner had described the events of that night with such amazing detail that Kyle had been quite eager to show him off to the jury. It wasn't often that he got to put on a witness with what appeared to be a photographic memory. *What in the daylights happened to THAT guy? That sure wasn't him in court today.*

As Kyle got to his office, Angela saw him and, with a panicked look, immediately asked, "Why are you back from court so early? Didn't Mr. Turner ever come back?"

"No, he didn't. I take it you haven't had any luck tracking him down?" Kyle asked in return.

"I've left several messages on his cell phone, and I've called every restaurant in town. I even checked with the police, the hospital, and the Piggly Wiggly, but no one has seen him."

"You called the Piggly Wiggly?" Kyle looked at her incredulously. "Why would you call the Piggly Wiggly?"

"I thought he might have stopped in for some snacks." Angela looked defensive. "It is a long trip."

Kyle just nodded, as if it made perfect sense that Mr. Turner would spend his lunch break stocking up on canned peanuts and beef jerky so that he wouldn't be troubled to stop on his long trip back to Calvert, Texas.

"Anyway, he hasn't called me back, and nobody's seen him anywhere around town," Angela continued.

"Judge Oaks gave us until the morning to find him," Kyle told Angela. "Maybe the highway patrol will track him down soon. Marcus said he'll work on it."

"Oh, that's good. Yeah, maybe they'll find him soon." Then, a thought occurred to Angela. "What'll happen if a state trooper finds him a hundred miles away, heading back to Texas? Will he be arrested?"

"Something like that," Kyle muttered as he flipped through his messages.

"Aren't you worried that he'll be so mad that he won't be a good witness?"

"Doesn't matter how mad he is. We've got to find him so that the defendant's attorney can cross-examine him or we'll end up with a mistrial and have to do this whole thing over again," Kyle said.

Then it dawned on him: a mistrial would be not necessarily be a bad thing. This whole fiasco could end abruptly, and he could get a do-over! Sharese would surely move for a mistrial the next morning if Mr. Turner didn't show up overnight. He'd put up only the mildest of opposition, and, even that, only for appearances. *She'll have to ask for a mistrial or else SHE will be flirting with "ineffective assistance of counsel."*

As Kyle mused the irony of the situation, he felt a sense of hope. He turned away so that Angela didn't notice that his expression had just changed from worry to mischievous delight. He knew it was best to slip completely from her sight as soon as possible, just in case. "I'll be in my office. Let me know if he turns up."

"Okay, I'll keep calling around," Angela said to Kyle's back.

"No, that's all right, Angela. You can stop now. Let law enforcement do their job," Kyle said. Thinking quickly, Kyle added, "Actually, you can take the rest of the afternoon off."

Angela gave him a puzzled look but apparently knew better than to question a rare opportunity to leave the office early. "Okay. Thanks a lot!"

"Yeah, you've been working really hard, and you deserve a little break."

"Try to get some rest yourself, Kyle." Angela shut down her computer while snatching up her purse. "It's not good to let this stuff get to you."

Kyle shut his office door without another word to Angela. *You have no idea, Angela. You have no idea.*

When he was sure Angela was gone, Kyle dialed the highway patrol office. He knew that Marcus had gone directly back to headquarters after court. "I was just wondering, have you issued that APB yet?" Kyle asked.

Marcus laughed into the phone, "It's only been a few minutes since we left the courthouse. Give me a little time, man!"

There was a long pause on Kyle's end of the line.

"Why don't we wait just a little while on that?" Kyle said.

"What?" Marcus couldn't believe what he heard.

"Yeah, he'll turn up, sooner or later, probably just got lost again, like he did the first time he came through here. Turned left instead of right out by the lumberyard and ended up headed out towards the armory instead of the courthouse.

Marcus lowered his voice. "What happened to 'find him and get him back here as soon as possible, Marcus?'"

"Why don't you swing by my office, and we'll talk about it, okay?"

"So don't issue the APB yet?" Marcus wanted to be clear.

Kyle hung up the phone without replying.

When Marcus drove up a few minutes later, Kyle was waiting for him. Marcus cast him a suspicious look, but he didn't object when Kyle opened the front door of the cruiser and got in.

"Let's go for a little drive, Marcus. Roaring River's mighty nice this time of year. What say we go do a little fishing?"

As the sun set in Maple Springs that evening, Kyle and Marcus sat on the front porch of Kyle's family cabin in straight-back chairs. A radio played low inside the cabin, and Kyle hummed along to "Clayton Delaney."

Marcus had cast off most of his state trooper uniform and was wearing only a white undershirt and tan pants. The legs were rolled up at the bottom above his bare feet, which were now splashed with mud. Kyle had shed the suit, button-down shirt, and necktie that he had worn to court that day. He was now sporting an old t-shirt and denim cutoffs he kept in the dresser drawer of the cabin's small bedroom. He, too, was barefoot. Neither man had too much to say to the other. Instead, they concentrated on the sun as it dipped closer and closer to the edge of the horizon and reflected itself upon the gently flowing water of the river.

"Better check our supper." Marcus sniffed the wafting smoke that drifted onto the porch. He walked out into the yard and peered at the fresh trout he and Kyle had caught earlier that afternoon. He gave it a flip, careful not to overturn the small charcoal grill that had seen its better days.

Kyle went into the house and returned with a bowl of baked beans he had warmed up in a saucepan on the stove. He set them directly on the porch and handed Marcus a platter. "For the fish. I'll go grab us some plates."

Marcus nodded at him but didn't speak.

In a few minutes, Kyle emerged from the cabin carrying plates, forks, and cups in one hand and a pitcher of sweet tea in the other.

Marcus was sitting on the porch beside the beans and a steaming platter of fish. His long legs were stretched out on the wooden stairs that led from the porch down into the yard.

Kyle, who was more relaxed than he had been in days, found himself ravenously hungry. He helped himself to several pieces of fish and a large serving of beans.

Marcus, too, ate eagerly. "Haven't had fresh trout in a while. It's good," he said.

After they had finished eating, they carried their dishes into the cabin. Kyle gave them a quick wash in the small kitchen sink. "My granddaddy only had three rules about this cabin: no drinking, no women, and wash your own dishes," Kyle said as he put the last dish into the drainer." He laughed lightly. "I've already broken one of those rules – best not to break another one."

"Yeah, about that..." Marcus started. He was leaning against the refrigerator and cleared his throat before he spoke further. "You know, you could have told me the truth about Sara on Monday. It might have made things a little easier."

"I'm a married man, Marcus. It's not easy to admit that I messed up that bad. I fell in love with another woman when my wife was pregnant."

"But you didn't know she was expecting. You thought it was over between you," Marcus replied.

"I thought so, yeah. She'd even filed for divorce." Kyle gave a long sigh. "Still doesn't make it right though, you know? I shouldn't have even talked to another woman until the divorce was final."

"We all make mistakes. I've made plenty of my own," Marcus looked Kyle directly in the eyes for the first time that afternoon. "I've got your back on this one."

"Thanks." Kyle returned the stare. "That means a lot to me."

The air again fell silent, except for the radio still playing softly.

"Guess we'd best be headin' back?" Marcus glanced around for his uniform shirt and gun belt.

"Yeah. Just give me a minute to lock up," Kyle replied.

Marcus headed out the front door of the cabin, letting the screen door slam behind him. He sat down in one of the straight-back chairs to put his shoes on.

A few minutes later, Kyle emerged from the cabin in his suit and tie. "Just drop me off at the office, okay? I left my car there."

"Whatever you say," Marcus replied.

They drove back into town in silence, leaving the windows rolled down and letting the heavy scent of jasmine in the night air take their minds back to simpler times.

CHAPTER 17

The next morning found Kyle especially chipper. A heavy burden had been lifted from his shoulders with his confession to Marcus the night before. It always lightened the load to share something with a friend, and Kyle knew his secret about Sara was safe with Marcus.

Kyle felt confident that Sharese would ask for a mistrial when it became evident that Larry Turner had disappeared into thin air and would no longer be available for cross-examination. Judge Oaks would have no choice but to grant the motion, sending Justin Hargis back to prison to cool his heels for a few months until the court could set another trial date. *A trial with a whole new slate of jurors.*

Kyle felt no guilt at this proposition, believing that this whole idea of a new trial on a three-year old case was nonsense anyway. Justin Hargis had killed Maria Flores, and he deserved all the punishment that had been laid upon him, if not more. *What difference did it make if the new trial happens this week or six months from now?*

When Kyle made his way into the courtroom, Marcus, Sharese, and Justin were already in their respective seats. Marcus greeted him with a confident nod, and Sharese gave him a quick smile as he passed the defense table.

"Any news?" Kyle asked Marcus loudly enough that Sharese was sure to hear.

"Not a thing. No one in the state has reported seeing Larry Turner in the last twenty-four hours," Marcus said. Technically, it wasn't a lie because no one had, in fact, reported seeing him.

"Oh, that's bad." Kyle tried to sound worried, shaking his head.

Sharese leaned across the aisle, "You mean you still haven't found that trucker?"

"Afraid not," Marcus said.

"What are you going do?" Sharese asked.

"I don't know." Kyle tried hard to look worried. As Sharese shared the news with Justin, Judge Oaks came into the courtroom, and court was called to order. "General, have you found that trucker yet?" the judge asked Kyle.

Kyle stood up and addressed the court with his head hung. "No, Your Honor, we have not been able to locate Mr. Turner." He looked at Sharese out of the corner of his eye, expecting her to make her motion for a mistrial, but she was busy talking to her client.

Judge Oaks looked down at Sharese, "What does the defense have to say about this?"

Sharese looked sideways at Justin and replied, "Your Honor, my client has nothing to say on this matter."

"What?" Kyle was confused. "You mean you—" Marcus gave him a tug on the cuff before he actually said the words "aren't going to move for a mistrial." They exchanged a look. *Don't be too obvious.* Kyle was relieved when Judge Oaks spoke up.

"Ms. Jackson, have you advised your client that he was the right to request a mistrial at this point due to the defense's inability to cross-examine the State's witness?" The judge peered down at the defense table.

Obviously offended and apparently past the point of caring what the judge thought about her, Sharese rose to her feet, "Of course I have, Your Honor. We discussed this very possibility yesterday afternoon after Mr. Turner failed to return to court. We also discussed it at length again this morning."

Looking down sympathetically at Justin, Sharese continued, "Mr. Hargis understands that he is giving up an important right here, but he wishes to proceed with the trial. He's been in prison for a long time, and he doesn't want to wait six months or a year for another trial date."

"Is that correct, Mr. Hargis?" the judge asked Justin.

Sharese motioned for Justin to stand up as he began to speak, "Yes, Judge. Miss Jackson done told me that I have a right to ask for another trial 'cause that trucker run off or whatever. Said I should have had the right to ask him questions in front of the jury, instead of him just answering what the State's lawyer ask him about. She said it's in the Constitution and all."

"Yes, that's right. And you wish to waive your constitutional right of confrontation?" Judge Oaks asked.

"Yeah, I do. I just want to finish the trial. I don't want to have to do this all over again later," Justin said.

Judge Oaks rubbed his eyes and blinked a couple of times before addressing the bailiff, "The Court could grant a mistrial *sua sponte*, but, in light of Mr. Hargis's waiver of his right to confront the State's witness Larry Turner, we will instead proceed with this trial. Ms. Jackson, you'll need to have your client sign a written waiver to that effect as soon as possible. Bailiff, bring the jury in, and let's get this thing going."

Kyle suddenly felt sick to his stomach. He was so sure that Larry Turner's sudden disappearance would buy him a mistrial – and an immediate escape from Sara – that he hadn't even bothered to prepare for any further witnesses. He looked at Marcus, obviously at a loss as to what to do.

"The brother, is he still here?" Marcus whispered.

Kyle nodded in the affirmative. "He's been here all week, just waiting around."

"Then get him in here," Marcus said low enough so as not to be heard.

"Yeah, that'll work. Thanks," Kyle said quietly to Marcus. "I guess we'll need to get the medical examiner over here after lunch, too. I'll need to call him during the first break."

As the jury was seated, Kyle addressed the court. "The State calls Mr. Homero Flores. He's the older brother of the victim, Maria Flores."

As the bailiff went to fetch Homero Flores, who had been waiting patiently in the hallway each day since the trial began, Kyle located the notes from his previous conversations with him.

After a minute or two, a young Hispanic man dressed in blue jeans and a red sport shirt walked into the courtroom. He had a strong, stout build and a look of youthful determination in his face. Still, he was obviously nervous and seemed to shrink slightly into his small stature as he approached the witness stand.

The clerk very subtly placed a box of tissues on the witness stand as she administered the oath.

"State your name, please, for the record," Kyle began.

"Homero Flores," the witness replied.

"Where are you from?"

"I was born in Mexico." Homero's Spanish accent was heavy. "We moved to Texas when I was small. I live here in Tennessee now, on the Holman Farm."

"Do you work there?"

"Yes, I do things for Mr. and Mrs. Holman around the farm or sometimes the house."

"How long have you worked for the Holmans?" Kyle asked.

"I work there six months last year, then I go back to Texas for the winter. I come back here in April this year."

"How old are you, Mr. Flores?"

"I'm twenty-two."

"Can you tell the jury how you were acquainted with Miss Maria Flores, the victim in this case?" Kyle asked.

Until that point, Homero Flores had an easy manner about him, a look of optimism on his face. With the dreaded question from Kyle, his face clouded over, and he stared at the floor. "She was my sister."

"Can you tell us a little bit about Maria?" Kyle was careful not to ask any leading questions. Sharese would be all too eager to put this sympathetic line of questioning to an abrupt halt with an objection.

Homero looked up and gave a sad smile to the jury. "She was a very sweet girl. Shy. Quiet. Very pretty, which worried my father a lot." He gave a small laugh with his last remark, and the jury joined in the sad joke. "She was two years younger than me. We were close growing up."

After grabbing a tissue and wiping his eyes, he went on. "She was a hard worker. Did whatever was asked." Homero looked away then. "She met a boy back home in Mexico when we went to visit relatives. She talked about him a lot after we come back here. She told our parents that she wanted to go and live with our grandmother in Mexico, but they would hear nothing of it. They say she was too young."

"So she ran away?" Kyle asked.

Sharese, who had been reticent up to that point, finally objected. "Your Honor, I've tried to be patient here out of respect for Mr. Flores's loss, but that last question calls for blatant speculation. Furthermore, the reason for Miss Flores's decision to separate from her family is not relevant to this case."

"Sustained." The judge barely looked up. "Let's rein it in a bit, General."

"How did you learn of your sister's death?" Kyle shifted gears. Sharese was right; the reason Maria Flores chose to run away was not important to the question of whether Justin Hargis was guilty of killing her.

"The sheriff came out to the farm where we were working and told my father that a young girl had been found dead. We had reported Maria missing a few days before that." A tear rolled down his face. "We – my father and my mother and my younger brothers – followed the sheriff into town to see the girl's body. We prayed the whole way there that it was not our Maria."

Tears began to stream down Homero's face in earnest.

Kyle gave the witness a minute to compose himself. "Can you tell us what happened next?"

"It was her. It was Maria. I went into the room with my father, and we tell the man, 'Yes, that is Maria.' She still had on the same clothes as when she ran away, but her face was bloody and her dress was torn and dirty." Again, Homero paused to wipe his eyes.

"They wanted to do an autopsy test, but Papi did not want it done. He did not want her body violated in that way." Homero looked down.

"My parents are very–" Homero looked up at Kyle, as if seeking help with finding the right word. "Very old-fashion where Maria was concerned. But the man say autopsy should be done because it was a criminal case. But Papi said, 'No. It does not matter. What's done is done.' So, we took Maria back to Mexico and buried her there in our family plot."

Kyle saw that Sharese was on the edge of her seat, poised to object to the hearsay evidence that Homero had let slip. The bit of testimony concerning the lack of an autopsy was actually more helpful than hurtful to Justin, so she remained quiet.

"My parents, they did not come back. They stay in Mexico. They live with my grandmother now. They will not come back to the United States again. They still grieve for Maria."

"But you came back?" Kyle asked.

"Yes, I came back last year with my uncle. I am of age now and can decide for myself what to do. The pay is good here, and I send money to help my family." Homero added, "My father cannot work now. My mother cares for him and my brothers and my grandmother."

Kyle looked down at his notes to see if he had missed anything. "Do you happen to have a picture of Maria before the accident?" he asked.

"Yes." Homero pulled out his wallet and showed Kyle a picture of a young girl in her teens. She had wide-set brown eyes and long black hair. In the picture, she was wearing a blue sundress and was smiling broadly. "This was about a month before she was killed. She wore that same dress when she ran away."

The court reporter marked the picture as an exhibit and returned it to Kyle. After showing the picture to the judge and to Sharese, Kyle went over to the jury box and handed it to the juror on his far left.

Kyle tried to avoid Sara's gaze, but their eyes met briefly as he walked in front of the jury box. He couldn't help but notice that she appeared very distraught. Not having any clue that she had been up most of the night worrying about Daniel, Kyle assumed that her emotional state stemmed either from Homero Flores's testimony or from Kyle himself. It hurt him to know that it could be the latter.

As much as he knew that their relationship was in the past, Sara's presence just a few feet away from him in such a high emotional state sent a shockwave through Kyle like he had not felt in years. *Three years to be exact.* He wanted to hold her, smooth that crazy hair of hers and tell her that everything would be okay. For just a moment, he closed his eyes and imagined doing exactly that.

Someone in the jury box sniffed loudly, causing him to open his eyes and come back to reality. *I couldn't offer her any comfort back then, and I sure can't now.*

Instead, he concentrated on the pattern of the tile and walked back to his seat. "Your witness, Ms. Jackson," he said without looking up.

***

Sharese took a few moments to gather up her notes before addressing Homero in the witness box. She knew she was on dangerous turf and did not want to come across as bullying this particular witness in any way.

"You were Maria Flores's older brother, is that correct?"

"Yes."

"How old were you when she died?" Sharese chose her words carefully. Saying Maria had "died" had a less damning ring to it than saying she was "killed."

"I was nineteen."

"You didn't actually see the accident during which she died, is that correct?"

"No, because she had run away from the farm where we were working. I think she hitchhiked to Maple Springs and then start walking again."

"Okay, but you were still at the farm at the time of the accident, correct?"

"Yes."

"And you didn't learn of Maria's death until a few days after it actually happened, right?"

"Yes."

"So," Sharese was careful to phrase her condemnation of the witness as delicately as possible and yet still get her point across to the jury, "you actually have no personal knowledge about this case, do you, Mr. Flores?"

"I identified her body. My father and I, we identified her body to the man." Homero was agitated. He clearly wanted to help prove the case against the person who had taken his sister's life, but he had a limited ability to do so under the circumstances.

"Yes, I know that you did," Sharese said kindly. "However, that was several days after the accident, isn't that right?"

"Yes, it was," Homero nodded reluctantly.

"And your family refused to allow an autopsy of Maria's body, even though you were advised that a criminal case was pending?"

Kyle interrupted, "Objection, Your Honor."

"Approach the bench, counsel," the judge said.

"The defense's question calls for hearsay, Judge," Kyle argued. The news that an autopsy had been refused was not helpful to the State's case at all. Kyle had not intended for Homero to bring up the autopsy and his doing so had created yet another unnecessary hole in the State's case.

"The witness testified as to this matter during direct examination, Your Honor. We have a right to follow up," Sharese said.

"I'll allow you a little latitude here, but let's wrap it up quick, Ms. Jackson," decided Judge Oaks.

"Can you re-read the question, please?" Sharese asked the court reporter.

The court reporter relayed the question from her notes, "And your family refused to allow an autopsy of Maria's body, even though you were advised that a criminal case was pending?"

Homero answered, "Yes. For reasons of – of – of modesty, my father refused the autopsy."

"No further questions, Your Honor," Sharese said.

As she turned to make her way back to her seat, Sharese felt Marcus's eyes following her and flushed. They gave each other a nod so slight that no one except Kyle even noticed. Sharese saw him whisper something to Marcus as she took her seat.

Judge Oaks asked Kyle if he had any redirect examination of Homero Flores, but Kyle did not. Sharese knew that, through Homero, Kyle had managed to formally identify the crime victim and put a face on her. The jury had seen her smiling face in the photograph and knew who it was they were to avenge with their verdict.

151

"You can step down, son," Judge Oaks said. Looking at the lawyers, he continued, "Let's have a ten-minute recess, counsel. Give the jury a chance to stretch their legs a bit."

Sharese knew what the judge really meant. Homero Flores's testimony had been emotional for everybody in the courtroom. The jury – and maybe even cranky old Henry Oaks himself – needed a few minutes to compose themselves.

***

During the break, Sara found a quiet corner outside the jury room and checked her cell phone to make sure she had not missed a call. Her first inclination after finding out about the earthquake was to go to Judge Oaks and ask to be excused from jury duty, but Andrew and Grams had encouraged her to go on to court. They said it would give her mind something to focus on besides worrying about Daniel. They'd promised to call if they heard anything at all about him or his mission group.

Sara hadn't thought through what she would have done if a call had actually come during the trial. Under normal circumstances, she would have loathed calling attention to herself by asking for a break. Of course, these were far from normal circumstances. As it happened, she hadn't felt the silent alarm in her pocket, and a visual inspection showed that she had indeed received no calls.

She considered calling Grams or Andrew just to check in and see if they knew anything, but she knew it was unnecessary. They would have called if they'd known anything. They had promised.

"What's wrong, child?" Sara's thoughts were interrupted by the concerned voice of fellow juror Fredonia Miller at her side. "You look a fright!"

Sara felt the tears welling and wiped at her eyes with the tissue she had put in her pocket earlier that morning. "It's my fiancé, Mrs. Miller. He's in Honduras on a mission trip. They had an earthquake there yesterday, and I haven't heard from him yet."

"I heard about that on the evening news. I didn't realize anybody from around here was down there or I would have been praying already." Fredonia put her arm around Sara and gave her a comforting embrace. "Now that I know, I'll be praying for your fiancé to come home safe to you. You two have a good life ahead of you, you know."

"Yes ma'am. I certainly hope so," Sara whimpered into Fredonia's shoulder. "Grams promised to call if she hears anything."

"Then don't you worry about it, child. Viola will make sure you get word if there's anything you need to know." Fredonia's tone was soothing. "No news is good news, right?"

"I suppose so." Sara's smile was weak. "Guess I'd better get a restroom break in before we have to get back in there. I'm sure I look a mess."

"You look fine, honey. Tired, but still as pretty as ever."

"Thanks." Sara didn't believe Mrs. Miller's words about her appearance, but she wasn't particularly concerned about her looks at the moment.

***

Back in the courtroom, Justin and Sharese's heads were huddled together at the defense table. "Do you think I'll get to testify today, Miss Jackson?" Justin asked.

"I'm not sure. The State still has to put on the medical examiner, and then we'll make a motion for a judgment of acquittal," Sharese responded.

"A motion for what?" Justin looked confused.

"Let's just say a motion to dismiss your case. We'll argue that the State has failed to present enough evidence to send the case to the jury."

"Will that work?" Justin seemed skeptical.

"No. Motions for a judgment of acquittal are rarely granted by the trial court." Sharese laughed lightly. "Judge Oaks has sat through three and half days of this case. No way he's going to turn you loose now."

Justin gave a little snort and nodded in agreement. "I know that's the truth."

"Anyway, the motion is basically a formality. Something to argue about on appeal," Sharese said. "Appellate courts do sometimes reverse a case on the basis that the motion should have been granted. Of course, they go on the cold record and aren't a part of the actual courtroom drama, so to speak, like trial judges are."

"Oh, okay. So, that medical examiner guy will testify, then we'll make a motion that we know we're gonna lose, and then I'll get to testify?" Justin asked.

"Uh, yeah, that about sums it up." Sharese tried not to laugh. For someone so young, Justin certainly had a way of getting to the heart of the matter. *He must have grown up fast in prison.*

An image flashed in Sharese's mind: a picture of her father, taken not long before he went to prison. Her grandmother still kept it on the piano. To Sharese, Tony Jackson was still that same kid with the shining skin and the cocky tilt of the head.

Shaking off the mixed feelings that the image stirred in her, Sharese forced herself to focus on Justin and the question that he had just asked her. "It could be tomorrow before you testify, Justin. It depends on how long the medical examiner's testimony takes. I've decided not to stipulate to his credentials. I'm going to make the State prove every iota of his CV."

"His what?"

"His curriculum vitae. His resume. It's a paper that lists where he went to school, where he's worked, and that kind of thing."

"Oh."

"Sometimes attorneys agree to stipulate that an expert is qualified to testify in their field. It speeds things along."

"So why don't we just do that, then?" Justin seemed confused again.

"They might leave something out if we make them work for it. Building reasonable doubt, Justin, is a process, not a one-time event."

"Okay, I get it." Justin nodded his head. "It's not one big thing. It can be a lot of little stuff all added up."

"Yes," Sharese said, "and the little stuff is starting to add up on the State rather quickly. Say a prayer, Justin. It's a long shot, but we could possibly win this case."

When court resumed after the recess, Sharese was true to her word and refused to stipulate to any of the medical examiner's qualifications. That made for a long and dry line of testimony that Judge Oaks finally interrupted when he could hear the jurors' stomachs' begin to growl all the way to the bench.

"General, I think you've gotten to the point where you can tender Dr. Walker as an expert. Let's take an hour for lunch here. I imagine the jury is getting hungry. I know I am," the judge said.

Kyle was relieved. "Alright, then. The State hereby tenders Dr. Trent Walker, Maple Springs Medical Examiner, as an expert witness in the case of *State v. Justin Hargis*."

Sharese remained in her seat, "No objection."

The judge cast a glare and a long sigh towards Sharese, and she knew he was thinking *I could be playing golf right now if you'd just stipulated to all that.* He didn't say it aloud, though, and was beginning to look reconciled to the fact Justin's case was indeed going to take the full week to try.

Sharese herself was relieved when Judge Oaks said in a tired voice, "The court hereby accepts Dr. Trent Walker as an expert witness. Let court stand in recess until 1 p.m."

"Justin. Justin!" Sharese whispered loudly to her client, who was about to drift off to sleep again in the chair beside her. She'd made good use of her elbow several times during the doctor's testimony, startling Justin awake each time he threatened to snore.

Justin woke up just in time to stand up as the jury exited the courtroom. "Thank goodness," Justin said as the door closed behind the last juror. "I thought that was gonna last all day."

"You know, Justin, it doesn't look good when you actually fall asleep during your own trial. Try to show some respect, will you?" Sharese said in a hushed voice.

Kyle and Marcus were clearing off their table and talking quietly. "Well, that was a lot of fun, huh?" Kyle said as he and Marcus finished gathering their things.

Sharese, who wasn't sure if she heard humor or sarcasm in his voice, just looked at him blankly. "You bet."

Kyle let out a small laugh and shook his head. He started to say something else to Sharese but thought better of it. Instead, he turned to Marcus. "Want to grab a sandwich at Eddie's?"

"Yeah, sounds good. Are you going to the office first?"

"Nah. I'll go after we eat," Kyle said.

"Want to join us?" Marcus looked at Sharese, who was still standing at the table with Justin and looking rather awkward.

Sharese was quite flabbergasted and stuttered her reply. "Uh, uh, no, I don't think, uh, so." She looked at Justin and continued, "We need to talk."

"Sure." Marcus was obviously embarrassed that his mouth had gotten ahead of his brain and invited her in the first place.

Kyle smiled mischievously. "Another time then, counsel. Another time," he said, shaking his head as he and Marcus walked out of the courtroom.

***

When they got out of the courthouse, Kyle began to laugh about what had just happened. "Wow, man, great timing. Last night we were conspiring to make her move for a mistrial, and now you're asking her out!"

"It was just lunch," Marcus corrected Kyle. "Not a date or anything. Anyway, she shot me down just like I told you she would."

156

"Yeah, she shot you down alright. Just like she shot down our big plan for a mistrial," Kyle said. Both laughed loudly, patting each other on the back as they tried to settle down. Finally, Kyle said, "It's not really funny, is it?"

"No, not really," Marcus said as they continued laughing all the way to Eddie's.

As they entered the restaurant, their laughter evaporated. "What do we do now, my friend?" Kyle said somberly as they waited to be seated in the small, crowded sandwich shop.

"Guess we could try a little harder to find that truck driver." Marcus lowered his voice. "I think we need him if we have any hope of pulling this one out of the bag."

"Let's do it," Kyle said.

***

After their quick lunch at Eddie's, Marcus went back to headquarters to process the APB for Larry Turner.

Kyle, meanwhile, stopped by his office and checked in with Angela. She presented him with a large stack of message slips as soon as he walked in the door. Some pertained to other cases, and a couple were from Elizabeth. There was nothing from Larry Turner. "I think you might need to call home," Angela said in her sweetest falsetto voice as Kyle looked at the messages.

From previous experience, Kyle knew what Angela really meant. *Your wife is ringing the phone off the hook, boss. Please make her stop so I can get my nails filed in peace.* He'd gotten home very late the previous night and had rushed out the door that morning without having a real conversation with Elizabeth or the children. Knowing he had to face the music sooner or later, Kyle reluctantly dialed home.

As expected, Elizabeth unleashed upon him immediately after hearing his voice. The baby had been crying off and on for two days, and Evan had been on his worst behavior. In a very tense voice, Elizabeth asked, "Do you think you might make it home before 10 p.m. tonight? I could really stand a little break here."

Kyle promised to try, feeling more than a little guilty about his little fishing trip with Marcus the night before. "I'll do what I can, hon. This case is turning out to be a lot harder than I thought it was going to be. It's just been one headache after another."

With that, Elizabeth shifted ever so slightly from haggard-mom-Elizabeth to would-be-professional-Elizabeth. "I thought it was a no-brainer, a new trial on a technicality."

"Yeah, that's what I thought too, going into it. It's just that a lot of stuff has come up that I didn't expect."

"Like what?" Elizabeth sounded less annoyed now that she was having a conversation with an actual adult.

Kyle stammered for an answer that didn't give away the real reason that *State v. Hargis* had turned him from a competent trial lawyer to a bumbling fool in a navy blue suit. "Well, there were some issues with seating the jury on the first day, some confusion about challenges and so forth," he began.

"But that was all worked out on the first day, right?" Elizabeth prodded.

"Yeah, yeah, that's all worked out now. For the most part anyway," Kyle said, trying not to stretch the truth too thinly. "But then some of the witnesses have had problems remembering things, stuff like that."

"I can see that. How long since the crime? Did you tell me four years?" Elizabeth asked.

"Three years," Kyle answered.

"Well, it's hard to remember things that far back," Elizabeth said.

Oh, how I wish that were true. Kyle shook away the image of Sara that had unwillingly popped into his mind. "We actually had one witness yesterday that didn't come back after lunch."

"Oh, that's bad!" Elizabeth sounded excited. "Did the defense attorney move for a mistrial?"

"I thought sure she would, but she didn't. Her client just wants to go on with the trial. Apparently, he needs 'closure,'" Kyle said, putting emphasis on the last word.

"Ah," Elizabeth chuckled. "That's a mistake. All he is going to get is closure on the door of a prison cell."

"Let's hope. I would hate to think I've spent all morning putting the victim's brother on the stand and then having to qualify a seventy-year-old medical examiner as an expert witness for nothing." Kyle sighed and then glanced at his watch. "Hon, I really gotta go now. I've got some other calls to return before I head back to court. I'll try my best to get home at a decent hour tonight."

"Thanks. I'm sorry I'm so crazy today," Elizabeth said. "It's just been a hard morning with the kids. Seems like Chelsea cries all the time these days. Can you hear her screaming right now?"

"Yeah, I can hear her. You'd better see about her." Kyle was anxious to end the call before Elizabeth got angry with him all over again.

"Okay. We'll see you tonight," Elizabeth said. "Good luck on your case."

"Thanks. Love you."

"Love you, too," Elizabeth ended the conversation.

Kyle knew that he should return his other calls, but instead he put his feet up on his desk, leaned back in his chair, and closed his eyes for a few minutes. Enjoying the relative calm and quiet of his office, he pondered how quickly it had become Thursday and how his world had been turned upside down in four short days. On Monday, he had thought he was sitting pretty, ready to put an easy notch in his belt with a slam-dunk conviction of an obviously guilty defendant. Then, he had looked around at the jury panel and seen that familiar face.

Seeing Sara again had affected Kyle much more than he liked to admit. Leaving her that summer was the hardest thing he had ever done. He had believed he was doing the right thing in returning to Elizabeth, given her condition. After all, he had never stopped loving Elizabeth, although being with Sara had almost made him forget.

He had known he was making a conscious choice, just as Elizabeth had made the decision to tell him about the baby. He knew there were other choices she could have made, and he was thankful she had chosen the path that included him.

As the years passed, Kyle had almost convinced himself that he hadn't really loved Sara, that it had just been a fling. Wouldn't it have been impossible for him to have truly loved two women at the same time, especially two women as different as Elizabeth and Sara?

Elizabeth was petite and blond and regal, intelligent in a way that was as intimidating as it was attractive. During their courtship, people had said they were a beautiful couple; that it was destiny for them to be together. Kyle had believed that, too, when they married. Unfortunately, their marriage had turned out to be a much bigger challenge than he had predicted. While he and Elizabeth were paired wonderfully in some ways, their marriage had a way of highlighting the areas in which they differed. She'd grown up in a privileged world that had included private school, vacations to Europe, and a Cadillac Escalade for graduation.

Kyle's own family had been blue collar, average. He had never thought much about it because they had a nice enough house and never seemed to struggle financially. If they were sensible and lived within their modest means, then that was the way that things were supposed to be. It wasn't until Kyle married Elizabeth that he began to see his background as somehow inadequate. Elizabeth never said anything derogatory about Kyle's family or their means, but – at least in Kyle's mind – she didn't have to. The difference was obvious.

Sara was the polar opposite of Elizabeth. She was tall and dark-haired, with an almost exotic quality to her. She came from a military family and had acquired a certain level of sophistication from the extensive travel her father's position had required of them. The frequent moves had also made her very practical. She was a light packer, both literally and figuratively.

When Kyle had first met Sara at her grandparents' cabin, she had only brought a few simple clothes with her, the materials for her thesis, and a camera. As they got to know each other that summer, Kyle realized Sara had a way of knowing what was really important. He never felt lacking in Sara's eyes because she made it clear that his presence and attention was all she required.

Kyle's thoughts of Sara and Elizabeth ended abruptly when Angela knocked on his office door. "Kyle, is everything okay? Doesn't Judge Oaks usually start back around 1 p.m.?"

"I'm fine," he called out to Angela. *What's one more lie in a week like this?*

Kyle checked his watch and saw that it was already 12:55 p.m. "Guess I'd better get back to court. Thanks for the reminder." He quickly gathered his things and headed for the door, leaving Elizabeth's messages scattered among the ever-growing pile of papers on his desk.

CHAPTER 18

As 1 p.m. approached in the jury room, Sara checked her cell phone for what seemed like the hundredth time that day. During the lunch break, she had called both Andrew and Grams to see if there was any news about Daniel.

The only significant development had been a television news report stating that several Americans were in the process of being evacuated from Honduras. No names had been given, and Sara could only pray that Daniel was among those who were safe and headed home.

"I hope I can stay awake in there," Fredonia said to Sara with a loud yarn. "That prosecutor may be handsome, but he was about put me to sleep this morning."

Sara didn't blush at the mention of Kyle. In fact, she didn't give him much thought at all as she replied to Fredonia. "Maybe it'll be over soon. I sure hope so, anyway."

"It must be hard to concentrate on all this with so much on your mind."

"Yes, it is. Try as I might, my mind keeps going back to Daniel. Forgive me for saying it, but I'm really hoping I get excused, seeing as how I'm only an alternate."

"Maybe you will, child. Did you call Viola during lunch?"

"Yes. She said there was a news report that some Americans were being evacuated, but they didn't give names."

"Well, let's just pray that your young man is on the first plane out." Fredonia patted Sara lightly on the back.

The bailiff opened the door and motioned for the jury to return to the courtroom. "You just punch me if I start to snore," Fredonia said.

Sara laughed politely at the joke, but she knew the last thing on her mind that afternoon was going to be whether Fredonia Miller was asleep in the chair beside her.

***

"Are you ready to proceed, General?" Judge Oaks asked Kyle after the jury members were seated.

"Yes, Your Honor, the State is ready," Kyle replied. "We ask that Dr. Trent Walker, medical examiner, return to the stand."

After Dr. Walker took the witness stand, Judge Oaks reminded him that he was still under oath and then explained to the jury that Dr. Walker had been qualified as an expert witness.

"Did you have an occasion to examine the body of Maria Flores, the victim in this case?" Kyle began.

"Yes. After her death, I was asked to examine the girl's body to determine whether her injuries were consistent with a vehicular homicide."

"Can you explain that a little further, please, Dr. Walker?"

"My job was to determine whether Maria Flores died as a result of being struck by an automobile."

"What was the result of your examination?" Kyle asked.

"May I refer to my notes?" Dr. Walker pulled a paper out of the manila file folder that he had carried with him to the stand.

"Were your notes made at the time of your examination?" Kyle knew he would have to go through all the formal steps necessary to ask that the witness be allowed to use his notes during questioning. Clearly, Sharese wasn't going to let anything slide today, not that he blamed her.

"Yes, they were."

"Without the notes, do you have any personal recollection of your examination of Maria Flores?"

"Very little."

"Have those records been kept by you in the regular course of your business as Maple Springs Medical Examiner?"

"Yes, they have."

"Judge, the State asks that Dr. Trent Walker be allowed to refer to his notes during his testimony in this case pursuant to Tennessee Rule of Evidence 803(5). That's the rule on past recollection recorded," Kyle said.

"No objection," Sharese said, even though neither Kyle nor Judge Oaks asked for the defense's position on the matter.

"Motion granted."

"Doctor, can you refer to your report and tell the jury about your physical examination of the body of Maria Flores, please?" Kyle said to the witness.

Dr. Walker glanced over his notes before beginning. "The victim was a Hispanic female, approximately fourteen to sixteen years of age. She was five feet, two inches tall, and she weighed one hundred and twenty-one pounds. Her identity was unknown at the time of the examination. The victim had abrasions and lacerations over most of her body. There was bruising on her arms, legs, and torso. Both of her legs were broken, as was her neck."

"Dr. Walker, were those injuries consistent with what you would expect to find if a pedestrian was struck by an automobile?" Kyle asked.

"Yes, the victim's injuries were consistent with having been hit by a car."

"Okay, doctor, thank you for summarizing your findings for the jury. Now, let's talk about Ms. Flores's injuries in more detail," Kyle said. "I understand that you took some photographs of the victim."

"Yes, I did." Dr. Walker produced a large stack of photographs from his file. "Some show particular injuries to the victim, and others show her entire body."

"If you would, doctor, let's start with the first photograph there. Please tell me what it shows."

Kyle spent the next ninety minutes questioning Dr. Walker about the photographs, stopping occasionally to ask detailed questions about Maria Flores's injuries as evidenced in the photos.

Sharese objected to the admission of some of the pictures on the basis that they were prejudicial due to their gruesome nature, but Judge Oaks allowed all of them into evidence. As each photograph was admitted, it was passed to the jury, who looked at Maria's injuries with a combination of interest and repulsion.

Finally, Kyle tendered the witness to the defense and the judge granted a short recess.

***

"I'm proud of you!" Sharese told Justin after the jury left the courtroom.

"What for?" Justin asked suspiciously.

"You stayed awake for every bit of Dr. Walker's testimony," Sharese teased.

Justin blushed. "I'm real sorry I kept dozing off this morning. I didn't sleep much last night."

"Worried about the trial?" Sharese asked.

"No. The guy they've got me sharing a cell with was snoring like a freight train."

Sharese laughed in spite of herself. "I guess you just can't catch a break."

"I guess not," Justin joined in the joke. "It's getting pretty late in the day. I'm probably not going to get to testify today, am I?"

"No, I don't think so. After the break, we'll cross-examine the medical examiner. I want to stress to the jury that no autopsy was done," Sharese said.

"Is that important? I don't remember anything about that from the first trial," Justin said.

"It doesn't necessarily destroy the State's case, but it does give us more room to argue reasonable doubt," Sharese said.

"You mean, like, they might have found out she died from something besides me hitting her?" Justin said, confused.

"Well, probably not," Sharese admitted. "But we'll never know now, will we?"

Justin nodded. "'Reasonable doubt.' I think I'm starting to understand what that means."

After the break, Sharese took her turn at questioning the medical examiner. "Dr. Walker, how long had Maria Flores been dead when you first saw her body?"

The witness looked at his notes before answering. "It was the morning after the accident."

"So several hours had passed since Ms. Flores had been pronounced dead at the scene?"

"Yes, that's correct."

"Just to be clear, you were not at the scene of the accident, is that correct?" Sharese asked.

"No, I was not at the scene."

"Have you ever spoken to my client, Justin Hargis, about this matter?" Sharese asked.

"No, I have not."

Sharese considered asking Dr. Walker whether he had spoken with Larry Turner about the case, but she wasn't entirely sure of the answer. She had been taught in law school that an attorney should never ask a question on cross-examination unless she already knew the answer. "So, you can't say for certain why or even if Mr. Hargis's vehicle may have struck Ms. Flores, isn't that true?"

"No ma'am, that's not entirely true. As I told the State's attorney, Ms. Flores's injuries were consistent with being struck by an automobile," Dr. Walker explained.

"Yet, you can't say with absolute certainty that it was Justin Hargis's car that struck Ms. Flores, can you?" Sharese asked. She knew she was going out on a limb a bit with the question, but she was prepared to cut off the witness promptly if he gave anything other than a "yes" or "no" answer.

"No, I can't say with one hundred percent certainty, but from what I understand–"

"Okay, you've answered my question," Sharese cut off the doctor before he could finish the statement.

The doctor gave Kyle a questioning look, and Kyle rose to his feet. "Your Honor, Dr. Walker has a right to explain his answer to Ms. Jackson's question."

"May we approach, Your Honor?" Sharese asked.

"You may," Judge Oaks said, and motioned for the court reporter to scoot closer to the center of the bench.

"Your Honor, Dr. Walker has answered the question that I posed to him, and anything further on his part would constitute hearsay and/or speculation," Sharese said as confidently as she could.

"Judge, it's an old rule, but a good rule: A witness has a right to explain a 'yes' or 'no' answer."

Judge Oaks scratched his head and thought a minute. "Well General, that depends on what the explanation is, doesn't it? What if she's right, that the good doc here is about to give us some hearsay testimony?"

"Maybe I need to phrase my objection in the form of a motion in limine – that is, a request to hear the witness's answer outside the jury's presence before proceeding further," Sharese said. "If the explanation is admissible under the rules of evidence, then we'll bring the jury back in and take it from there."

Judge Oaks looked at Kyle.

"Sounds good to me," Kyle said.

"Very well," Judge Oaks said. After Sharese and Kyle had returned to their seats, he spoke directly to the jury. "Hate to do this to you folks, but we're going to have to ask you to step back to the jury room for a few minutes. We have a little procedural matter we need to take care of."

**

"Why in the world did they send us right back in here?" Fredonia Miller said in a loud voice as they entered the jury room. "We'd no more than sat down in that courtroom."

"Maybe it won't take long." Sara tried to be reassuring.

"The worst of it was, I had just got my seat warmed up good," Fredonia said.

Sara let out a small laugh, but she knew Fredonia wasn't really kidding about the seat. It was icy cold in the courtroom. With all that was on her mind, Sara kept forgetting to bring a sweater.

"This case is a crock," a male juror said. "That Hargis boy is as guilty as sin. He never was nothing but trash."

A couple of the other men nodded their heads in agreement, and Sara was sure that Fredonia would add her two-cents worth any minute. She wasn't sure whether to remind the others of Judge Oaks' instructions not to discuss the case among themselves or whether to try and ignore the talk around her. Luckily, she didn't have to do either one.

The bailiff came into the room, asking if anyone needed anything. No one did, as it had only been a few minutes since the lunch break. The interruption did the trick, though, and the jurors resumed the standard talk about the weather, the Vols, and the best fishing holes around Maple Springs.

Although the judge had expressly forbidden them to talk about the case until all the evidence was in, it was nearly impossible. Sara was glad the bailiff had put a stop to it before it got out of hand. He had developed a friendly rapport with the jurors over the course of the week, and the mere sight of him put them back on the right track.

Still, the men's comments had gotten Sara thinking about the case. With the sudden reappearance of Kyle in her life and then news that an earthquake had struck the country where Daniel was on the mission field, Sara hadn't given much thought to the guilt or innocence of Justin Hargis. As an alternate, she was still hoping to be dismissed from the jury before the deliberation. It wasn't a sure thing, though. One of the women had been talking at lunch about her mother being in the hospital. *What if she has to be excused for a family emergency?*

Sara separated herself from the other jurors without being obvious. She strode over to the small window, turning her back to the others and closing her eyes. Silently, she prayed. *Please let me be excused from this jury, Lord. I don't think I can do what needs to be done here, not with so much on my mind. I'm sure I haven't heard half of the testimony. It wouldn't be fair to that young man to send him to prison when I can't even remember the evidence against him.*

An unsettling feeling came over Sara as she struggled to remember something about the defendant, something that the checkout clerk had said in the grocery store. *Did she say he was already in prison? But how could that be when he hasn't been convicted yet? What did Elizabeth Copeland say? Oh, yes: something about this being a new trial.*

The clerk's knock at the door interrupted Sara's thoughts. As the bailiff announced that it was time to return to the courtroom, Sara finished her prayer with a plea for Daniel's safety, then mouthed a silent "Amen" before joining the other jurors in line.

***

During the next hour, Sharese cross-examined Dr. Walker as vigorously as she could, given her lack of experience and the doctor's limited examination of the victim.

"Dr. Walker, is it true that the victim's family refused permission for an autopsy?"

"Yes. They objected quite vigorously, actually. It was clear that they did not want their young daughter's body handled in that manner."

"There are other ways of obtaining an autopsy, aren't there, Dr. Walker? A court order, for example?"

"Well, yes, that is sometimes done, but we felt this family had suffered enough."

"You knew that a criminal investigation was pending, did you not, Dr. Walker?"

"I knew that, yes."

When it was over, Sharese felt that she had scored a few points. Dr. Walker held to his opinion that Maria's death was consistent with being struck by Justin's automobile but admitted that he did not actually witness the accident and he did not see Maria's body until the next day. She knew those admissions would likely form part of her reasonable doubt argument later on.

Still, Sharese was haunted by something that had come out during the motion in limine. After the jury had left the room, she had again asked Dr. Walker whether he could say with absolute certainty that Justin's car had struck Maria.

As expected, the doctor gave a hearsay answer. "Yes. I'm sure that it did because it is my understanding that there were pieces of Ms. Flores's clothing attached to the front of the defendant's automobile."

Because Dr. Walker had not personally inspected Justin's car and could not recall how he learned about the clothing fragments, Judge Oaks had granted Sharese's motion and instructed Dr. Walker to give a simple "yes" or "no" answer when the jury returned.

What bothered Sharese was that this was the first time she had heard about Maria's clothing being found on Justin's car. There had been no reference to it in the first trial. She had read the entire transcript several times, and there was nothing mentioned about clothing fragments.

Photographs of the accident scene had been admitted at both trials, but Sharese did not recall seeing anything that looked like clothing fragments on Justin's car in the pictures. *Why is this just now coming out? Is it too late for the State to bring it up? No. The State hasn't rested its case yet; they could recall the trooper to testify about the fibers.*

Sharese rested her head in her hands and sighed. After Justin had told her that he couldn't remember hitting Maria with his car, she had begun to form a theory in her mind. The only thing that she could think of that would reconcile the facts as they had been presented was that a second, unknown driver had hit Maria and then caused Justin to lose control and crash his car.

It had been a plausible theory, but clothing fibers on Justin's car would definitely put an abrupt end to such an argument. *Too bad we can't ask Larry Turner if he saw any other cars that night.*

As Kyle asked Dr. Walker a few follow-up questions on redirect examination, Sharese made some notes in anticipation of the motion for judgment of acquittal hearing that would follow Dr. Walker's testimony. On her yellow legal pad, she scribbled, *"No eye witnesses = reasonable doubt. Trooper didn't see accident. Trucker only saw car before/after accident, not during. Brother only saw body days later. Medical examiner didn't go to scene, didn't do autopsy. Only person at scene was defendant – unconscious."*

Stealing a glance at Justin in the chair next to her, Sharese wished that he would give up his stubborn insistence on testifying on his own behalf. She knew that she could make a decent argument about reasonable doubt in the absence of an eyewitness, and it just might fly if Kyle didn't recall Marcus to the stand and ask him about the clothing fibers on Justin's car.

He's so convinced that he'll remember something about the accident if he gets up on that stand. What if he remembers something that neither of us really wants to know?

***

After Kyle's redirect of the medical examiner, Judge Oaks called a quick bench conference. "Is that your last witness, General?"

Kyle wasn't sure what to say. He had hoped Marcus would have some word about Larry Turner by now. "Could I have a minute to confer with Trooper Thompson, Judge?"

"Make it quick," Judge Oaks replied.

Kyle walked back to the table and leaned over to the trooper. "Can you check with headquarters and see if they've tracked down Larry Turner?"

"No need to. Someone would have called me if he'd turned up." Marcus pointed to the cell phone strapped to his gun belt. "We'll just have to do without him – or ask for a continuance."

Kyle winced at the mention of the word "continuance." First of all, the only thing Judge Oaks hated more than continuances were Florida Gator football fans. Second, a continuance would drag out the case – and Kyle's interaction with Sara – even longer. *Do I want to win this case or do I want to get out of here as soon as possible?*

With mixed emotions, Kyle returned to the bench. Bracing himself, he said, "Judge, the State moves for a continuance. I'm afraid we need some more time to find that truck driver and get him back here to finish his testimony."

Before Judge Oaks could respond, Sharese interjected, "You want a continuance to find the State's witness? No way, not after my client waived his right to cross-examine the witness so that we could get this trial finished this week."

Kyle could feel her I-can't-believe-you-even-said-that glare even though he avoided looking directly at her.

"I take it the defense opposes the State's motion, Ms. Jackson?" Judge Oaks asked.

"Your Honor, the defense *strongly* opposes the State's motion for a continuance. We move for a judgment of acquittal in this case."

"Is your client still insisting on testifying, Ms. Jackson?" Judge Oaks asked. "That is, if the court were to deny both of these motions, the State's motion for a continuance and the defense's motion for an acquittal."

"Yes, sir. Mr. Hargis intends to testify, against the advice of counsel, of course."

Judge Oaks let out an annoyed sigh but seemed resolved to the task that lay before him. "Okay, then." Judge Oaks said. "We'll dismiss the jury for the day and then take a ten-minute recess before hearing arguments on these motions.

"Looks like you folks get to get out of here a little early today," Judge Oaks said to the jury as the attorneys returned to their seats. "Got a little business to take care of. Be back at 9 a.m. sharp in the morning, and we'll see if we can't get this thing wrapped up."

***

Sara was relieved to be getting out of court early. She was cold from the overzealous air-conditioning in the courtroom and exhausted from lack of sleep the night before. The truth was she hadn't slept well in days, and news of the earthquake in Honduras had just turned the matter from bad to worse. Her stomach had grown increasingly queasy during the course of the afternoon, and her head had been throbbing for the last hour.

As soon as she was out in the hallway, she checked her cell phone for messages about Daniel. There was nothing. She took the stairs down from the third floor of the courthouse as usual and was the first juror out of the building.

She didn't know whether the others had stopped by the restroom or were hanging back to continue the conversation that they had started in the jury room before the bailiff intervened. If it was the latter, she wanted no part of it. *Please Lord, spare me from the deliberation.*

The heat was intense as she walked out of the cool courthouse into the hot July sun. An uncontrollable shiver passed over her, and she stumbled on the sidewalk as she walked toward her car. She caught herself before she actually fell, but she knew she needed sleep. *I'll just drive by the church and talk to Andrew for a minute, and then I'll go home for a nap if there's no news.*

She arrived at the church within a couple of minutes and walked into the office to talk to Andrew. He was sitting behind Daniel's desk and apparently didn't hear her come in. For a moment, Andrew's resemblance to Daniel almost took Sara's breath away. She thought about telling Daniel goodbye in that same office just a few days earlier.

Sara let out a small cry, and Andrew looked up. "Sara! Are you okay?" He was surprised to see her in the doorway.

"No, I'm not okay at all. I didn't sleep much last night, and I've been thinking about Daniel all day long." Her tears fell. "Have you heard anything?"

"Not really. I've called the mission board a couple of times, but they haven't been able to give me any definite news. All they'll say is that the earthquake damage is concentrated in and around the capital city of Tegucigalpa, Honduras."

"I don't know if that's good news or bad news. I wish we knew whether Daniel got out of Tegucigalpa before the quake hit." Sara seemed frustrated.

"Yes, so do I. All we really have to go on is that last phone call Daniel made to you on Monday saying that he would be there for a day or two."

"So he could have still been there when the earthquake happened, or he could have already left for the mountains," Sara said, repeating the words she and Andrew had said to various members of the congregation the evening before. "We just don't know."

Both Sara and Andrew let out long sighs.

"Did you sleep?" Sara asked.

"Not much. I kept the television on all night, just hoping to see something," Andrew said. "Mom and dad are worried sick, too. They keep calling me every little bit."

"I'm just so tired," Sara said. "I can't even think straight anymore. I hadn't even thought about your parents."

"They're struggling with it all just like we are, Sara. And praying," Andrew said. "It's really all we can do at this point."

"Yes. I've been doing that all day," she said with a weak smile. "He has to be okay. Right?"

"Yeah, he's probably fine. He'll have a big laugh when he finds out we worried over nothing." Andrew returned Sara's smile. "Go home and get some rest. I'll call you if I hear anything at all."

"I'm so exhausted that I don't think I have much choice," Sara said. "To think, I was worried about something like a jury trial just a few days ago. This really puts things into perspective, doesn't it?"

"It certainly does," Andrew said. "How's the trial going, by the way?"

"Well, the judge instructed us not to talk about it until was over, but I think it's okay to tell you that I'm only an alternate. Hopefully, I'll be dismissed before the deliberation. I'm praying that's what happens, anyway."

"That would be hard, wouldn't it? To sit through an entire case and then not get to vote?"

"Actually, it would be a wonderful thing. I haven't heard half the testimony."

"I'm sure this thing with Daniel has had you pretty distracted."

"That's part of it." Sara wished for an instant that she could tell Andrew the whole story. Of course, there was no way she could admit to her fiancé's brother that she had an affair with a married man and was now a juror on a case in which he was serving as a prosecuting attorney. *What would he think of me?*

"Go on home and get some rest. I'll call you the minute I hear something."

"Thanks." *That's what I need. Some rest and some time to think.*

Sara stopped by Grams' house before heading to her apartment. Like Andrew, Grams had been watching the television all day, hoping for more news about the earthquake in Honduras. She didn't know any more than Andrew did, though, as the news had only been showing the same footage over and over. Grams also urged Sara to try and get some sleep, so Sara drove home after just a few minutes at her house.

When Sara got home, an irate Callie met her at the door "Oh, no! I hope I didn't forget to feed you this morning!"

The cat meowed loudly and rubbed herself against Sara's legs.

Sara checked the food dish and found it empty. "I'm sorry, Callie. I'll get that taken care of right away!" Sara filled the empty food dish and changed the water.

Sara checked to see if she had any messages on her home phone. There were none. She hadn't really expected any, as Daniel usually called her on her cell phone. She grabbed a couple of ibuprofen tablets for her headache, headed to the couch, and turned on the television, flipping through the news channels until she found coverage of the earthquake.

As Andrew had told her, the damage was most severe in and around the capital city of Tegucigalpa. According to the latest reports, there had been quite a bit of structural damage to smaller buildings, but larger, more solid buildings such as churches and schools appeared to be intact. The news anchor said the death toll in the capital was climbing into the hundreds, but there had been very few deaths outside that particular city.

Callie jumped up on the couch beside Sara. Sara stroked the cat's head, feeling her purr growing louder. "Did you get your belly full, girl?"

Callie remained silent. She wasn't the kind of cat who went about meowing over nothing.

Sara spoke softly to her, "Sorry I forgot your food this morning. You wouldn't believe the crazy week I've had."

Callie stretched out on the couch and looked up intently as Sara spoke to her.

"First, I was worried about being on a jury. You see, Callie, I was afraid it would be too hard to judge somebody else's guilt or innocence when I've made so many mistakes myself. But then, you know all about that, don't you, girl?"

Callie continued to purr and look up at Sara.

"Callie, it was him. It was Kyle. You remember, the one who rescued you when you wandered onto his porch out at the river? You were just a baby kitten. Well, now you're a big, grown kitty cat, and he's a lawyer, the prosecutor for the State. He's trying the case this week, and I'm on the jury. What kind of crazy luck is that? It took me so long to get over him. Then I finally did, and here he is again."

Callie's eyes were growing smaller as Sara continued to talk.

"He's married. Of course, we already knew that part. He has two kids now. That explains a lot, doesn't it, girl? He left us because his wife was going to have a baby." Sara nodded her head up and down thoughtfully. "And that's okay. That was the right thing for him to do."

Callie's eyes were closed, and she blinked them open only with a great effort.

"It was hard at first, seeing him again. It brought back all those old feelings, the hurt, the anger. Then I found out that Daniel was in trouble, that there was this earthquake down in Honduras, and I didn't think about Kyle anymore. I thought I truly loved him, but now I don't know. It felt real at the time, but I knew something wasn't right."

Callie's head was now lying flat on the couch, and she no longer made any effort to look at Sara.

"I understand it better now. Kyle was never mine. But you know what? That's okay, Callie. I have Daniel now. It's real this time, with Daniel. It's right. I feel it in my heart."

Sara rested her hand on Callie's soft, warm head. Her eyes were growing heavier as she concentrated on the television. The news reporter was still talking about death tolls and earthquake intensity, but there was nothing that Sara hadn't already heard. She turned down the volume on the television and bowed her head, praying silently.

When she was done, she stretched out on the couch beside Callie. After a minute or two, she pulled a thin quilt over them both and fell soundly asleep.

***

Back at the courthouse, Kyle and Sharese were heatedly debating the State's motion for a continuance.

"Judge, Larry Turner is a crucial witness, and it would pose no hardship on the defendant if the court gives the State a couple of days to locate him," Kyle pleaded. "The defendant has been in prison for three years. A few more days in the county jail aren't going to hurt him." *I guarantee they won't hurt him any more than they'll hurt me.*

"Your Honor, the defendant has waived his Constitutional right to cross-examine Mr. Turner so that we could finish this trial this week. He wants to get this matter behind him as soon as possible," Sharese said.

Judge Oaks didn't say anything for a long moment. Finally, he peered down at Kyle. "You've had your chance, General. I don't see how delaying this matter will make or break the State's case. The witness testified on direct that the defendant passed him at a high rate of speed, and he even identified the witness in the courtroom. What more could you want?"

What Kyle wanted was to make sure that the "conduct creating a substantial risk" portion of the vehicular homicide statute was covered. To do that, he needed Larry Turner to get back up on the witness stand and testify that the road had been dangerous and curvy.

Of course, he knew that the judge had a point in saying that Mr. Turner had already testified that Justin passed him, speeding, just a few minutes before he struck Maria. The State also had the testimony of Sharon White to argue that Justin was intoxicated at the time of the accident, even if his BAC was slightly below the threshold for a presumption of intoxication under the DUI statute.

Kyle looked back at Marcus, not sure what to do. Marcus gave a small shrug, which Kyle took to mean that it didn't really matter much whether they found Larry Turner or not. The case was at a point where it could go either way, depending on the disposition of the jury. Kyle wondered which way Sara would vote if she ended up deliberating with the other jurors rather than being excused as an alternate.

"Well, General? What else do you hope to prove if we get Larry Turner back here?" Judge Oaks asked.

Kyle realized he had lost his train of thought again. "Uh. Oh. You know, Judge, I think the State's going to go ahead and withdraw its motion for a continuance." Both Sharese and Marcus gave him a questioning look.

As Kyle sat down, Marcus leaned over and whispered, "Just because we were losing the game didn't mean you had to just hand the ball to the other team like that. What's happened to you? Sara's not even in here, man!"

Kyle didn't say anything for a minute. He just let out a long breath and stared straight ahead. As Sharese began to argue her motion for an acquittal, Kyle whispered to Marcus, "It doesn't matter whether she's in the courtroom or not. She's in my head, and I can't get her out."

CHAPTER 19

As expected, Judge Oaks denied Sharese's motion for a judgment of acquittal. As she gathered up her things and made her way out of the courtroom, she gave Justin a knowing smile. They knew the motion was a long shot, just part of the procedural foundation for an appeal if there was a conviction, and neither was particularly disappointed at the outcome.

After the judge left the bench, Sharese had a slight feeling of buoyancy, knowing that she had done the best that she could for her client thus far in the trial. She had gone from a completely green, weak-in-the-knees newbie to – well, not a veteran trial lawyer by any stretch of the imagination, but she was certainly a different person on Thursday afternoon than she had been on Monday morning.

"All right then. So you're still going to try and ruin all my hard work by getting on that stand and throwing yourself to the wolves?" Sharese grinned at Justin.

"Well, ma'am, I do still want to testify, if that's what you mean."

"Yeah. I was afraid of that. I need to go by my office for a few minutes and check messages, that kind of thing. Then, I'll come over to the jail, and we'll go over your testimony, okay?"

Justin looked confused. "But I don't really know what I'm gonna say tomorrow. How can we practice when I don't know what I'll say?"

Sharese was quick with a reply. "That's the point, Justin. It's not what you *are* going to say that will make us or break us, but what you are *not* going to say."

"Oh, okay. Gotcha," Justin replied. "See you at the jail."

Sharese waited until the deputy took Justin out of the courtroom and then made her way to her office. The heat was stifling, and she quickly shed her suit jacket as she exited the courthouse.

When she got back to the public defender's office, she found the door locked. Checking her watch, she saw that it was a little past 5 p.m. She fumbled through her purse and found her office key.

At the receptionist's desk, she collected a stack of messages. At the top was one written in red. *Sharese, your Grandma Eloise has been calling all day. Says she can't reach you on your cell. She needs to talk to you today!*

Seeing the familiar Memphis telephone number, Sharese felt simultaneous waves of guilt and frustration. She usually returned her grandma's calls with the same promptness with which one would respond to blue lights in the rearview mirror. But, this was different.

This call wasn't really about her grandma. It was about her father and his parole hearing. She had hoped that, if she ignored her grandma long enough, Eloise would give up on her attempt to get Sharese to write a letter on his behalf. *Guess that plan is not working out too well.*

With a sigh of resignation, Sharese dialed the number. She braced herself for the fight she knew was coming. Two rings and three heartbeats later, she heard Eloise say, "Hello?"

"It's me, Grandma."

"Sharese, baby! I've been calling you all day! Why didn't you answer your cell phone?"

"I was in court, Grandma. Been trying my first case this week. Today was the fourth day of trial."

"Goodnight! What did your client do that it's takin' that long to sort it out? They ain't startin' you out with some big murder case, are they?"

"No, Grandma. It's a vehicular homicide case."

"A what? That still means they killed somebody, right? You be careful, girl!"

"I'm fine, Grandma. I'm a lawyer, remember? This is what I'm doing for a living."

"Well, I know that, but I just can't help worrying about you. Who'd he kill, anyway?"

Sharese drew her breath and tried to focus on staying calm. "According to the State, he hit a young girl with his car. He didn't do it on purpose, but he'd been drinking and was speeding."

"Oh, well, I guess that's not too awful then. A shame and all, but at least he's not an ax murderer."

"No ma'am. The State wouldn't let an ax murderer off with less than first-degree murder charge."

"Well, that's good. Anyway, I've been calling, tryin' to tell you that the letters are due on your daddy's behalf earlier than I told you before. They moved the deadline up a week because of some change in the parole board schedule or something."

There was silence on the phone for a long minute.

"Sharese? Baby, you are gonna write a letter, right?"

"I don't know if I can, Grandma."

"He's your daddy."

"No. I don't have a 'daddy.' Tony Jackson is my biological father. And he's in prison for homicide." Sharese rarely back-talked her grandmother, but this time she couldn't help herself. "Two minutes ago, you were worried about the mere possibility of me representing some random killer in court, and yet here you are wanting me to write a letter on behalf of a convicted murderer. Have you forgotten that his gang killed a cop?"

On the other end of the line, there was a long pause. "You know I ain't forgot that. I won't ever forget, anymore than that policeman's mama will forget. We both lost our sons that night."

Sharese heard her grandmother sniffle on the other end of the line. She felt a surge of love for her and regretted the harsh words she had spoken. "I'm sorry, Grandma. I shouldn't have talked to you like that. I know you love him."

Eloise responded, "Yes, I love him, just like I love you. I know he's been bad. You child, you don't know any different side of him, but there is a good side, too. I saw that side of him when he was a little boy, 'fore he got into all that gang mess, and I been seeing that good side for a few years now when I go visit him at the prison. You go see him, and you'll see it, too."

Sharese tried to conjure up some sympathetic image of Tony Jackson, convicted cop-killer, that she could think of as "good." Something that would give her a reason to try to help him, but there was nothing. When Sharese thought of Tony Jackson, all she had was a vague sense of loss. Try as she might, she could think of nothing about the man that gave her any sense of responsibility to try to help him.

Still, she was moved by the urgency and heartbreak in her grandmother's voice as she pleaded with her to give her father a chance. The words were out of her mouth before she could stop herself. "I'm not going to promise to go and see him, Grandma, but I'll write a letter if it will make you happy."

"Thank you, baby girl. You don't know what it means to me," Eloise said.

And you don't know what it means to me, either. "I really have to go now, Grandma. I've got to go see my client and get ready for his testimony tomorrow." They quickly said their goodbyes, and Sharese was left to think about what she had just agreed to do.

A good side and a bad side. Where Tony Jackson was concerned, Sharese had lived her entire life as the carnage of the bad side. Part of her wanted to believe that Eloise was right, that there was good in him, too, but it was hard.

Sharese thought about Justin. Certainly, the Justin Hargis she had come to know over the last few weeks was not the same young man who had been driving down that country road the night that Maria Flores died. She accepted that there was a good side and a bad side to him, and she was willing to try to help the good triumph over the bad.

It was different between her and Justin, though, and Sharese knew it. She was Justin's attorney. She liked him and hoped his case went well, but she wasn't personally vested in the outcome. At the end of the day, it would be Justin, and Justin alone, who would have to live with whatever happened in the courtroom. If she agreed to help Tony Jackson, she knew it would be a very different story.

***

After court, Kyle and Marcus walked out of the courthouse together. Marcus's tan and black Tennessee Highway Patrol cruiser was parked in front of the courthouse in one of the spots reserved for law officers.

Marcus opened the door and started the car so the air conditioning could cool it down before he got inside. With the door open and the engine running, he leaned against the front fender and looked at Kyle. "You've got to let it go, man. Shake it off before you go home to your wife and kids."

Kyle, who had not spoken since the two men left the courtroom, was staring at his feet. With his head still hung, he cast his eyes upward at Marcus. "Tell me something I *don't* know, man."

Marcus let out an uneasy chuckle and looked around the court square to make sure there weren't any curious eyes on them. "Three years is a long time. Surely, you're over her."

"It's not that. I don't love –," Kyle stopped abruptly.

"Three years, man. Three years."

"Yeah, three years. In some ways, it seems like a lifetime ago. Back before there were kids and mortgages and crazy trials like this. You still think we got a shot at this one, Marcus? Tell me straight."

Marcus sighed. "I wish we had gotten more out of the trucker before he split. He said Hargis was driving too fast before the accident, but he wasn't an actual eyewitness to the wreck. I'm sure the P.D. will argue that creates reasonable doubt. I hate to say it, but the best thing we've got going is Hargis himself, if he's really crazy enough to take the stand."

Kyle nodded. "Yeah, we still have that, I guess. Good thing we drew that brand new P.D. She'll figure out soon enough what a mistake she's making, letting him testify on his own behalf."

"Oh, she knows better already," Marcus said. "She's no fool, just a got a fool for a client."

"So you're starting to notice the lovely Ms. Jackson after all," Kyle teased Marcus.

"Well, four days of all day, every day, and a man can't help but notice a woman like that," Marcus admitted.

"It's about time," Kyle answered. "And you're right; it's not her fault. Judge Oaks always lets a defendant testify if he insists on it. To tell you the truth, I think he likes giving them enough rope to hang themselves."

"They don't call him 'Hang 'em Henry' for nothing." Marcus stifled a yawn. "I'd better check in at headquarters and then head home."

"No b-ball tonight?" Kyle asked.

"Nah. I'm wiped out. I'll be lucky to stay awake to watch the news tonight. All this mess is catching up with me."

"All right, man. See you in the morning," Kyle said as Marcus got into his cruiser and drove off.

Kyle stopped in his office to check his messages and read his mail. It only took a few minutes to reconstruct the major dramas of the day as recorded by Angela, but he wasn't ready to go home just yet. Instead, he got into his car, rolled the windows down, and turned up the radio.

He soon found himself driving the familiar route towards Roaring River. He didn't really know why he was doing it – after all, he'd just been there the day before – but somehow he couldn't seem to help himself.

He didn't stop as he passed his family's fishing cabin. Instead, he continued on the narrow gravel road to the small, white clapboard cabin two doors past his own. The one where he had met Sara. As he crept along the road at a snail's pace, his mind traveled back in time.

"Josie? Josie, open up the door." He knew she would not be expecting him so early in the day, and he hadn't wanted to startle her.

When she answered the door, she was wearing a white cotton shirt and denim shorts. Her wild hair was tangled up in a knot on top of her head, and a camera hung around her neck.

"Can I come in?"

"Of course. Hey, do you want to see that picture I took last night of you and your big fish? I printed out a copy of it. I'm thinking of using it as a visual aid for my thesis," she joked.

Kyle didn't laugh. "We need to talk, Josie."

Josie tilted her head, trying to read him. "Talk about what?"

"My wife called me this morning. I'm going back to Knoxville tonight. I'm sorry, but I won't be back."

Just then, a deer ran out in front of Kyle's car, snapping him out of his daydream. He hit the brakes and watched as several more charged blindly ahead, just inches from his front bumper. The first few were oblivious to anything except getting to the other side of the road, but the last one, a young doe, was different. For some reason, she glanced sideways before she proceeded across.

Maybe it was the sound of the car's engine or perhaps it was just a case of youthful curiosity that made her pause. Whatever it was, it startled her enough that she stopped dead center of the road. It was obvious that she didn't know what to do with herself once she had stopped. First, she looked at Kyle through the windshield, and then she took a quarter of a turn back towards the path behind her. That didn't seem quite right to her either, so still she stood in the middle of the road.

Growing impatient, Kyle yelled out the window, "Make up your mind! Don't you know that standing in the middle of the road is crazy?"

The deer reacted immediately, running with all her might into the safety and sanctity of the forest ahead.

Kyle looked from the spot where the deer had disappeared up to the cabin where he had left Sara crying on the porch when he went back to Elizabeth that fateful summer day. The feeling of conflict that had burned in his stomach as he said goodbye had eased during the intervening years, but he knew deep down that it would never completely go away.

That deer made it look so easy. All she needed was someone to point out the obvious, that the middle of the road is a dangerous place.

The deer was long gone and could no longer hear the rumble of the car's engine as it idled in the road.

CHAPTER 20

A sudden crash of thunder shortly before dawn on Friday morning brought Kyle out of a deep sleep. It also awoke Chelsea, sending Elizabeth to her crib to try and soothe her.

As long as the baby was only fussing quietly in Elizabeth's arms, Kyle could pretend he was still asleep. As the storm grew closer and louder, Chelsea became inconsolable, and Kyle knew it was time to get up and face the consequences of his broken promise to come home early the night before.

There was ice in Elizabeth's voice when they met in the hallway. "Where were you last night? You said you'd be home early."

"I drove out to Roaring River. I wanted to take a look at the accident scene before closing arguments." Kyle was both impressed and disgusted with how easily the lie had come. The truth was he hadn't given any thought to the fact that the accident had happened only a mile or so from his family's cabin until that moment.

"I waited up until 11 p.m."

"The accident happened at night, so I thought I should wait until dark to get an accurate impression." *Trust me, I'm a lawyer.*

"So you just sat out there in your car for hours?"

"I, uh, hung out at the cabin for awhile. I was going over the file."

"You could have called."

"I lost track of time. By the time I realized how late it was, I was afraid I would wake the baby if I called."

Elizabeth checked the time on the grandfather clock at the end of the hallway. "Could you please just hold her long enough for me to take a shower?"

Kyle saw that her hands were shaking as she handed him the baby. "Sure. Take your time."

Kyle took the baby downstairs, turned on the Weather Channel, and watched a squall line move through the area on radar. After a few minutes, Chelsea settled down. "You're a sweet girl when you want to be, now aren't you? Will you do me a favor and be extra nice to your mommy today? Between you and me, she seems pretty close to the end of her rope."

By the time court started at 9 a.m., the initial thunder and lightning had moved through, and what remained was a dark, dreary mess of a day. Kyle and Marcus sat at the defense table, both bleary-eyed.

"What'd you do last night, man?" Marcus summoned the energy to start a conversation. "I think I was asleep before sunset. Sure could have used another couple of hours sleep this morning."

Kyle was still looking at the window. "Let's just say I went deer hunting."

"What? It's not deer season," Marcus said.

At first, Kyle just shook his head, indicating to Marcus that it was not a story worth telling.

"You've piqued my interest now." Marcus refused to let it slide. "Tell me what you meant by that."

Looking around to make sure no one was within earshot, Kyle explained. "I drove out to the river again. Nearly hit a deer right in front of her cabin."

"You what? *Her* cabin? Did she see you?" Marcus was alarmed that Kyle had taken such a risk.

"No. She wasn't out there, not that I know of, anyway," Kyle spoke in a low voice.

"So what happened?"

"I just sat there, feeling like that deer caught in the headlights," Kyle said.

"You've got to let it go." Marcus gave Kyle a serious look. "You don't want to blow what you've got now. You made a choice back then, remember?"

Kyle didn't say anything for a minute. Marcus peered at him expectantly.

After giving the matter some thought, Kyle responded, "Okay, I made a choice. I just didn't count on Sara ever coming back into my life again, that's all."

"It's not easy when your past mistakes come knocking on the door like that, but, believe me, it could be a lot worse."

"I don't see how," Kyle replied.

Before Marcus could explain, the bailiff sounded, "All rise for the Honorable Henry Oaks."

"Right on time," Kyle said.

"At least something's predictable around here," Marcus replied.

***

On the other side of the aisle, Sharese found her hands shaking almost violently. She thought she had shaken the nerves that had plagued her during the first day or two of the trial, but apparently she was wrong.

She'd never much believed in omens, but the thunderclap before the break of dawn had not suggested that it would be a good day.

"Is the defense ready, Ms. Jackson?" Judge Oaks asked. "I assume your client still wishes to testify."

Sharese cleared her throat as she stood to address the court. "Yes, we're ready for Mr. Hargis's testimony, Your Honor."

"Come on up to the witness stand then, young man. We need to get a few things on the record before we bring the jury in." Judge Oaks motioned Justin up to the front of the courtroom.

The court reporter sat poised and ready, watching Justin as he carefully made his way to the witness stand in his leg irons.

"Now, Mr. Hargis, has your attorney advised you that you have a right under the Fifth Amendment to the United States Constitution to remain silent in this case, that is, to refuse to testify in your case so as not to offer incriminating evidence on your own behalf?"

"Yes, sir, she done that." Justin didn't hesitate.

"Do you understand that the State of Tennessee does not have a right to call you as a witness in this trial but that, if you testify on your own behalf, the district attorney general will then have a right to cross-examine you about your testimony?" Judge Oaks continued.

"Yes, Miss Jackson explained all that to me real clear." Justin looked directly at the judge as he spoke.

"Very well then," Judge Oaks said. "Do you wish to waive these rights?"

"Yes, sir, I do. I want to tell my side of things, at least as best I remember," Justin spoke softly.

Judge Oaks asked Justin a few other questions, making sure he had created enough of a record to survive an appeal on the issue of the defendant's voluntary waiver of his Fifth Amendment rights. When he was finished, he turned to look at Justin, meeting Justin's steady and certain gaze. Speaking to the attorneys, the judge said, "I think that about covers the waiver issue. Think we'll get this case to the jury today, folks?"

"Probably so, Your Honor," Sharese said, "unless the State has a lengthy rebuttal." *Is it too late for him to recall Trooper*

Thompson to question him about the clothing fibers found on Justin's car?

"I don't anticipate that at this time, Your Honor," Kyle said.

"Very well, then. Let's bring in the jury." Judge Oaks motioned for the bailiff to go back to the jury room. "You can stay where you are, Mr. Hargis. It'll just be a minute."

***

On the way to court, Sara had stopped by the parsonage and talked to Andrew about Daniel. Andrew hadn't heard any news during the night, but he had promised to request an update from the mission board, who had been attempting to locate Daniel and the others since the earthquake struck.

As Sara was waiting in the jury room for court to begin, she had received a text from Andrew. *Mission board has spoken to local pastor at mountain mission site. Daniel and party had not arrived there as of 8 a.m. this morning. Communication still sporadic in Tegucigalpa.*

Fredonia noticed Sara's worried look and came over to her. "Honey, are you okay? I hope you haven't had bad news about your fiancé."

"Not bad news exactly, but not good either," Sara replied. "I just got a text from Daniel's brother saying that he and the other missionaries didn't make it up to the Honduran mountains before the earthquake like we'd hoped. They must still be in the capital city where the quake hit hardest."

"Oh, honey, I'm so sorry." Fredonia gave Sara a comforting hug. "He's probably fine though. I saw a report on the news last night saying that phone lines are down all over the place there."

"Yes, Andrew's text said that, too."

"We'll just keep praying. It's gonna be all right; I just know it is," Fredonia said with a degree of conviction that Sara wished was contagious.

When the bailiff came to escort the jurors into the courtroom, Sara put her cell phone on vibrate and slipped it into the pocket of her slacks. She smiled despite herself as she whispered to Fredonia, "While we're praying, do you think we can ask that the judge not send me to jail if I answer this cell phone during court?"

"I think that would be just fine, honey," Fredonia chuckled.

CHAPTER 21

When the jurors arrived in the courtroom, Justin was still seated in the witness box. Judge Oaks reminded him that he was still under oath, and Sharese began her direct examination.

"State your name for the record, please," Sharese began.

"Justin Alvin Hargis."

"Where were you born?"

"Maple Springs, Tennessee."

"How old are you?"

"I turned twenty-one this summer."

"Do you understand that you are on trial for the vehicular homicide of Maria Flores?"

"Yes, ma'am, I understand that."

"And you have chosen to waive your right to remain silent, a right guaranteed to you under the Fifth Amendment to the United States Constitution, in order to tell your side of this case to the jury?"

"Yes, ma'am, I have."

"Can you tell me what you remember about the day of the accident?" Sharese said a silent prayer that Justin would, through his testimony, find the peace that he sought. *Please, Lord, let him remember what happened that night. All of it – the truth, the whole truth, and nothing but the truth.*

"Yes, ma'am. I'll try my best." Justin shut his eyes. Sharese knew he was willing himself to remember as many details as possible about the day Maria Flores died. "I don't remember anything about the early part of the day. It was the middle of the summer. I probably slept pretty late, messed around the house. You know, that kind of stuff."

"What about later in the day? Do you remember anything about that afternoon or evening?" Sharese asked.

"Well, ma'am, the first thing that I can remember was going over to my friend Danny's house. We played a video game – Call of Duty, I think – and watched a ballgame and a movie."

"What time did you get to Danny's house?"

"It was late afternoon when I went over there, but I don't know the exact time."

"Tell me what you remember about being at Danny's house."

Justin's eyes were still closed as he listened to Sharese question him. "Like I said, we watched some television and played video games. After awhile, we got sorta bored and decided to head out to the river and party."

"Party?" Sharese asked him with a raised eyebrow.

"Well, party some more, you might say." Justin hung his head as he spoke.

"Had you and Danny been drinking or doing drugs during the time that you were at his home playing video games and watching the ballgame?"

"No, ma'am, we didn't do no drugs, but we did drink a few beers."

"How many beers did you have?"

"Danny took a six-pack out of his old man's fridge in the garage. We split that, so I guess three apiece?" Justin opened his eyes and looked up at Sharese, as if asking her whether he had correctly divided six by two.

"Three apiece then," Sharese felt obliged to answer back. "Over how many hours?"

Kyle voiced an objection, and the attorneys approached the bench. "Your Honor, she's leading the witness. For all we know, they knocked back the entire six-pack in ten minutes instead of several 'hours' as defense counsel indicated."

"Technically, General, I agree, but surely you can't complain about this line of testimony, can you? How often do you get a defendant to admit on the stand that he'd been drinking at all?" Judge Oaks gave Kyle a look that clearly told him to sit down and shut up. "You can follow-up on the particulars on cross-examination."

Kyle nodded. "Okay, the State will withdraw its objection."

Sharese took her place back at the podium and continued questioning Justin. "As I was saying, can you tell me how many hours it took you and your friend Danny to consume the three beers apiece?"

Justin shook his head. "No, ma'am, not exactly. I don't remember what time it was when we took the beers out of the fridge or what time it was that we left the house."

Knowing that the longer it took the boys to consume the beers, the better off Justin would be, Sharese thought for a minute of how she might be able to help her client remember more. "Do you recall much about the ballgame? For example, do you know what inning it was when you started drinking?"

Justin closed his eyes again and thought about it for a minute. "You know, I'm pretty sure that it was the second or third inning."

Sharese had asked him about it before, but he had never remembered much about the game. This new detail seemed to surprise even Justin, and his eyes flew open.

"Yeah, now I remember. We missed the first inning for sure. It was like the bottom of the second or the top of the third when we turned the game on. The Braves had lost the two games before that, and we were really hoping they'd pull that one out. But when we turned it on, they were already down by two runs. Danny was real ticked off, and that was why he went and got the beer. He hated it when the Braves lost." Justin smiled sheepishly at the jury as some of the men nodded their heads in agreement.

"We kept watching the game, hoping they'd turn it around. But after about the seventh inning, it was gettin' real bad. They were down by about ten runs, so we turned it over to a movie."

"Do you remember the name of the movie that you watched?" Sharese was pleased that Justin seemed to be remembering some things that had previously eluded him.

"Well, ma'am, I'm not sure." Justin closed his eyes again and bowed his head. He reached up and rubbed his head as he concentrated on answering Sharese's question. "I know it was an old movie. One my mama used to watch when I was a kid. It was set back in the 1950s, and there was a dude that was in a gang. There was this girl who was real shy, but they got together at the end at some carnival or something."

Grease. Although Justin didn't actually name the movie, Sharese recognized it immediately, and she was sure that most of the jury did also. She considered whether to say the name of the movie aloud to Justin, but she knew that it would trigger an objection from Kyle.

Not wanting to disrupt the flow of Justin's testimony, she opted to continue the questions without actually naming the movie. "Did you and Danny start watching the movie at the beginning or had it been on awhile?"

"It wasn't at the beginning. I think when we turned it over to the movie, it was at that part where the girl has pink hair and there's this dude singing to her about being a high school dropout. No, a beauty school dropout, that's it." Justin laughed a little to himself, apparently remembering the humorous image from the movie.

"Did you watch it to the end?"

"Yeah." Justin smiled at Sharese. "I remember Danny ribbing me pretty hard for wanting to watch the part at the end where they dance at the carnival. Hey, I think the dude in the movie was named 'Danny' too - yeah, Danny Zippo or Zuko or something like that." Justin looked over at the jury box. "Anyway, I didn't care if Danny – my friend Danny – made fun of me. That's the best part of the movie, and I made him wait 'til it was over."

Sharese was pleasantly surprised that Justin's memory of the ballgame and the movie had given her a few new details to help firm up the time line of his consumption of alcohol on the night of the accident.

"Can you estimate how long it was from the time that you began watching the ballgame to the time that you left your friend Danny's house after the movie?"

Counting up the time in his head, Justin mumbled to himself before telling Sharese, "I think probably three hours or so?" He said it more like a question, again asking Sharese's opinion on the accuracy of his estimate.

"How do you figure that?" she asked, wanting Justin to explain his response and hoping the jury was aware of the general rule that it takes one hour for the body to process one alcoholic beverage. If the jury believed that Justin was sober enough to drive that night, it might establish some reasonable doubt as to whether his intoxication contributed to the accident. Of course, there was still the question of his speeding, but that would have to be explored later.

"Well, ma'am, a baseball game lasts about 3 hours, I'd say. We missed the first inning for sure and the last two, too, I think. If we watched six innings out of nine, that's two-thirds, and two-thirds of three hours is two hours, right?"

"Yes, I believe that's right." Sharese felt a little sorry for Justin that he needed her help with a fourth grade math problem.

"Okay, so that's two hours, and then probably another hour for the movie. That adds up to three hours."

"Do you remember what time you left Danny's house?"

"Yeah, it was about dark. Probably between 8 p.m. and 9 p.m."

"What were your plans when you left Danny's house?"

He hung his head as he said, "We were gonna buy some dope and head out to the river."

"Are you talking about methamphetamine?" Sharese asked.

"Well, we was gonna buy grass – marijuana – but we ended up with meth. Crystal, methamphetamine, crank, whatever you wanna call it," Justin said shamefully. "Danny had been smoking it for about a month and told me I should try it, too."

"Where did you buy the meth?"

"We drove out to Cotton's and bought some from a guy Danny knew. We seen him in the parking lot right after we got there."

"Who drove to Cotton's, you or Danny?"

"I did, ma'am. It was my car, my Blazer that we was in."

"Did anything significant happen while you were at Cotton's, other than you purchasing drugs?"

"Well, Danny seen his old girlfriend Brianna. He took off with her and left me by myself. Nothing too exciting except that, I reckon."

"What did you do then?"

"Well, I had the meth, and I was really wantin' to see if it was as good as everybody said it was. I thought about doing in the parking lot, but I was a little worried that the cops might pull up. They hit Cotton's pretty regular. So I took off and headed out to the river. There's usually some kids out there at night in the summer. I figured I'd meet up with them and smoke the meth out there."

"Did you actually make it to the river?"

"No, the accident happened before I got there," Justin said.

"Tell us what you remember after you left Cotton's." Sharese hoped Justin would not destroy the seeds of reasonable doubt that she had worked so hard to plant. She struggled to silence the competitor in her who wanted to win the case at all costs, even if that meant that Justin didn't remember another single thing about the accident. *Peace, Lord. Justin wants peace. Help him remember.*

Justin was silent for a long minute, and several of the jurors shifted uncomfortably in their seats. Sharese was sure that he was about to say that he couldn't remember anything else, but then he looked down at his hands. An odd look came over his face, and he fingered the blue necktie that his mother had bought him for court.

"Blue," he whispered. "Hands. Something blue and someone's hands."

"I'm sorry, Mr. Hargis, can you repeat that? I didn't quite understand you," Sharese said, wondering what in the world he was talking about. Up until that point, Justin had claimed no recollection of anything at all after he left Cotton's.

A look of confusion passed over Justin's face. "I just – I thought I remembered something blue. And something about hands. I just – I don't –" Justin began to breathe heavily and break into an obvious sweat.

Sharese had never seen him like this. "Your Honor, I think we might need to take a break." She knew the timing was bad, as Justin seemed on the verge of remembering something important, but he also looked as if he were about to pass out in the witness box.

Judge Oaks, who had been riveted to Justin's testimony, agreed with Sharese's assessment of the situation and asked Justin, "Do you need a break, Mr. Hargis?"

"No," Justin said quietly. "Just give me a minute." He wiped his face with his hands and closed his eyes again. "There was a song on the radio, 'Blue Suede Shoes.' Not Elvis, but the dude that wrote it, Carl Perkins. I like his version better, and I turned it up."

"Is that what you meant by 'something blue,' Justin, the song title 'Blue Suede Shoes'?" Sharese asked, even more confused than before. *He said the other day that a 1950s song was on the radio.*

Justin took a deep breath before continuing. He closed his eyes again, willing himself to remember more. "No. That song just happened to be on the radio. I saw something blue in the road. I don't know what it was though. Then, hands waving. A flash of light."

The courtroom was completely silent except for the tapping of the court reporter on her machine. Even the judge was holding his breath.

"What happened then?" Sharese asked, though she wasn't sure she wanted to hear the answer.

Justin sat silently in the witness chair.

"Justin, what happened next?" Sharese repeated, a bit louder. A pained look came over his face, and he looked up at Sharese.

"I don't know, Miss Jackson. I can't remember anything else."

There was another question she wanted to ask, one that delved into dangerous territory. It was risky, but at that moment she thought that it was the only hope she had of proving that someone other than Justin killed Maria Flores. "The flash of light that you mentioned, could it have been from another car – another car that could have struck Ms. Flores?"

Justin shook his head in the negative. "No, ma'am, I don't think so."

Sharese winced at Justin's response. Had she been able to think clearly, she might have thought more quickly of another question that would have shifted the jury's attention away from what had just been said. As it was, the seconds of silence ticked by and Justin's answer lingered in the air until it was almost palpable.

Then, Sharese reminded herself of what Justin had said to her a few days before. *He doesn't expect to walk out of here a free man. He just wants to know what really happened. More than anything else, he needs closure.* As the competitive side of Sharese cowered under the table, the compassionate side asked, "Do you remember hitting Maria Flores with your car, Justin?"

Justin shook his head again, a blank look on his face. "No, ma'am. I don't remember hitting her. I don't remember seeing a face or a body. Just something blue and hands. And then the flash of light."

"What's the next thing that you remember?"

"Waking up in the hospital the next day and talking to Trooper Thompson," Justin answered, looking across the courtroom at Marcus.

Sharese tried desperately to think of another question, something that would trigger Justin's memory of that night, of the accident. Something that would make him realize the truth of what had happened and to accept it.

Sharese looked across the aisle at Kyle as he furiously scribbled notes on his legal pad, and it dawned on her. *It's not my job to convict Justin Hargis of vehicular homicide.* Bracing herself for the thing that she had been dreading all week, she drew a deep breath and said, "Thank you, Justin. That's all the questions that I have for you. Your witness, General."

CHAPTER 22

As Sharese took her seat, Kyle and Marcus leaned their heads together, exchanging thoughts about Justin's testimony in hushed voices. "I think that might have saved us," Marcus said. "He as much as admitted to killing the Flores girl."

"Yes. I think we're going to be okay." Kyle's relief was evident.

Kyle started to get up, but Marcus put his hand on his arm and stopped him. "Just one thing worries me."

"What?" Kyle asked impatiently, not particularly wanting to hear any bad news Marcus might be about to offer.

"Well, the jury's seen a picture of the girl in the blue dress, so we all know what the 'blue' was about. What bothers me is that thing about the light. That was just strange, don't you think?" Marcus replied.

"No, the only strange thing is that you fell for that line of bull." Kyle brushed off Marcus's concern with a smirk. "He just made it up."

"Maybe. It just sounded odd, that's all," Marcus said. "If he was making it up, why wouldn't he have said that the light was from another car? His lawyer even asked him if there could have been another car involved. He said, 'No.'"

"It's fine, man, really. We're in the best shape that we've been in all week." Kyle cast a mischievous grin to Marcus, then rose to his feet to begin his cross-examination. "Now, the real fun begins." Kyle took his place at the podium and cleared his throat. "Mr. Hargis, I represent the State of Tennessee in this vehicular homicide case. I just have a few questions for you."

"Yes, sir, I understand," Justin responded politely.

"On direct examination, you said that you had consumed approximately three beers before getting behind the wheel of your Chevy Blazer on the night in question, is that correct?"

"Yes, sir. That's the best I remember, anyhow."

"And you told us that, based on your recollection of a ballgame and a movie that you watched some three years ago, while intoxicated, you're pretty sure that you consumed those three beers over a period of about three hours, correct, Mr. Hargis?"

"Yes, sir. That's right."

"That's a lot of threes, isn't it?"

"Objection. Argumentative," Sharese called out.

"I'll withdraw the question." Kyle didn't miss a beat. "Mr. Hargis, you also told us what inning you began watching the ballgame, what inning you stopped watching it, and the plot of the movie, all of which occurred three years ago, correct?"

"Yes, sir, I did," Justin replied.

"Mr. Hargis, can you tell the ladies and gentlemen of the jury what you ate for supper on Tuesday night?"

Justin's mouth opened, but he didn't say anything. He looked around, obviously trying to remember.

Kyle gave a confident look to the jury and let Justin's silence sink in for a minute. "Sorry, Mr. Hargis, I don't think we heard your response."

Justin shook his head. "No, I can't. I don't remember."

"You don't remember what you ate for supper three days ago, but you expect us to believe that you can remember a ballgame and a movie from three years ago?"

"Yes, sir. I do remember it now, but I haven't always."

Kyle's eyebrows shot up in surprise. "So you just remembered all of this today, Mr. Hargis?" The incredulous tone of his voice was not lost on the jury. Several of them were shaking their head in disbelief at the proposition of Justin's sudden burst of memory.

"Well, I remembered a little about Danny's house when I was in pris—"

Sharese was talking in her loudest voice before she was even completely to her feet. "Your Honor, I think we need to take a break!"

Kyle knew she was hoping to drown out the word "prison" as it had come out of Justin's mouth.

Judge Oaks gave a weary nod. "Counsel, approach the bench please."

When Sharese, Kyle and the court reporter were in place before the judge, he continued. "We're not taking a break, Ms. Jackson. We're getting this thing wrapped up today. If you haven't already advised your client not to tell the jury that he's been in prison for this crime, then it is too late!" With that, Judge Oaks gave the gavel a thunderous pound, causing Sharese to jump as she went back to her seat.

Kyle continued with his questions, lightened by what had transpired during the bench conference. "Mr. Hargis, I believe you were telling us about the recent return of your memory. You can continue with that."

Justin had, in fact, gotten Sharese's hint. "What I meant, sir, was that some of it I remembered a while back, and some of it I remembered today."

Kyle crossed his arms and peered across the podium at Justin. In a voice reserved exclusively for homicide defendants – and his son on the rare occasions that he really misbehaved – he asked, "When exactly did you remember killing Maria Flores, Mr. Hargis? Was that a while back or did it just come back to you today?"

207

Justin met Kyle's gaze without looking away, "Like I told Miss Jackson, I don't remember seeing the girl, and I don't remember hitting her. I just remember hands waving and something blue. And then a flash of light."

A smile broke across Kyle's face, although it was clear that he was not a happy man at the moment. "Ah, yes, the mystical light. The one that you told us was not from an oncoming car, correct?"

"Yes sir. I mean, no sir." Justin shook his head. "I don't remember any other car being on the road that night."

Kyle went for the shot. "So, there was no one there except you and someone dressed in blue, waving her hands at you?"

Justin said quietly, "I didn't say it was somebody dressed in blue. I just remember a flash of something blue, and I remember waving hands. And then the light."

Kyle gave an amused look to the jury. "I didn't mean to twist your words, there, Mr. Hargis. Let's move on. Tell me how fast you were driving that night."

"I don't know exactly."

"Did you listen carefully to the testimony of Larry Turner, the truck driver whom you passed on the road that night?"

"Yes, sir, I heard what he said."

"Do you deny that you passed him at a high rate of speed?"

Justin closed his eyes and thought about it before responding, "I can't say for sure, sir. I don't remember it if I did. I just can't remember anything after I left Cotton's."

Again, Kyle moved in for the easy shot, "You remember the song on the radio – even the singer's name – but you don't remember passing an eighteen-wheeler on a dark, curvy, country road that night, is that correct?"

Justin had to know that things were looking bad, but he showed no anger as Kyle attempted to discredit him. "That's right, sir. I do remember the song, and I remember turning the radio up to listen to it. But, no, I don't remember passing Mr. Turner's truck that night."

"And you don't recall how fast you were driving either, is that, right? Kyle asked. "Could have been thirty-five or one hundred and thirty-five, for all you know?"

"Objection, Your Honor," Sharese began.

Before she finished her thought, Kyle threw his legal pad down on the table by Marcus. "I'll withdraw that last question and tender the witness back to the defense, Judge. I think the State's already made its point."

Sharese looked up at Justin as he sat on the witness stand. She knew the damage had already been done and that she could only make it worse with a re-direct examination. "The defense rests, Your Honor."

"General?" Judge Oaks asked. "Anything further from the State?"

"No, Your Honor. I think we're ready for closing arguments," Kyle replied with the most confidence he had managed to muster all week.

The judge looked at his watch and then at the jury. "It's a little early, but I'm going to send you folks on to lunch. We'll meet back around 1 p.m., and the attorneys will give their final arguments."

After the jury left the courtroom, the judge addressed the attorneys. "You all need to be back around noon. We need to firm up these jury instructions and take care of any last minute motions."

"Yes, Your Honor," Sharese said.

Kyle nodded his understanding. *We still have thirteen people on the panel, so there should be no need for an alternate. Judge Oaks will have to let her go. I may survive this week yet.*

CHAPTER 23

After the jury was out of the room, the bailiff led Justin off the witness stand and over to the defense table. "So what happens now, Miss Jackson?" Justin asked.

"The attorneys will deliver closing arguments, and then the judge will give the jury their instructions."

"Did I do okay up there?"

Sharese gave an uncertain smile. "Well, it was good that you remembered at least something about the accident. I know you wanted to do that. But…"

"But I still didn't remember killing the girl."

"Yeah. You still didn't remember killing the girl. The thing is, you didn't offer any other explanation as to how your car came to be wrapped around a tree and her dead body laying in the ditch, either."

The pained look on Justin's face told Sharese that her words had been too harsh. "I'm sorry, Justin. That wasn't a good way to put it."

"It's okay, Miss Jackson. Like they say, 'The truth hurts.'"

"Yeah," Sharese said, noticing the bailiff's impatient look. "Looks like it's time for you to go back to the holding area. I'm going back to my office to make some notes for the closing arguments."

"Okay. Thanks, Miss Jackson."

"No problem. Closing arguments are just part of my job."

"No, I mean thanks for letting me testify. I know it probably didn't help my case none, but I feel better knowing I've remembered all that I can and that I've said my peace."

"You're welcome, Justin. I know that's worth a lot to you."

"And one other thing, Miss Jackson."

"Yes?"

"It really is okay if they find me guilty again. I'm expecting it, so don't think I'll be mad at you or nothing."

"Let's just stay optimistic, Justin. We still have closing arguments. Maybe something will strike a chord with the jury, and they'll find enough reasonable doubt for an acquittal."

"Do you really think that could happen, Miss Jackson?"

Sharese didn't have to answer. She knew Justin saw the truth in her eyes.

***

Kyle and Marcus remained in the courtroom after the others left. "So what do you think, Marcus? Did I make the shot?"

Marcus didn't answer for a minute. "I don't know. I just don't know."

"Don't you think Hargis hung himself with his own rope? All that crazy stuff about seeing blue and waving hands? You said yourself that had to be the girl – her blue dress and her hands."

"You asked him about that, and he said he didn't know if it was the girl or not."

"I still say he was just shooting us a line of bull with all that."

"What if he wasn't?"

Kyle scratched his head. "Hmm. Maybe the blue was from your cruiser lights, and the hands were you trying to wake him up."

"He said it was before the impact."

"Yeah, but it was three years ago, and he's just now remembering it. Maybe he's got it all mixed up."

"Could be."

"It sounds plausible enough to use in my closing argument, don't you think?"

"If you're on, Copeland, they'll believe anything you say." Marcus laughed. "Trouble is, I don't think you can look into that jury box and stay focused for more than a minute or two."

Kyle let out a long sigh. "Let me worry about that, Marcus. Go get some lunch."

"Want me to bring something back for you?"

"Nah. I'll grab something out of the vending machine downstairs if I get hungry."

"All right, then. See you in a little while."

Kyle was already busy making notes on his legal pad before Marcus was out of the courtroom.

***

Sara and the other jurors were crowded together around the largest table that Eddie's Sandwich Shop had to offer. As she checked her phone yet again to see if there any more texts from Andrew, she heard two of the men at the far end of the table talking about the case.

"Did that boy say he'd been in prison?"

"Sure sounded like he was about to, at least before his lawyer up and cut him off."

"Wonder what he's been in prison for?"

The bailiff coughed loudly behind the men. "Fellows, you remember what the judge said? You need to save that kind of talk for the deliberation."

As the men's conversation shifted from the trial to the weather, Sara's mind went back to the conversation that she had heard between Elizabeth Copeland and the clerk at the grocery store two days earlier. *Yes, now I remember. The clerk said the defendant went to prison some time back, and Elizabeth said Kyle*

213

was retrying the case on a technicality. What exactly does that mean, and why didn't it come out in court?

"Something wrong, honey?" Fredonia Miller asked.

"Umm... No, Mrs. Miller, everything's okay. I was just thinking about something."

"I'm sure you've got a lot on your mind with your fiancé down in Honduras. Have you heard any news?"

"Nothing since the text from his brother a few hours ago. All we know is that he isn't in the mountains. That must mean he was still in the city when the quake struck."

"That doesn't mean anything bad has happened," Fredonia offered. "The odds are in favor of him being just fine."

"You're right. I'm probably worrying for nothing."

"Let's talk about something else, then. Get your mind off all that. Let's see, now what can we talk about? Oh, I know! Did Viola ever tell you that she stood up with me when I got married?"

"No, but it sounds like a great story."

The waitress interrupted to take their orders.

"Ham and cheese sandwich with fries," Fredonia said.

"Tuna on whole wheat," Sara told the waitress. "You were going to tell me about your wedding," Sara reminded Fredonia.

"Oh yes. It was the summer of 1953. My Jimmy had just got home from the war in Korea. He had proposed to me before he left the year before, but I turned him down. I had no intention of marrying a soldier and being left a widow like my cousin Idaleen."

"That's understandable."

"But then the war ended, and Jimmy was discharged. One day, he just showed up at my house in a brand new, red Chevy Bel Air. The windows were rolled down, and 'Crazy Man, Crazy' was playing on the radio."

"I don't think I know that song."

"Some people say it was the first rock n' roll song. Bill Haley and the Comets sang it."

"The group name rings a bell. What else did they sing?"

"You might remember 'Rock Around the Clock,' but it didn't come out until later."

"Oh, I do know that one."

"So, anyway, Jimmy got out of the car and walked up to the porch. I was breaking up beans and fanning away the June bugs. I remember it like it was yesterday."

"Did he propose again?"

"Yes, he did, and I knew better than to refuse him twice."

Sara laughed lightly. "I guess you'd had some time to reflect on turning him down the first time, huh?"

"Yes, I had, and I realized that it was a mistake. I threw those beans down, ran inside to leave my mama a note, and was a married woman by the end of the day."

"What about blood tests and licenses?"

"I don't remember much about that. Somebody down at the courthouse might have fudged a few rules that day." Fredonia winked.

"So where does Grams fit into the story?"

"Well, we knew we'd need witnesses, so we stopped by and picked up Viola – she lived down the street from me over on Sycamore. Then, we went and got Jimmy's friend Frank to be the second witness."

"Grandpa Frank?"

"Well, yes, eventually, but back then he was just plain old Frank Anderson. He lived down the road from my Jimmy out on Route 3 when we were all growing up. A year later, Jimmy and I were standing up for Viola and Frank at their wedding."

"Ah, what a great story!" Sara smiled at the thought of her grandparents on their wedding day.

"I thought you might like it," Fredonia said.

"I hope that Daniel and I have a tale to tell like that someday."

"You will, child. Somehow, I just know that you will."

CHAPTER 24

Promptly at 1 p.m., Judge Oaks instructed the bailiff to bring in the jury. Kyle watched as they filed back into the courtroom one by one. *Look at her. Look at her now, and then get her off your mind. Once you go up to that podium, she's nobody to you. And she never will be again.*

Judge Oaks began, "Hope you folks had a good lunch break. While you were out, the court settled a few procedural matters so that we can get you all back to the jury room for the deliberation as quickly as possible.'

"As you probably know, all the evidence is now in, and both the State and the defense have rested their cases. Now comes the part where the lawyers get to make a statement to you – some call it closing arguments, some call it summation – where they will attempt to go over the case from their client's point of view and tell you to vote guilty or not guilty, depending on their perspective.'

"While these arguments can be, and often are, quite convincing, you need to remember that they are not evidence in the case. Only the witnesses' testimony and the exhibits are evidence. The arguments of counsel are just that: simply the attorneys' arguments as to how the case should go.'

"Ultimately, it will be up to you – twelve of you, anyway – to decide whether the defendant, Justin Hargis, is guilty of the crime of vehicular homicide in the death of the victim, Maria Flores. You can use the attorneys' statements to guide you in that process, but you are not obligated to do so.'

"Once the attorneys are finished with their arguments, I will give you a set of instructions concerning the law of the case and how you are to conduct yourselves in the jury room. If there are still thirteen of you present at that time – and I certainly hope that nothing happens this afternoon that would prevent any of you from participating in the deliberation – then we will dismiss our alternate."

Another hour or two, and Josie – Ms. Sara Anderson, that is – will walk out of here, and my life will get back to normal. Kyle's sigh caught Marcus's attention, but Kyle's ever-so-slight nod toward the jury box told Marcus all he needed to know.

"General, is the State ready?" Judge Oaks asked.

"Yes, Your Honor," Kyle said. As he picked up his legal pad and walked to the podium, he willed himself to make a closing argument that would atone for the ineptitude that had plagued him since he had first seen Sara in the courtroom on Monday morning.

Before he began to speak, he closed his eyes and pictured Maria Flores's bloody, tangled body. *That's what this case is about, not some stupid affair that happened years ago.* Opening his eyes, he took a deep breath and began.

"Ladies and gentlemen of the jury, I have a confession to make. I haven't been my best this week. I've had a lot on my mind. For one thing, my baby daughter's been keeping my wife and me up late at night, so I haven't been sleeping well.'

"And some other things have come up this week, too. You don't need to know all the details, but I just haven't been myself. I apologize to you for that." Kyle paused just long enough to look each juror in the eye. He flinched ever so slightly as his eyes met Sara's.

"You folks have taken a week out of your lives for this case, and you deserved better than what you saw from me this week. Maria Flores deserved better. I apologize to her family for not being on top of my game." Kyle turned to look at Homero Flores, who was sitting on the first row of the audience section of the courtroom.

Looking back at the jury, he continued, "As guilty as I may be of bad lawyering, the thing is, it wasn't me who was on trial here this week. Nothing that came out of my mouth – however lacking in eloquence it may have been – was evidence. My job was only to ask the right questions, and I hope that I at least did that much.'

"When you're back in that jury room this afternoon and the judge's instructions and the coffee cups are spread out on that long, wooden table, it's not the questions that you will need to remember. It's the answers.'

"Remember the words of Trooper Marcus Thompson telling you he found the defendant, Justin Hargis, passed out at the wheel of his car with the radio blaring, on the night of the accident. Remember Sharon White from the TBI telling you that the defendant's blood alcohol content that night was 0.07 percent, which, while not enough to convict him of driving under the influence, is enough to cause a loss in depth perception, distance acuity, and peripheral vision. Remember Larry Turner telling you that the defendant passed him – 'left me in the dust' were his exact words – shortly before the accident. Remember Dr. Trent Walker telling you about the horrible injuries that caused Maria Flores's death. Remember the pictures Dr. Walker showed you.'

"There was one other witness whose testimony you especially need to remember during your deliberation – the defendant himself, Mr. Justin Hargis." Kyle paused, turning to look at Justin. "I have to admire Mr. Hargis for having the decency to get up on that witness stand and face the consequences of his actions. He didn't have to do that, you know. The Constitution guarantees him the right to refrain from self-incrimination. He could have 'pled the

Fifth' like most defendants do, but he chose to tell his side of things, at least what little he remembers about that awful night.'

"He didn't shy away from telling you that he'd had several beers before getting behind the wheel, and he didn't mind telling you that his intention that night was to drive out to the river and party with his friends. He even admitted that he could have been going thirty-five miles per hour or one hundred and thirty-five miles per hour that night, for all he knows. He seemed to be telling the truth up there on the stand.'

"Then, he told us that there was a light, something blue, and waving hands. I thought that was a rather odd set of things to remember at first. I even thought he might have made it all up. After I thought it over, though, I think I understand. 'The light and the something blue' were the lights of Trooper Marcus Thompson's cruiser. You folks have seen state troopers stopped on the road, right? Spotlights? Blue lights flashing everywhere? The waving hands were just Trooper Thompson reaching into the car to try and awaken the defendant at the scene.'

"That makes sense, doesn't it? The defendant woke up just long enough to see the flashing blue and white lights that were no doubt lighting up the entire area that night. He saw Trooper Thompson's hands as he attempted to wake him." Kyle was silent for a few moments, gauging the jury's reaction to his argument. Several of them were nodding in agreement with his theory.

"In most criminal cases, the hardest part of the jury's job is resolving the conflicts in the testimony – deciding whom to believe, in other words. In this case, that job is going to be easy because everybody told the same story. Justin Hargis drank a few beers, took a drunken ride out to the river, and struck and killed Maria Flores as she walked alongside the road. All you have to decide is whether he deserves to be punished for that."

Kyle had another page of notes prepared to use in his closing argument, but he was seasoned enough to know when he had made his point. He looked into the eyes of each of the jurors, and every face except one told him that he had won their trust. As for the last juror, she would be out of his life soon enough.

"The State rests, Your Honor," he said as he tossed his legal pad onto the table and took his seat beside Marcus. "I have nothing more to say."

CHAPTER 25

The courtroom was silent as Sharese made her way to the podium. As she passed behind Justin, he whispered, "Good luck, Miss Jackson." Sharese gave him a weary smile, but her heart was full of doubt. *I don't think luck is going to cut it, today, Justin. We need divine intervention.*

Sharese had kept her nerves under control for most of the week, but her knees were wobbly and her hands were shaking as she faced the jury to deliver her closing argument. A couple of the jurors shifted in their seats, waiting for her to begin. *Please, Lord, just let me find the right words, the words that will convince this jury that Justin Hargis doesn't deserve to go back to prison.*

Looking down at the notes she had prepared during the lunch break and during Kyle's closing argument, she read silently:

1. Thank the jury for their time and attention.

2. Read the statutes on vehicular homicide and recklessness.

3. Define the State's burden of proof.

4. Read the definition of reasonable doubt.

5. Summarize the witnesses' testimony.

6. The State says this case is easy – not true!!

Sharese's eyes kept going to the bottom line. *The State says this case is easy.* The rest of the page faded into a blur, and she knew what the gist of her argument had to be. "Ladies and gentlemen, the State says that your job here is easy. I don't see it that way, and I hope you don't either.'

"A teenage girl died three years ago. Her family lost a beloved sister and daughter. Death, especially the death of a young person like Maria Flores, makes us want revenge; we want someone to pay for the senselessness of it all. Revenge is an easy concept: an eye for an eye, and a tooth for a tooth. But, the law isn't designed to exact revenge. The law is more complicated. The law seeks justice.'

"What is 'justice?' Let's start with what it's not. Justice is not revenge. Justice is not sympathy. Justice is not taking the easy way out. So, what exactly is justice? In law school, the professors told us that justice is part reason, part rectitude, and part righteousness. It is a precious thing and a fundamental building block of the American judicial system."

Sharese glanced down at her notes again. *Thank the jury for their time and attention.* "The quest for justice is why we have taken a week of your time to present this case. You have been very attentive this week, and I can tell that you have taken your job as fair and impartial jurors very seriously. On behalf of Mr. Hargis, I sincerely thank you for that. It's not an easy thing to sit on a jury."

Read the statutes on vehicular homicide and recklessness. "The question that you are ultimately going to have to decide in this case is whether justice requires that you convict Justice Hargis of the vehicular homicide of Maria Flores.'

"Under Tennessee law, the crime of vehicular homicide is defined as a reckless killing arising from the operation of an automobile. It happens when a driver engages in conduct that creates a substantial risk of death or serious bodily injury to others. There are three parts to the statute; two of them specifically address cases where there is a DUI charge or the defendant was drag-racing.'

"Mr. Hargis is not charged with driving under the influence or drag-racing, so the sole issue here is whether this was a reckless killing in the operation of an automobile. In other words, did Justin Hargis's reckless behavior result in Maria Flores's death? Let's read the statutory definition of the word 'reckless.'

"According to Tennessee Code Annotated § 39-11-106(a)(31), a person acts recklessly with respect to circumstances surrounding the conduct or the result of the conduct when the person is aware of, but consciously disregards, a substantial and unjustifiable risk that the circumstances exist or the result will occur.'

Sharese saw that several of the jurors' faces bore confused expressions as she read the statute from the Code. "Nothing easy about that, huh?" A couple of the jurors chuckled lightly, and Sharese began to feel a bit more at ease.

"It's just a complicated way of saying that reckless conduct occurs when a person consciously disregards a substantial risk that a certain result will happen. In this case, the question is whether Justin Hargis consciously disregarded the risk that his behavior on the night of the accident might cause someone's death."

Define the State's burden of proof. Read definition of reasonable doubt. "The burden of proof in this case is on the State. In a criminal case, the burden is always on the State. It's a high standard of proof – beyond a reasonable doubt.'

"At this point, I should mention that, when we attorneys are finished with our closing arguments, the judge is going to give you a set of instructions to use back in the jury room. The instructions will tell you that reasonable doubt hinges on whether or not the jurors' minds can rest easily as to the certainty of guilt."

Summarize the witnesses' testimony. "In order to reach a verdict that will allow your minds to rest easily – that will allow you to sleep at night when this case is over – you're going to have to listen very carefully to the judge's instructions, to the criminal charge against the defendant, to the presumption of the defendant's innocence, to the State's burden of proof, to the definition of reasonable doubt, and to all the other instructions that the judge gives you.'

"When you go back into the jury room for the deliberation, your job will be to apply the judge's instructions to the evidence as it was presented to you. The State's attorney said that all the witnesses told the same story, so your job is easy. I don't know what Mr. Copeland heard – maybe the acoustics are different over there at his table – but the story that I heard was not one that will make your job easy.'

"I heard Trooper Marcus Thompson say that he arrived at the scene of the accident to find Justin Hargis unconscious. His head was on the steering wheel of his vehicle, which had crashed into a tree and was blocking part of the roadway. The trooper said that he attempted to wake Mr. Hargis but that Mr. Hargis was out cold."

Sharese glanced over her shoulder at Kyle. "People who are out cold don't see waving hands or flashes of blue or light as suggested by Mr. Copeland. Whatever Justin Hargis saw that night, it was not Trooper Thompson's hands or the flashing lights of his cruiser." Sharese brushed off the feeling of warmth that came over when she said Marcus's name aloud. *Girl, get that off your mind!*

"The next witness that we heard from was Sharon White from the Tennessee Bureau of Investigation crime laboratory. Ms. White didn't specifically remember testing Justin Hargis's blood, so she read us a report that said Justin Hargis had a blood alcohol content of 0.07 percent on the night of the accident. She told us that was below the level for a presumption of driving under the influence, which is why Mr. Hargis is not charged with DUI in this case.'

"Next, we heard from Mr. Larry Turner, the Texas truck driver who was passing through Maple Springs around 10:30 p.m. on the night of July 20, three years ago. He told us that Mr. Hargis passed him as the two of them were headed in the direction of Roaring River. The State's attorney emphasized that Mr. Turner said the defendant 'left him in the dust,' and, to the best of my recollection, Mr. Turner did say that. But, what does that mean exactly?'

"Mr. Turner didn't tell us how fast he was going, how fast Mr. Hargis was going, or where exactly on the road out to the river Mr. Hargis passed him. When you get right down to it, Mr. Turner didn't tell us very much of anything. And then, he left the courtroom and didn't come back and allow me, the defendant's attorney, to cross-examine him. For whatever reason, he decided that this case wasn't worth any more of his time."

Sharese saw a look pass over some of the juror's faces, a look that suggested that they had not realized that Larry Turner had left the trial prematurely. *A lot of important business happens out of the jury's presence. Too bad you have no way of knowing some of the things that have gone on here this week.*

"The State presented two other witnesses, Homero Flores and Dr. Trent Walker. Neither of these men witnessed the accident. All that Mr. Flores could tell us was that his sister had run away from home – probably attempting to go back to Mexico because of a boyfriend there – and that his parents had refused an autopsy of Ms. Flores's body following her death.'

"Dr. Walker told us that, while Ms. Flores's death was consistent with being hit by an automobile, he could not say with certainty that it was Justin Hargis's automobile that struck her." *What about the clothing fibers that he mentioned during the motion in limine hearing? The jury didn't hear those words, but you shouldn't twist what he said so much that you make yourself into a liar.*

Sharese knew there was only one more witness left to discuss. "Finally, we heard from Justin Hargis himself about what happened on the night of Maria Flores's death. As the State's attorney pointed out, Mr. Hargis didn't have to testify, but he wanted to do it anyway. He wanted to tell you his side of things.'

"Mr. Hargis told you he drank approximately three alcoholic beverages on the night in question. He said that happened at a friend's house over a period of about three hours. He also admitted to purchasing methamphetamine that night but said that he didn't use it. You don't have to take his word for that, by the way. Sharon White would have told you if there were any drugs in his system.'

"The last thing that Mr. Hargis told you was that his recollection of the accident is limited to the sight of something blue, waving hands, and a flash of light. The State's attorney suggested that Mr. Hargis had the timing wrong, that he saw those things after the accident rather than before. That's just not the way that it happened, ladies and gentlemen. We have three witnesses – Mr. Hargis, Trooper Thompson, and Larry Turner – who said that Mr. Hargis was totally unconscious following the accident.'

"So, what did that mean, Mr. Hargis's statement about blue, hands, and light? Ladies and gentlemen, I have to admit to you that I have no idea what it means. All I know is that it must mean something."

The State's attorney says your job is easy – not so!! "The State's attorney said that you have an easy job here today. I disagree. If we knew what the blue, the hands, and the light meant, your job might be easier. If we knew more about the moment when Justin Hargis passed Larry Turner on the road, your job might be easier. If we had an autopsy, your job might be easier. But, we don't have any of those things.'

"The burden of proof is on the State of Tennessee to prove guilt beyond a reasonable doubt. Did the State do that in this case? Is the evidence against Justin Hargis such that your minds can rest easy as to his guilt?" Sharese looked at Kyle. "That's not going to be an easy decision, ladies and gentlemen."

Sharese looked across the jury panel, silently imploring each juror to take the task at hand very seriously. *Don't send this young man back to prison. It won't bring Maria Flores back.* "Once again, I thank you for your time and attention in this case. I hope you make the right decision, even if it isn't easy."

When the courtroom grew silent except for the rhythmic clicking of Sharese's heels as she walked back to her seat, Judge Oaks looked up from whatever he was reading on the bench. "General?"

"Nothing further," Kyle said.

Sharese was pleasantly surprised. *Seriously? Perry Mason isn't going to seize the opportunity to discredit every word I just said? He must have a hair appointment this afternoon.*

"Let's take a 15-minute recess, folks. When we come back, I'm going to give you some instructions and then let you get to the deliberation."

CHAPTER 26

After the jury left the room, Judge Oaks addressed the attorneys. "I'm assuming that you're both in agreement with the standard Tennessee Pattern Jury Instructions for Criminal Cases being given in this case. If there's something specific that you want included, now's the time to say so."

Sharese, whose confidence had returned, spoke up. "The defense requests that the court instruct the jury on the law of an absent material witness."

Judge Oaks flipped through the large book on his desk that contained the pattern jury instructions for criminal court. "Are you talking about Instruction 42.16, Ms. Jackson?"

"Yes, Your Honor."

"I believe that's what we commonly call 'the missing witness rule.' Let me read it from the pattern instructions. 'Absent Material Witness. When it is within the power of a certain party to produce a witness who possesses peculiar knowledge concerning the facts and who is available to one side at the exclusion of the other, and the party to whom the witness is available fails to call such witness, an inference arises that the testimony of such witness would have been unfavorable to the side that should have called such witness.'

"Yes, Your Honor," Sharese said. "The defense requests that the instruction that the court just read be given to the jury."

"What do you say to that, General?"

"The State objects to the instruction, Judge. First of all, it was not within the State's exclusive power to call Larry Turner as a witness. The defense could have called him if they had wanted to. Secondly, the State didn't fail to produce Mr. Turner as a witness. We got him here. For whatever reason, we just couldn't seem to make him stay."

Sharese had a moment of panic. *Uh-oh. Did I mess up in not subpoenaing Larry Turner on Justin's behalf? No, that's not right. He didn't have anything helpful to say for the defense, so there's no reason I would have called him.* "Your Honor, the defense would argue that it was the State's job to keep the witness here once they called him."

"We looked for him, Judge, but we haven't been able to find him. And, anyway, the defendant waived his right to cross-examine Mr. Turner."

"Yes, I recall that," Judge Oaks said. "I want to make sure the verdict sticks this time, so, out of an abundance of caution, we'll include the instruction, Ms. Jackson. Anything else?"

"Nothing from the State, Your Honor," Kyle said.

"Nothing further from the defense." Sharese sighed. *The judge is so sure there'll be another conviction that he's making sure there are no grounds for an appeal. Is there really no hope?*

"Let court stand in recess for ten minutes," Judge Oaks said. In a barely audible voice, he added, "Maybe I can still get a few holes in this afternoon."

***

Back in the jury room, Sara's stomach in a knot. Although she was still praying to be dismissed from the jury, she had listened carefully to every word that Kyle and Sharese had said. As the attorneys had pled their respective cases, Sara had realized just how much she had missed during the trial.

The trooper had testified on the first and second days of the trial, during the time that her emotions were still raw from seeing Kyle again. Try as she might, she could barely recall his testimony. She also had trouble remembering much of what Sharon White, Homero Flores, and Dr. Trent Walker had said.

The only witness who she recalled in vivid detail was Larry Turner, the truck driver. *There was something about him. Something...familiar? Maybe it was just hearing a Texas accent again. It reminded me of those years when my father was stationed at Fort Hood.*

"Any news about your fiancé?" Fredonia interrupted Sara's thoughts with a gentle pat on the arm.

Sara reached into her pocket for her cell phone and double-checked that she had not missed a message during the closing arguments. "No, apparently not. I'm just praying that no news is good news."

"I'm sure it is, honey," Fredonia said. "Looks like you may get to go home here in a little bit."

"I certainly hope so. I'll gladly leave the deliberation to you and the others. I just hope no one gets sick in the next hour or two."

"You know, my rheumatism has been acting up. Maybe I'll ask the judge if I can go home," Fredonia teased.

"You wouldn't dare!" Sara said.

Fredonia gave a big whoop. "Child, Viola Anderson would have my hide if I stuck her grandbaby in a jury room to deliberate on this silly old case when she should be home planning a wedding."

"No, that wouldn't do at all," Sara teased back.

Fredonia gave another chuckle and then took on a more serious tone. "You know, weddings are a lot of fun, but don't forget to look a little further down the road. Your wedding day will only last a few hours, but you'll be married for the rest of your life.

Spend some time planning how to *be* married, not just how to *get* married."

Sara nodded. "That's good advice, Mrs. Miller. I guess brides-to-be have a tendency to focus on just that one big day."

"Getting married is the easy part. Living happily ever after is the part that takes work."

"Yes, ma'am, I'm sure you're right."

"If there's anything that you know of that might come between you and your fiancé, get it settled before your wedding day."

Does she know about Kyle? Did I give something away this week, something she picked up on? "What do you mean, Mrs. Miller?"

"Well, I don't know your particular situation, but I saw on one of those daytime talk shows where a young lady neglected to tell her fiancé that she had filed bankruptcy before they met. He didn't find out until they tried to buy a house and couldn't get credit. It just about ruined their marriage."

"Yes, that would be bad, all right."

Fredonia gave Sara a questioning look.

"Oh, no, Mrs. Miller, I've never filed bankruptcy."

"Well then, you should be fine."

If only it were that simple. If only.

***

As they waited for Judge Oaks to return to the bench to deliver the jury instructions, Kyle leaned over and quietly asked Marcus, "So, what do you think, my man? Guilty verdict in less than an hour?"

Marcus shrugged, not looking up from the table where he was nervously tapping an ink pen.

"Come on, Marcus, don't you want to play? We always bet on how long it'll take the jury to come back."

Marcus stopped tapping but still didn't answer.

"Okay, two hours. Three, tops," Kyle said. "Don't make me bid against myself, Marcus. You're shaking my confidence."

Marcus finally looked Kyle in the eye. "Five bucks says they'll come back at midnight with a hung jury."

Kyle raised his eyebrows. *Ouch.* "That bad, huh?"

"Yep," Marcus said, tapping his pen on the desk again. "You had to lose one sooner or later, right?"

"Oh, come on, Marcus." Kyle glanced over his shoulder at Sharese and then grinned at Marcus. "You just want *her* to win, don't you?"

With that, Marcus threw the pen across the desk and hissed at Kyle, "You just don't get it, do you? It's not about her, it's not about you, and it's not about the pretty lady on the jury. It's about whether or not that boy over there deserves to go back to prison."

"What's happened to you, Marcus? When you sat in my office on Monday morning, you were sure he was guilty."

"I can't explain it. Something is not right here."

"The blue-hands-lights thing?"

"Maybe. I don't know." The two men sat in silence for a few minutes before Marcus spoke up again. "Don't you wonder what happened to that truck driver? Why he skipped like that?"

Before Kyle could answer, Judge Oaks came into the courtroom. "All right, folks, let's get this jury charged and let them do their job."

Thank goodness. Another hour or so, and Ms. Sara Josephine Anderson will go back to being just a memory.

CHAPTER 27

Sara took her seat in the jury box for what she hoped would be the last time. She looked across the courtroom at Justin, who was whispering something in Sharese's ear. Sara couldn't hear the words, but she saw Sharese smile at Justin, nod her head, and mouth, "Yes."

Sara wondered what Justin's question had been. *Is it almost over, Ms. Jackson? Do you feel good about the case? Do you think they'll find me guilty again?* Sara flinched, remembering Elizabeth *saying that the defendant had already been convicted once before and that this was a new trial. 'On a technicality,' she'd said.*

Sara glanced around at her fellow jurors. If she had to deliberate on the case with them, she would certainly keep that bit of information to herself. As the trial had progressed, it had become obvious that several of the jurors had ignored the judge's admonishment not to form an opinion until all of the evidence was in and were already leaning toward a guilty verdict. *How will I vote if I have to deliberate?*

Judge Oaks cleared his throat and then looked toward the jury box. "Ladies and gentlemen of the jury, the defendant, Justin Hargis, is charged with the crime of vehicular homicide. He has entered a plea of not guilty. The evidence and arguments in this case have been completed, and it is now my duty to instruct you as to the law.'

"The indictment in this case is the formal written accusation charging the defendant with the crime. It is not evidence against the defendant and does not create any inference of guilt.'

"Statements, arguments, and remarks of counsel are intended to help you in understanding the evidence and applying the law, but they are not evidence. If any statements were made that you believe are not supported by the evidence, then you should disregard them."

Sara's mind was racing as she tried to take in all that the judge was saying. *Does that include Kyle's statement in the stairwell?*

"You are the exclusive judges of the facts in this case. You are also the exclusive judges of the law under the direction of the court. You should apply the law to the facts in deciding this case."

Please, Lord, let me off this jury. I can't remember enough of the facts to give that young man a fair verdict.'

"You should consider all of the evidence in the light of your own observations and experience in life."

Sara struggled to breathe normally as the judge droned on the instructions. *But it was my 'observations and experience' with the attorney for the State that caused me to not remember the evidence!*

"The law presumes that the defendant is innocent of the charge against him. This presumption remains with the defendant throughout every stage of the trial, and it is not overcome unless from all the evidence in the case you are convinced beyond a reasonable doubt that the defendant is guilty."

Is it overcome when a juror hears the prosecutor's wife tell the clerk at the Piggly Wiggly that the case is being retried following a previous conviction?

"The State has the burden of proving the guilt of the defendant beyond a reasonable doubt, and this burden never shifts, but remains on the State throughout the trial of the case. The defendant is not required to prove his innocence."

Why did the defendant take the stand? He didn't have to, but he wanted to. Why would he do that unless he wanted to prove his innocence?

"Reasonable doubt is that doubt engendered by an investigation of all the proof in the case and an inability, after such investigation, to let the mind rest easily as to the certainty of guilt. Reasonable doubt does not mean a doubt that may arise from possibility."

What about the possibility that the defendant was telling the truth about seeing something blue and seeing hands waving? Kyle said it was the trooper trying to wake him up, but that doesn't seem right. Could it have been Maria Flores in her blue dress?

"Absolute certainty of guilt is not demanded by the law to convict a defendant on a criminal charge, but moral certainty is required, and this certainty is required as to every proposition of proof requisite to constitute the offense."

Moral certainty? Is that another name for the sureness that I felt after seeing Elizabeth? Certainty that Kyle went back to her because she was carrying his child – certainty that I am absolutely over him, that Daniel is my future?

"For you to find the defendant guilty of the crime of vehicular homicide, the State must have proven beyond a reasonable doubt the existence of the following essential elements: first, that the defendant killed the alleged victim by the operation of a motor vehicle, second, that the defendant acted recklessly, and third, that the killing was the proximate result of conduct creating a substantial risk of death or serious bodily injury to a person."

Risk of death or serious bodily injury! I told Daniel not to go to Honduras. I just knew something bad was going to happen.

"'Recklessly' means that a person acts recklessly with respect to circumstances surrounding the conduct or the result of the conduct when the person is aware of but consciously disregards a substantial and unjustifiable risk that the circumstances exist or the result will occur. The risk must be of such a nature and degree that its disregard constitutes a gross deviation from the standard of care that an ordinary person would exercise under all the circumstances as viewed from the accused person's standpoint."

Did Justin Hargis 'disregard a substantial and unjustifiable risk'? How would he know that someone would be walking along the road at night? I was staying just a short distance from where the accident happened, and I didn't see any hitchhikers that summer. In fact, I hardly saw anyone except Kyle, Callie, and the man in the cabin between my grandparents' and Kyle's family's.

"The requirement of 'recklessly' is also established if it is shown that the defendant acted knowingly or intentionally."

No one has said that Justin acted intentionally. He would have had no reason to kill the girl. He just wanted to go down to the river and get high. That's wrong in and of itself, but this isn't a drug case; it's a homicide case.

"You must consider all the evidence pertaining to each issue, regardless of who presented it."

I had so much on my mind that I couldn't really listen to either side. Please, please, please Lord, let me off this jury!

"During the trial, you heard the expert testimony of Dr. Trent Walker, who was an expert in the field of forensic medicine. The rules of evidence provide that, if specialized knowledge might assist the jury in understanding the evidence or in determining a fact in issue, a witness qualified as an expert may testify and state his opinions concerning such matters."

I can't even remember what the doctor said. All that I remember are those awful pictures he showed of the girl's body. At least she died instantly.

"Merely because an expert witness has expressed an opinion does not mean, however, that you are bound to accept this opinion. The same as with any other witness, it is up to you to decide whether you believe this testimony and choose to rely upon it."

The judge paused, and Sara saw the court reporter holding her hand up. "Hold on a second, folks. The court reporter needs to change the paper in her machine."

As the court reporter took care of business, Sara stole a fleeting look at Kyle. He was leaning on the table, head in hands. He must have felt her gaze and looked up. For a moment, their eyes met. Sara felt sweet tears in her eyes and looked away. *You have a great wife and kids who love you and need you. You did the right thing three years ago. If there's anything to forgive, I forgive you. Goodbye, Kyle.*

Judge Oaks saw that the court reporter had finished her job and went back to the jury instructions. "Let's see, now. Where were we? Ah, yes. The guilt of the defendant may be established by direct evidence, by circumstantial evidence, or by a combination of both. 'Direct evidence' is defined as evidence which proves the existence of the fact in issue without inference or presumption.'

"'Circumstantial evidence' consists of proof of collateral facts and circumstances which do not directly prove the fact in issue but from which that fact may be logically inferred."

Sara tried to concentrate on the judge's words again, but she found it difficult. Not because of the momentary distraction with Kyle but simply because she wasn't accustomed to all of the legalese that the judge was spouting. He had already been talking for a good thirty minutes, but he showed no sign of letting up anytime soon. *Please let me out of here.*

"When the evidence is made up entirely of circumstantial evidence, then a guilty verdict requires you to find that all the essential facts are consistent with the hypothesis of guilt. The facts must exclude every other reasonable theory or hypothesis except that of guilt, and the facts must establish such a certainty of guilt of the defendant as to convince the mind beyond a reasonable doubt that the defendant is the one who committed the offense."

I just don't know if I could go along with a guilty verdict; but what about that poor girl's family?

"Before a verdict of guilty is justified, the circumstances, taken together, must be of a conclusive nature and tendency, leading on the whole to a satisfactory conclusion and producing in effect a moral certainty that the defendant, and no one else, committed the offense."

Who else could have killed Maria Flores except Justin Hargis? There was no one else there.

"You are the exclusive judges of the credibility of the witnesses and the weight to be given to their testimony. If there are conflicts in the testimony of the different witnesses, you must reconcile them, if you can, without hastily or rashly concluding that any witness has sworn falsely, for the law presumes that all witnesses are truthful."

I believe Justin was telling the truth.

"In forming your opinion as to the credibility of a witness, you may look to the reasonableness of his statements, his appearance and demeanor while testifying, and his contradictory statements as to material matters if any are shown."

The only witness whose appearance and demeanor caught my attention was Larry Turner. Ms. Jackson said that he left before she could cross-examine him. Why would he do that?

"The defendant having testified in his own behalf, his credibility is determined by the same rules by which the credibility of other witnesses is determined, and you will give his testimony such weight as you may think it is entitled."

Even Kyle said Justin Hargis appeared to be telling the truth, at least as best as he remembered it.

"Before the defendant can be convicted of vehicular homicide, the State must have proven beyond a reasonable doubt that the death of the deceased was proximately caused by the criminal conduct of the defendant, Justin Hargis. The 'proximate cause' of a death is that cause which, in natural and continuous sequence, unbroken by any independent intervening cause, produces the death and without which the death would not have occurred."

He was just driving out to the river. It was a remote area, and it was well after dark. I don't think that drinking three beers over three hours is enough to send him back to prison. How fast was he going? That's the real question, isn't it?

"The defendant's conduct need not be the sole or immediate cause of death. The acts of two or more persons may work concurrently to proximately cause the death, and, in such a case, each of the participating acts or omissions is regarded as a proximate cause. It is not a defense that the negligent conduct of the deceased may also have been a proximate cause of the death."

Does that mean that, even if Maria Flores was negligent in walking along the road at night, that's not a defense to vehicular homicide? I guess so, or Ms. Jackson would have argued that during her closing.

"However, it is a defense to homicide if the proof shows that the death was caused by an independent, intervening act of the deceased or another which the defendant, in the exercise of ordinary care, could not reasonably have anticipated as likely to happen."

Was there some independent, intervening act by Maria Flores? The flash of blue was probably her dress. Maybe it was her hands that Justin saw. Maybe she was waving at him, hoping he would give her a ride. But, if that was the case, why couldn't he have just stopped?

"If some other circumstance caused the victim's death, unrelated to the defendant's actions, then that would be a defense to vehicular homicide unless the circumstance was the natural result of the defendant's act."

The defendant's act was speeding. Drinking and speeding. Nothing that Maria Flores did would be a natural result of that, would it? I'm so confused.

243

"If you find that the defendant's acts, if any, did not unlawfully cause or contribute to the death of the deceased, or if you have a reasonable doubt as to this proposition, then you must find him not guilty."

I don't want to send that young man back to prison, but I can't imagine any way that Maria Flores could have died that wouldn't have been his fault.

"When it is within the power of the State or the defendant to produce a witness who possesses peculiar knowledge concerning facts essential to that party's contentions and who is available to one side at the exclusion of the other, and the party to whom the witness is available fails to call such witness, an inference arises that the testimony of such witness would have been unfavorable to the side that should have called or produced such witness."

What does that mean? Is he talking about Larry Turner?

"The verdict must represent the considered judgment of each juror. In order to return a verdict, it is necessary that each juror agree thereto. Your verdict must be unanimous."

Let me off the jury, let me off the jury, let me off the jury! Please, Lord!! I cannot deliberate on this case!

"It is your duty, as jurors, to consult with one another and to deliberate with a view to reaching an agreement. However, each of you must decide the case for yourself, but do so only after an impartial consideration of the evidence with your fellow jurors."

Am I the only one who is struggling with a decision? Have the others already made up their minds?

"In the course of your deliberation, do not hesitate to re-examine your own views and change your opinion if convinced it is erroneous. But, do not surrender your honest conviction as to the weight or effect of the evidence solely because of the opinion of your fellow jurors or for the mere purpose of returning a verdict."

Some of the other jurors have been so overbearing this week. I don't want to have to argue with them about this case for hours on end. I just don't have the strength. I'm worried about Daniel, and I want to get out of this courtroom away from Kyle so I can think about my future.

"You can have no prejudice or sympathy, or allow anything but the law and the evidence to have any influence upon your verdict. You must render your verdict with absolute fairness and impartiality as you think justice and truth dictate."

I feel so sorry for both sides. The defendant has already paid for his sins by serving time in prison, but the girl paid with her life.

"When you retire to the jury room, you will first select one of your members as foreperson who will preside over your deliberation. When you have reached a verdict, you will return with it to this courtroom, and your foreperson will announce it." Judge Oaks looked up from the instructions at Sara.

Please let me go!

"Ms. Anderson, it looks like we've made it through the week with our twelve-person jury intact. Since you were serving as our alternate, you are free to go at this time. The rest of you may now retire for the deliberation."

Oh, thank you, Lord! Thank you, thank you, thank you!!

CHAPTER 28

When all of the jurors had left the room, Justin turned to Sharese. "How long do you think it'll take them to decide, Miss Jackson?"

"I don't know, Justin. I hope we gave them enough to talk about for a few hours, anyway." She noticed the bailiff waiting to take Justin back to the holding cell. "Just so you know, I think you made the right decision in taking the stand. I thought it would be a mistake, but, overall, I think it went fairly well."

"I wish I could have remembered more up there. What did come back to me was real vague. Like a dream or something in slow motion."

"Do you have any idea what it means?"

"No, not for sure. But I know it wasn't like the D.A. said. The blue wasn't the highway patrol's lights. The blue and the light were two different things. The flash of light wasn't blue. It was just regular, white light."

Sharese shook her head. "How did you feel when you remembered something about that night?"

Justin thought for a minute. "I don't know that I felt much of anything as I was remembering it up on the stand. Fear maybe. I was real scared about testifying."

"And now?"

247

"Now? Hmm." Justin shut his eyes. "'Blue Suede Shoes' on the radio. Carl Perkins singing 'One for the money, two for the show.' I had it up real loud, just blasting it. I love that song, especially his version of it."

"What else?"

"I saw just a split second of something blue. Then hands. Hands waving in the air." Justin's eyes were still closed. "A flash of light, and then – nothing."

"Nothing?"

"No, there's nothing else," Justin opened his eyes. "Nothing until the next morning when Trooper Thompson came to the hospital."

Sharese sighed. "I wish you could remember more."

The bailiff signaled that it was time for Justin to return to the holding cell to await the jury's verdict.

"What if there's not anything else, Miss Jackson?"

"Maybe there isn't."

"I may never know for sure what happened that night, but I think I can be at peace with it now. I've told my side of things, and that's all that I can do."

"You can keep praying for some divine intervention," Sharese said.

"I will if you will." Justin grinned as the bailiff led him away.

Oh, I will, Justin. You'd better believe I will.

***

After Justin left the courtroom, only Kyle, Marcus, and Sharese remained. "Are you going to wait it out here?" Kyle asked Sharese. "It may be a late night."

"I think I'll head back over to my office. I have some things that I really need to take care of. The clerk has my number." Sharese picked up her things.

"Personally, I can't accomplish anything in the office while I'm waiting on a jury. What about you, Marcus? Are you going hang around here with me?"

"I need to go over to headquarters for a bit. Got a little business to take care of."

"Well, if neither of you are going to keep me company, I guess I'll just go home and wait it out there. See if my wife's still speaking to me after this crazy week." He picked up his briefcase and headed toward the door. "Marcus here kept me out late every night."

"Don't be telling lies on me, Copeland," Marcus said. "You're the one that decided to go deer hunting last night."

Kyle shot Marcus a look, worried that Sharese might ask why he was deer hunting in July.

Sharese just laughed, apparently oblivious to the true meaning of Marcus's remark. "Sounds like you'd better get home and make amends with your wife, then."

"Yeah, I definitely should," Kyle said. *But where do I start?*"

CHAPTER 29

As Sara got into her car, a strange feeling came over her, a feeling that she could not quite understand. All week, she had hoped and prayed that Judge Oaks would excuse her from the deliberation, and now he had done just that. Instead of the exuberance that she had expected to feel, there was emptiness within her, a kind of loneliness that had no name.

I'm just tired from sitting in that courtroom all week. She turned on the radio for a distraction. The Beatles were singing, "Yesterday, love was such an easy game to play; now I need a place to hide away…" *Oh, gee whiz. I don't need to hear that right now.*

Sara was going to change the station, but the song faded out, and the announcer came with the week's sales at the Piggly Wiggly. *Hmm. A sale on Sara Lee pound cakes. I should pick one up for Daniel. Oh, Daniel, how I miss you!*

Sara closed her eyes, remembering the night that she had first met Daniel. Grams had scolded her for bringing a store-bought dessert to the welcome dinner for the church's new pastor, but Sara had been unashamed.

"I'm sure the women in the kitchen can find something juicier to gossip about than my lack of culinary skills," Sara said.

"Maybe so, but it wouldn't hurt you to learn your way around the kitchen, Sara Josephine. The way to a man's heart is through his stomach, you know."

"Maybe I don't want a man in my life. Maybe I'm happy just as I am."

"I saw how you looked at Dr. Parker when he came in a few minutes ago. I may be old, but I remember that look. It's how a woman on the third day of a diet looks at a box of Godiva chocolates."

Grams had been right, of course. To say that Sara's heart skipped a beat when she saw Dr. Daniel Parker walk into the church fellowship hall that night would be like saying Atlanta suffered a small fire when General Sherman marched through town during the Civil War. As every Southerner knows, the fire began suddenly, spread quickly, and was all-consuming.

"Okay, so maybe he is an attractive man, but that doesn't mean I want to date him. Being a preacher, he's probably very pious. Besides, he's probably already seeing someone. A nice wholesome girl who can bake a pecan pie while reciting the Beatitudes."

"Not that there's anything wrong with piety – he is a man of God, after all – but he seemed very humble when he came for the trial sermon last month. Leeann Speck on the pulpit search committee told me that he's anxious to find a nice girl and settle down."

"I'm not sure I'm the kind of girl he's looking for. I have, um, dated before, you know," Sara said, not elaborating and not looking her grandmother in the eye.

"Sara Josephine, no one said he was looking for the Virgin Mary. Besides, you're the only single woman in the church even close to his age. I think the pulpit committee may have even included you in the benefits package."

"I hope you're kidding," Sara said as she covered her face with her hand. *"If you're not, I don't think I want to hear anymore."*

"There's just one other thing, dear."

"What's that?"

"He's standing right in front of you," Grams whispered.

When Sara had removed her hand from her face, she saw that Daniel was indeed standing right in front of her. He was even more handsome up close, and Sara felt all of her concerns about his occupation and his piety slip away.

"Hello, ladies. I'm Daniel Parker. And you are–?"

"I'm Viola Anderson, and this is my granddaughter, Sara Josephine. We're so glad to have you as our new pastor, Dr. Parker." She gave him a friendly handshake and then said, *"Now, if you'll excuse me, I think I'm needed in the kitchen."*

As Grams disappeared into the crowd, Daniel asked, *"Was it something I said?"*

Sara gave a nervous laugh. *"Not at all. She just doesn't specialize in subtlety, that's all."*

"I see." Daniel's deep blue eyes danced as he extended his hand to Sara. *"It's nice to finally meet you, Sara Josephine. I've heard a lot about you. You're the kindergarten teacher, right?"*

"That's me. And, it's just Sara. Only Grams still adds the 'Josephine.' It was her mother's name, so she's quite attached to it."

"Okay. It's nice to meet you then, Just Sara," Daniel said with a smile.

When Sara took Daniel's hand and looked into his eyes, all of her embarrassment about the search committee's attempt at matchmaking evaporated. In its place came a warm and intoxicating sensation that swept over her and caused her knees to sway beneath her wool skirt.

"Welcome to Maple Springs, Dr. Parker."

"Thank you," Daniel said, slowly letting go of Sara's hand.

An older woman with silver, back-teased hair interrupted their conversation. "We need for you to ask the blessing, Dr. Parker. You should know the desserts are a little limited tonight. For some reason, everybody brought green bean casserole or potato salad. If you've got a sweet tooth, you'd best get something on your first trip through the line."

"You didn't happen to see any pound cake over there did you? It's my favorite," Daniel replied to the woman.

"Actually, Dr. Parker," Sara interrupted, "I brought a pound cake. Hope you don't mind, but it's the store bought kind – Sara Lee."

"Please, call me Daniel. And Sara Lee sounds great to me. The homemade ones can be a little dry sometimes." Noticing the crowd starting to gather around them, Daniel said, "Looks like it's time for me to get back to work. Maybe we could have coffee sometime?"

"Yes, I'd like that," Sara said. "I'd like that very much."

A beeping horn snapped Sara back to reality, and she knew she needed to stop daydreaming and concentrate on her driving. *Daniel took me out for coffee the following week, and we've been together ever since. Daniel Parker is a man of his word. He'll come home safe to me from Honduras. He said that he would, and he will. I know he will.*

As the Everly Brothers crooned "Bye Bye Love," Sara remembered Fredonia Miller's words about how a bride-to-be needed to be preparing herself for marriage and not just planning her wedding day. Sara had intended to stop by the parsonage to see if Andrew had heard any news, but instead she drove past the parsonage and headed out to her grandparents' cabin at the river.

There's something I need to do before Daniel comes home. Something that will put Kyle completely in my past and not in our future.

CHAPTER 30

As Kyle walked to his car, he was glad to see that, although the early morning rain had passed through, the day remained overcast, and it was pleasantly cool for July. He put his briefcase on the front seat and placed his suit jacket over it, tossing his cell phone on top of the pile so he could get to it quick if the clerk called. *Marcus is probably right. This one will take awhile.*

As he drove home, he went over the trial in his mind. *Voir dire* was nothing but a blur. Seeing Sara again after three years had opened up a deep and painful wound, and it had taken all of his strength not to run to her and take her in his arms when he had first seen her in the courtroom.

News of Sara's engagement had stung him, even though it had been his choice to end their affair. After he reconciled with Elizabeth, he had almost convinced himself that the affair had never happened, and thus he had never fully mourned the loss of his relationship with Sara. *I never really got over her. Maybe I never will.*

He tried to shake off the memories of Sara and focus on his internal analysis of the trial. His opening statement had been a total disaster, but Marcus had been a strong enough witness to undo most of the damage that had occurred up to that point. He had done as well as could be expected with Sharon White. The testimony of Homero Flores and Dr. Walker had gone well, too. His cross-examination of Justin Hargis was the highlight of the trial. *Score!!*

There was just one witness whose testimony and behavior he could not reconcile in his mind: Larry Turner. *When I talked to him on the phone, he seemed to have a picture perfect recollection of the night of the accident, but on the witness stand he stammered around like he could barely remember anything. Weird.*

Kyle was still thinking about Larry Turner when he got home. As he got out of the car, he saw that Elizabeth was buckling Evan into his car seat. "Y'all going on an errand?" Kyle asked.

"The pediatrician. Chelsea has been crying non-stop since right after you left this morning. Dr. Bradshaw likes to leave early on Friday, but I convinced the nurse to work us in. I think she took pity on us when she heard Chelsea screaming over the phone."

Kyle could hear the baby, apparently still inside the house, wailing at the top of her lungs. "Want me to bring her out to the car?"

"That would be great. She's already strapped into her basket, just inside the front door."

When Kyle got inside, he saw that Chelsea's face was very red, almost purple with the intensity of her rage. She was screaming louder than she ever had before, and her legs and arms were flailing. When he patted her on the head to try and soothe her, he could feel that she was burning with fever. "Did you take her temperature?" he called to Elizabeth over the baby's cries.

"One hundred and four," Elizabeth shouted back.

"That's really high. Are you sure we shouldn't go to the emergency room instead of the hospital?"

"They're right across the street from each other. I'm sure the pediatrician will send us there if he thinks it's necessary."

"Oh," Kyle said. "I didn't know Dr. Bradshaw had moved his office."

"You would have, if you'd been to any of Chelsea's doctor appointments. He moved a year ago."

Guilt washed over Kyle. Had he really not been to any of Chelsea's check-ups? With Evan, he had been to almost every one of them up until he was a year old. "Do you want me to go with you?"

"It would really help," she said. "I guess the jury didn't take long to come back, huh?"

"Actually, they just went out. The clerk has my cell number. She'll call me when they reach a verdict."

"Okay. Will you drive us, then? I'd like to ride in back with Chelsea."

"No problem," Kyle said.

When Elizabeth was safely wedged in the backseat of the SUV between the children's car seats, Kyle started the car. He flipped off the Laurie Berkner CD and turned up air-conditioning for the baby's sake, even though it wasn't particularly hot inside the car. "I feel like I'm forgetting something," he said to Elizabeth. "Did you notice if I locked the front door?"

"What?" Elizabeth said as Chelsea's bawling filled the car.

"Nothing, hon," Kyle replied as he glanced up and saw that he at least closed the door even if he had forgotten to lock it. *Everything will be okay. It's a safe neighborhood, and my car is in the driveway.*

***

As Sara neared the turn-off that would take her to the cabin, she slowed the car down and pulled off of Winningham Road. *This must be where the accident happened. This is the only place with a clearing big enough for a semi-truck.*

She shut off the engine and got out. Fog was rising up from the river nearby, and there was a peaceful quiet. *So, this is where Maria Flores died.* She bowed her head and prayed. *Heavenly Father, so much has happened in my life this week that I haven't given much thought to that young girl or her family. I just pray that she's in Heaven with you. Please give her family peace and comfort. Amen.*

Sara took one last look around, got back into her car, and drove the short distance down the gravel road that led to her grandparents' cabin. As she passed Kyle's cabin, she wondered if he still came out to the river. *I'll bet he brings his wife and children here to fish. Grams said that Kyle came here as boy. He'd want to pass that legacy on to his son.* Sara smiled as she pictured Kyle and the little boy that she had seen at the grocery store standing side by side on the dock in front of the cabin.

When she arrived at her own family's cabin two doors down, she took a deep breath before opening the door and walking up the steps. Since Grandpa Frank had died, the cabin was seldom used, but it wasn't yet showing the signs of neglect. *Grams must be paying someone to keep the yard mowed.*

Reaching under the empty flowerpot on the third step, Sara found the key. A memory of Kyle on the front porch of the cabin flashed into her mind, but she shook it away as she unlocked the door and went inside. The furniture had a thin layer of dust but otherwise had a familiar, rustic charm. *Just like I remember it.*

Sara shut the door behind her and made her way to the small room in back that her grandparents had set aside for her visits when she was just a little girl. The metal footlocker – a hand-me-down from her father's early years in the Army – was still at the foot of the bed. She carefully opened the locker and laid aside the quilts and blankets that were near the top.

A tear ran down her cheek as she pulled out the small wooden box that had been stored beneath the quilts for three years. *This is crazy. I shouldn't be crying. I should be happy to be starting a new life with a wonderful man.* The tears continued to flow as she carried the box out to the front porch. *It should end in the same place it began.*

She set the box down on the arm of the rocker that flanked the front door and went back inside. When she returned, she had a tissue in one hand, and a book of matches in the other. *Oh, gee whiz, stop crying!* She laid the matches beside the box, and then used the tissues to wipe her eyes and blow her nose.

When she had regained her composure, she sat down in the rocker and put the box in her lap. *Okay, I'm ready now.* She opened the box and first pulled out a small, leather book. *The journal I kept the summer that I met Kyle.* She struck a match, fanned the pages of the journal, and lit them on fire. When the pages were nothing but ashes, she shut the book to snuff out the fire and then tossed the book over the wooden porch railing out into the yard.

Next, she pulled out a stack of letters. *The ones I wrote to Kyle, begging him to come back to me. At least I had the decency not to mail them.* With another swift strike of the match, the letters were ablaze. Once they were consumed, Sara fanned out the fire and threw what was left of them into the yard beside the torched journal.

And last but not least, the photographic evidence. Sara pulled out the small handful of pictures that she had taken during her summer with Kyle. *It's a good thing Grams never looked in here.* She struck a third match, but a sudden breeze blew it out. The same thing happened with two more matches, and then the matchbox was empty. *I guess I'll just have to rip them up.*

Sara had not read the journal or the letters before she destroyed them, and she willed herself not to look at the pictures as she took them out of the package and shredded them one by one. She was almost finished when thunder rumbled in the distance. The breeze picked up, blowing the last picture out of her hands and into the yard.

She sprinted towards the picture but grabbed only air. As the ashes and shreds of all that she had destroyed circled around her in the wind, Sara chased the last tangible reminder of her summer with Kyle around the yard. Just as she would almost reach it, the wind would pick it up again and toss it farther away. When she finally caught hold of it, she found herself in front of the cabin between her family's and Kyle's.

There was a chill in the air as rain began to fall in sheets. Sara tucked the picture under her arm and ran back to the porch. Drenched but not to be undone, she opened the door and went inside. She threw the picture on the table and went in search of dry clothes. *Grams always keeps a few things out here. We're about the same size.*

After she hung her wet clothes to dry and carefully placed her cell phone in the pocket of her grandmother's faded jeans in case there was news about Daniel, she sat down at the table. Out of curiosity, she flipped the picture over to see what image had caused her so much trouble.

When she did, she saw Kyle smiling into the camera and holding up a large mouth bass. There was a man in the distance, and Sara strained to make out the face. *Oh, yes. That was the man who had stayed in the cabin between ours that summer.* Sara's hand flew to her mouth and the picture fell to the floor as she realized that she had seen that face again recently. *That's Larry Turner!*

CHAPTER 31

Sharese ripped the top page off her legal pad and wadded it into a tight ball. *How can I write a letter in support of someone that I don't even know?* She tossed the wad into the trash can with the others, picked up the phone, and dialed her grandmother in Memphis. "Hi, Grandma."

"Sharese, baby," Eloise Jackson replied, "I was just thinking about you."

"You were?"

"Yes, I was. I'm making a caramel cake, your favorite."

"Yum. Wish I was there to have a slice."

"I wish you were here, too, but I'd have to shoo you away from this fine dessert. Got to take it over to your Aunt Ellen's house. She fell and broke her leg. Got a cast clean up to her hip."

"I'm sorry to hear that. Tell her I'll be praying for a quick recovery."

"While you're at it, you can pray for that little ole rat dog of hers. She was chasing it around inside the house, and that's what made her fall. She says she's gonna have it put down."

"That doesn't seem very fair." Sharese tried not to laugh. Aunt Ellen had been threatening to put that dog to sleep since the day she got him. Every time he wet the rug or chewed a favorite shoe, she started talking about the doggie death penalty. "I'm sure she'll get over it."

"Yeah, she always does." Eloise chuckled into the phone. "She'll probably be loving on him and giving him a bite of this cake as soon as I'm out the door."

Both Sharese and her grandmother laughed at the mental image of Aunt Ellen, casted foot propped up on the coffee table, pinching off pieces of Eloise's caramel cake and feeding it to her misbehaving Chihuahua.

When their laughter quieted, Eloise asked, "So, is that big trial finally over?"

"Sort of. All the evidence and arguments are in, but the jury is still out for the deliberation."

"How did it go? Do you think you won?"

"I don't know, Grandma. The jury's been out for a few hours now. I think that's probably a good sign."

"Sounds like my baby girl gave them something to talk about."

"Yeah, I hope so. I really like my client, and I don't think he deserves to go back to prison."

"Speaking of prison," Eloise began.

That didn't take long. "I haven't written the letter yet, Grandma. That's why I'm calling, to tell you that I don't think I can do it."

"You can defend some boy that you don't even know, but you can't write a letter on behalf of your own daddy? I thought I raised you better than that, girl!"

The words stung Sharese. "I appreciate everything that you've done for me, Grandma, I really do. When I was growing up, you were all that I had. You were my grandmother, my mama, and my daddy all rolled up into one. For your sake, I tried to write the letter. I really did. But I just can't write a letter for someone that I have absolutely no connection with."

There was silence on the other end of the phone, then a sniffle.

Don't cry. Please. "I'm sorry, Grandma. If I could, I would. I just can't."

"It's okay if you can't write a letter, Sharese baby," Eloise said. "They'll probably deny his application anyway."

"Yeah." *Cop killers aren't favorites of the parole board.* "I guess I should go now, Grandma. I should probably get back over to the courthouse."

"Will you at least promise me that you'll drive up to the prison and visit Tony some time? He'd love to see you."

Sharese sighed heavily. "I don't think that I can promise to do that."

"Will you at least pray about it?" Eloise asked.

"Yes, Grandma. I'll do that," Sharese agreed. "I love you. Bye now."

***

As dusk began to fall, Sara was pacing the worn wooden floor of the cabin. *I knew I recognized him from somewhere. With seeing Kyle again and worrying about Daniel in Honduras, I just couldn't place the face. I only saw him a few times that summer, but I remember that scar across his face and that heavy Texas accent.*

Sara picked up the picture and looked it again. *That's him, all right. He must have been out in his yard when Kyle caught the fish and brought it up to the cabin. I remember Kyle coming up from the dock with the fish and me telling him to wait outside until I could grab the camera.*

She tossed the picture back on the table. *His testimony during the trial is so fuzzy, but I'm almost sure that he told Kyle that he was just passing through town on the night Maria Flores was killed.* Sara wracked her brain, trying to remember exactly what Larry Turner had said on the witness stand. *If he lied about how long he had been in town, what else might he have lied about?*

Sara's thoughts were interrupted by the ringing of her cell phone. *Please let it be good news about Daniel.* "Hello?" she said without checking the caller identification on the phone.

"Hi, honey," Grams answered. "Are you out of court?"

"Yes. I got dismissed from the jury."

"You what? Why?"

"I was only an alternate, and the judge let me go because the jury was still intact when it came time for the deliberation."

"Oh, I see. Have you heard anything more about Daniel?"

"No, not since this morning. All I know is that the mission board said his party never made it the mountains."

"You must be worried sick. I know I am."

"No, Grams, actually I'm not worried anymore. I just know that Daniel is going to be okay. He told me that he would come home safe, and he will."

"That's showing a lot of faith, Sara Josephine. I'm proud of you for that."

"Thanks." Glancing back at the picture, Sara wrapped up the call, "I was sort of in the middle of something, Grams. I'll stop by and see you in the morning, okay?"

"That'll be fine, honey. I'll say an extra prayer for Daniel tonight."

Sara switched off the phone and laid it on the table beside the picture. *I need to stop worrying about Larry Turner. It doesn't make any difference now, anyway. The evidence is all in, and the jury is out for the deliberation.*

Still, something stopped her from destroying the photograph as she had all the other tangible reminders of Kyle. She pictured the jury, huddled around the large conference table at the courthouse repeating Larry Turner's words about Justin's driving on the night of the accident. *He left me in the dust.*

Then, she pictured the exchange at the Piggly Wiggly. *The cashier said that she thought that Justin was already in prison, and*

Elizabeth said that he was but that he got a new trial on a technicality.

Sara ran her fingers through her hair, trying to think what it all meant. *Justin Hargis has already served time in prison, but what if Larry Turner was lying and Justin wasn't really speeding that night? This picture proves that he lied about at least one thing.*

Sara thought back to Sharese's closing argument, the part where she had said that Larry Turner left before he could be cross-examined. *I remember thinking that he was acting strange that day, even if I didn't remember who he was. Why would he leave like that?* Sara eyed the photograph again. *Did he recognize me in the jury box? No, probably not, but maybe he remembered Kyle? Wouldn't they have met during the first trial? Maybe Kyle didn't try the case the first time.*

A sinking feeling came over Sara as she came to the realization that she had to show the picture to Kyle. *I have to let him know that Larry Turner might not have been telling the truth on the stand.* She picked up the picture and put it in her shirt pocket.

As she looked around for her keys, doubt began to set in. *I came here to put the past behind me, not find a reason to see Kyle again. If I go to the courthouse to show him this picture, everyone will wonder why I'm there. How will I explain why I have a picture of Kyle and Larry Turner from three years ago?*

She put the keys back on the table and sat down at one of the chairs. *Maple Springs is a small town. If word gets out about Kyle and me, my reputation will be ruined. Daniel is a minister; he'll be embarrassed in front of his congregation.*

Sara pictured Kyle's children. *If people find out about us, it might even end his marriage. And what about the fact that neither of us told the judge about our relationship during the jury selection? What kind of trouble will we get into? Could he be disbarred? Could I go to jail?*

She ran her fingers through her wet hair, making it even more of a tangled mess. Then she bit her lip as she picked up the picture again. *I should just rip this to pieces right this minute and forget I ever saw it.*

Sara's hands began to shake at the prospect of destroying the only piece of evidence that could save Justin Hargis if Larry Turner had indeed been lying on the witness stand. As the picture fell out of her trembling hands, she slid out of the chair and onto her knees in prayer. *Father, I don't know what this picture means. It might not mean anything at all. But Daniel said that maybe you were putting me on the jury for a reason.*

She wiped her eyes and picked up the picture from the floor. *Is this the reason, Lord? This picture? If it is, I don't know if I can obey Your will. It could cost so much to so many if I come forward with this picture. It could cost me Daniel. It could cost Kyle his family, his job. It might even get me into some sort of legal trouble for not saying I knew Kyle during jury selection. Give me strength, Lord. Give me wisdom.*

CHAPTER 32

Sharese walked the short distance from her office to the courthouse in a rainy mist. As she entered the building and began shaking off her umbrella, she noticed a janitor mopping the floor. She looked about the same age as Sharese's grandmother and even had a similar build. "Good evening," she said to the woman.

"Be careful ma'am. Floor's wet."

"I will. Thank you." There was a smell of food in the air, and Sharese's rumbling stomach reminded her that she hadn't had dinner. "Something smells good in here."

"Pizza," the janitor said. "The jury was getting hungry, so they called some in."

"It'll be awhile then, I suppose?"

"Don't know. You'd know more about that than me, ma'am."

Sharese started to say that the janitor probably had more experience than she did around the courthouse but thought better of it. *No use advertising your weaknesses.* "I guess I'll wait it out upstairs in the courtroom. You have a good night."

"You, too, ma'am." The janitor nodded to Sharese and then went back to her business of mopping.

As she carefully walked across the wet tile floor, Sharese could hear the janitor whistling an old gospel song that she remembered from childhood. When she was inside the elevator, she sang a bar of the song. *Like a bird, from these prison bars has flown, I'll fly away.*

When the elevator door opened, she was surprised to see Marcus Thompson standing right in front of her. "Trooper Thompson," she said in higher pitch than she would have liked.

"Ms. Jackson," Marcus replied. "The jury's still out, if you were wondering."

"Yeah, the janitor told me they just ordered some pizza."

"I was just about to check out the vending machines myself," Marcus replied, patting his stomach.

"There are vending machines?" Sharese's stomach growled loud enough for both of them to hear. "Where?"

Marcus laughed. "Downstairs. Stocked with the finest junk food Maple Springs has to offer. Can I bring you back something?"

"Yes, that would be wonderful. Let me give you some money."

"It's okay; I have plenty of change." Marcus stuck his hand in the pocket of his uniform pants and jingled some quarters. "What's your pleasure – peanuts, chips, or candy?"

"Hmm. It's been a week that calls for chocolate, but I guess I should be sensible and say peanuts. At least there's a little nutrition in them."

"Whatever you say. And some coffee?"

"Definitely some coffee."

By the time that Marcus got back from the vending machines, Sharese had made a quick check on Justin in the holding cell. He had his head down on the table, snoring away. *How can you sleep without knowing the jury's verdict?* The deputy offered to wake him, but Sharese just shook her head and said, "Let him sleep. It's been a long day."

Marcus set Sharese's coffee on the defense table and placed his own on the State's table before reaching into his pockets for two packages of chocolate covered peanuts, one for him and one for Sharese. "The best of both worlds."

Sharese smiled. "Perfect. You're sure I can't pay you back?"

"I've got it." Marcus opened his snack. "You haven't seen Copeland around, have you?"

"No. Didn't he say he was going home for awhile?" *Sorry Robin, but it's not my day to watch Batman.*

"That's what he said, but I've called there a couple of times and there was no answer. No answer on his cell either."

"Hmm." Sharese munched her peanuts. *Why would he need to talk to him when he just saw him a couple of hours ago? And men say women are on the phone too much. Geez.* "You two are pretty tight, huh?"

Marcus put down his coffee cup and looked squarely at Sharese. "I like to think we're friends."

Sharese raised an eyebrow. *I'm getting about tired of these two and their shenanigans. They've whispered and pointed and conspired against me all week.* "Friends, huh? Y'all going to play basketball again? Go deer hunting?"

Marcus huffed, "It's about the trial, thank you very much."

Ohhh. They're up to their tricks again. "Did something come up with the jury that I need to know about?"

"No, nothing like that. I just wanted to talk to him about – " Marcus trailed off before finishing his sentence.

"Talk to him about what?"

Marcus studied Sharese for a minute before answering. "Nothing." Sharese could tell that Marcus was struggling to regain his composure. "Can I get you some more coffee, Ms. Jackson?"

"No, *Mr.* Thompson. I'm fine." *He's acting really strange.* "Are you sure you didn't need to talk to him about the jury?"

"No, I don't need to talk to him about the jury," Marcus said firmly. "The jury will decide what the jury wants to decide, and there's nothing any of us can do about it at this point."

"Then what?" *I'm not giving up. You two are up to something, and I'm going to find out what it is.*

"Really, it was nothing you need to know about. We're not on the same team you know, you and me."

Yeah, no kidding. "Well, all right then. I hope he shows up before the jury gets back or you might have to go to the Good Ole' Boy Cotillion all by yourself."

"Whatever," Marcus mumbled. "I'm going to get some more coffee."

When he had gone, Sharese felt very alone in the courtroom. All she could hear was the clock ticking on the wall and the hum of the florescent lights overhead. *Marcus Thompson, you are a strange man. Unbearably handsome, but very strange. Quite rude, too.*

CHAPTER 33

Sara sat at the table inside the cabin, her cell phone in one hand and the photograph of Kyle and Larry Turner in the other. *I can only think of one person who might be able to clear this up and possibly keep me from embarrassing myself for nothing.* She took a deep breath and punched the numbers into the phone.

"Hello?" Grams answered.

"Hi Grams," Sara began. "I need to ask you a question. It might not make any sense right now, but just hear me out, okay?"

Grams cleared her throat. "Okay. What is it, honey?"

"It's about the cabin next door out at the river, the one between yours and the Copelands'."

There was nothing but silence on the other end of the phone. "Grams? Are you still there?" *Maybe the reception is bad out here. I'll try outside.* "Is that better? Can you hear me now?"

"I can hear you fine, Sara Josephine."

"Oh, well, what I wanted to know is, who owns that cabin?"

Silence.

"Grams?"

"I'm here, Sara Josephine."

"So, who owns the cabin? Do you know?"

"Why would you ask me about that cabin?"

Grams' voice was strained, and Sara was starting to regret making the call. *What am I going to say now?* "Um, it has to do with the trial."

"I thought you were excused from the jury."

"I was."

Grams gave an exasperated sigh. "I don't understand why you're asking me this, Sara Josephine."

Wow, three 'Sara Jospehines' in less than two minutes. I've really struck a nerve with her about something. "It's just that, um–" *Oh, just say it, already!* "I think I might have recognized one of the witnesses during the trial. He reminds me of a man that I saw at the cabin next door that summer that I was working on my thesis."

"You saw someone at the Turner cabin?"

The Turner cabin! "Yes. A middle-aged man, sort of heavy-set. Thinning red hair."

A gasp on the other end of the line.

"Grams, are you okay?"

In a gravelly, almost unrecognizable voice, Grams said, "Lawrence."

"Lawrence? Lawrence Turner?"

"Yes. But–"

"But what?"

"Lawrence Turner died forty years ago."

A chill ran up Sara's spine. "No, I just saw him a couple of days ago, at the trial."

"I assure you, Sara Josephine Anderson, you most certainly did not see Lawrence Turner two days ago or three years ago or ever! He died before you were born."

This is getting more bizarre by the minute. "It was the same man, Grams. I'm sure of it. He has a deep scar across his cheek and a very heavy Texas accent."

"Oh." Grams was still a little uncertain. "That wasn't Lawrence, then. He didn't have a scar, and he wasn't from Texas."

Lawrence, Larry. Oh, wait – if Lawrence died forty years ago, maybe he was Larry's father. That would explain the resemblance.

"Did Lawrence Turner have a son?"

"Good grief, Sara Josephine, will you please stop asking me these infernal questions?"

Another 'Sara Josephine' and now 'infernal.' What has gotten into her? "Look Grams, I can tell that I've upset you – and quite frankly, I don't know why – but I really need to get this straight in my head. Can you please just tell me if Lawrence Turner had a son named Larry?"

A long, heavy sigh on the other end of the line. "All right, if you're insistent on knowing about the Turners, I guess I may as well start the story at the beginning."

"Okay." Sara sat down on the front porch rocker. "That sounds like as good a place as any."

***

Sharese sat alone in the courtroom for as long as she could stand it. Finally, she ventured out into the hallway in search of some form of human companionship or at least another snack. *Now, where did that annoying man say the vending machines were?*

A sudden noise at the end of the hallway startled Sharese. *What in the world?*

The stairwell door flew open, and Sara Anderson exploded into the hallway. "Ms. Jackson!" She looked as surprised to see Sharese as Sharese was to see her.

"Ms. Anderson, what are you doing here? The judge excused you from the deliberation."

"Has the jury returned a verdict yet?" Sara puffed.

"No, not yet." Sharese took another look at Sara. Her hair was wet, she was wearing a pair of jeans that looked older than she was, and she was obviously quite winded. *And I thought Marcus Thompson was acting odd tonight. I may owe that man an apology.* "Are you okay, Ms. Anderson?"

"Thank God! I'm not too late then."

"Too late for what?" *I'm beginning to think I've moved into The Twilight Zone.*

Sara looked past Sharese towards the courtroom door. "Are the others in there?"

"No." *What in the world is going on here?*

"Do you know where they are?"

"Who do you mean by 'they'? The judge? The clerk?

"Kyle. I mean, Mr. Copeland."

"Kyle?" *Why would she call the D.A. by his first name?*

"Yes, Mr. Copeland."

"You said 'Kyle.'"

Sara glanced around nervously. "Please, Ms. Jackson, do you know where he is? It's really important that I see him before the jury comes back."

"When the jury retired a few hours ago, he said he was going to wait it out at home," Sharese began. "But why would you–"

"Home? I can't go there," Sara interrupted. A look of confusion passed over her face. "I don't even know where he lives."

For a long minute, neither woman spoke.

"Why would you call the D.A. by his first name if you don't even know where he lives?"

Sara's shoulders drooped. "Look, Ms. Jackson, I know you must think this is strange, me coming here, but–"

"Yes, Ms. Anderson, I must say that I am quite interested in not only why you're here when the judge told you to go home but also why you're suddenly on a first-name basis with the prosecutor." *Am I just being paranoid or is this as crazy as it seems?*

Before Sara could answer, the elevator light came on, signaling that someone was on the way up. At the same time, they said, "Maybe that's him."

When the doors parted, Marcus Thompson stepped out. He looked from Sharese to Sara and back again. "What's going on here?"

"Ms. Anderson here was just looking for the district attorney."

"Do you know where he is, Trooper Thompson?"

Marcus looked back and forth between the women again. "Umm, uh. I uh, I think he went home," he stammered.

"You said that you called him there, and there was no answer," Sharese said.

"Yeah. That's right. No answer."

"Do you have his cell phone number?" Sara asked.

"Now, what in the world would you need with the prosecutor's telephone number, Ms. Anderson?" Sharese asked. *Okay, I know I am not just being paranoid. These people are crazy.*

"He's not picking up on it either," Marcus said. "You know, Ms. Anderson, the judge released you from the jury, so you can go home now."

"Well, duh, Mr. Thompson, she's obviously been home. She's changed clothes, and she's soaking wet from coming back here in the rain." *Men never notice anything.*

"Why don't you let me walk you to your car, Ms. Anderson," Marcus said, pushing the down button on the elevator.

"Oh, no, you don't!" Sharese said. "Whatever is going on here, I need to know about it."

Sharese and Marcus stared at each other, but no one moved as the elevator opened and closed.

"I didn't want to do it this way, but–" Sara began.

"But what?" Sharese turned to face her.

"Is there some place that we can talk, all three of us? Somewhere private?" Sara asked.

"There's a small conference room downstairs. It's at the back of the General Sessions courtroom. No one will be in there this time of night," Marcus said.

"Well, aren't you handy?" Sharese said.

Marcus ignored Sharese's remark and led the two women down the stairs to the first floor. He glanced around and, seeing no one, opened the door of a small courtroom. Flipping on a single light near the bench at the far end of the room, he motioned, "Back there, in the corner."

When Sara and Sharese walked to the doorway that Marcus had indicated, he said, "Open the door and flip on the light in there."

Sharese did as Marcus instructed, and Marcus turned off the switch in the courtroom and joined the women, closing the door behind him and leaving the courtroom dark to anyone who walked by.

"It's about Larry Turner." Sara pulled the photograph from her shirt pocket and placed it on the table. "I think he may have had something to do with Maria Flores's death."

CHAPTER 34

Kyle and Elizabeth walked out of the emergency room into the damp night air. Evan was asleep in Elizabeth's arms, and Chelsea was cooing peacefully against Kyle's shoulder. "Do you have a blanket for the baby?" Kyle asked.

"It's eighty degrees out here. She'll be fine," Elizabeth answered.

She'll be fine. How relieved Kyle had been when he had finally heard those words. "I guess I'm just still worried about her, that's all."

"The emergency room doctor said it's just an ear infection. Babies get them all the time."

"Not *my* baby," Kyle said, patting Chelsea's downy hair. "My baby is a strong, healthy girl. She's not going to get sick and scare her daddy half to death ever again, are you, sweetheart?"

"Oh, for goodness sake, the ER was only a precaution. Dr. Bradshaw just wanted to rule out meningitis because one of his other patients came down with it last week. He never said Chelsea actually had it."

"I know, but it was still terrifying. Meningitis can be fatal."

"Yes, Kyle, I know that," Elizabeth said as she struggled to get Evan into his car seat without waking him. "You know, you could have carried the heavy one."

"Oh, sorry. I guess I should have, but I just don't want to let this little girl out of my sight right now. I'm so grateful she's okay."

Elizabeth sniffed and bit her lip. "Oh Kyle," she said, falling into his arms, "What if we'd lost her? What if it really had been meningitis? What if I'd waited too long to take her to the doctor?"

Kyle put his free arm around Elizabeth and kissed her cheek, baby Chelsea in between them. "She's going to be fine, honey. We're all going to be just fine."

Elizabeth wiped her eyes. "I'm sorry. I'm just such a mess these days. It seems like all I do is worry and complain. And fill sippy cups and change diapers. And pick up toys and wash baby clothes. And–"

"It's a lot for one person to do. I'm sorry I haven't been home much lately. Work has been–"

"It's okay. You had that big trial this week." Elizabeth felt around in her purse for a tissue and blew her nose. "You know, the jury sure is staying out a long time, aren't they?"

The jury! I'd almost forgotten. Kyle checked his watch. "Wow, it's later than I thought. Maybe I should call over to the courthouse and check on things." He reached for his cell phone but found nothing in the case on his belt where he usually kept it. "Where's my phone?"

"You don't have it?"

"No, it's not in the case."

"Did you take it out while we were in the hospital?"

"No, I don't think so."

"Maybe it's in the car."

Kyle felt around in the driver's seat and floorboard. "It's not in here, either."

"Did you leave it at the office?"

"I couldn't have. I drove straight home from the courthouse. Oh! Now I remember. I took it out and put it on the seat, so I could get to it quick if the clerk called about the jury."

"You can use mine." Elizabeth reached into her purse and pulled out her phone.

"I don't know the clerk's number. I have it programmed into my phone."

"Is there someone else there that you could call?"

"I'll call Marcus. I have his number memorized." Kyle chuckled and quickly dialed Marcus's number. "Hey Marcus, is there any word from the jury yet?"

"Where are you?" Marcus's tone alerted Kyle that something was amiss.

"Hang on a minute," Kyle said. "Hon, will you go ahead and put Chelsea in the car. I'll be there in a minute."

Elizabeth took the baby, and Kyle walked far enough away from the car that Elizabeth would be unable to hear Marcus's words. "What's up? You don't sound right."

"Why haven't you answered your phone all night?"

"I accidentally left it in my car. When I got home, Chelsea was sick, so I drove her, Elizabeth, and Evan to the doctor's office in Elizabeth's SUV. He was afraid it might be meningitis, so we've been in the ER all night."

"Is she going to be all right?"

"Yes. Luckily, it turned out to be just an ear infection."

"Are you back home now?"

"No, we're in the hospital parking lot getting ready to head that way. Why?"

"Take your wife and kids home, and then come straight to the courthouse."

"Is the jury back?"

"They've been back in for an hour, but the judge hasn't asked them for the verdict yet. We've been waiting on you."

Kyle cursed. "I'll be there as soon as I can."

"There's something else you need to know."

"What's that?"

"Sara's here. She has a picture of Larry Turner from three years ago. You're in it."

Kyle shook his head. "What? I know I must not have heard that right."

"You heard it right. You need to get over here, now."

Kyle looked at Elizabeth, who was strapping Chelsea into the car. *Sara. At the courthouse. With a picture of me and Larry Turner. How could that be possible?* "How could she have a picture of me and Larry Turner when I just met the guy on Monday?"

"Meet us in the conference room at the back of the General Sessions courtroom, and we'll explain everything."

"She's with you?"

"Yes. Sharese Jackson is here, too."

"I'll be there as soon as I can." As he walked back to the car, Kyle felt his world slipping away from him – his family, his career, his political ambitions. *Just when I thought it was completely over with her, it starts all over again.*

CHAPTER 35

Sara was wringing her hands and pacing beside the small conference table as she listened to Marcus end his call with Kyle. "So, he's on his way?" *Dear Lord, please give me strength.*

"He was at the hospital. His little girl was sick, but she's okay now. He has to take Elizabeth and the kids home, and then he'll be here."

"How long will that take?" Sharese asked.

"Maybe twenty minutes," Marcus said.

"Do you think we should tell the judge he's on his way?" Sharese asked.

"No. We need to talk to Copeland first," Marcus said.

"You've just got to help your buddy cover his tracks, don't you?" Sharese commented.

"Can you please just try to look at the bigger picture for a minute?" Marcus said.

"I knew you two were up to something this week. I may be new around here, but I'm not totally clueless, you know," Sharese said.

Please stop arguing. This is hard enough without you two bickering. "Ms. Jackson, if it means anything to you, I thought you did a great job for your client this week," Sara said. "If I'd had to participate in the deliberation, I would have a lot of trouble deciding which way to vote."

"I thought you did a great job, too," Marcus said.

Sharese softened. "You did?"

"I've been involved in this case for three years, and I've never had any doubt whatsoever that Justin Hargis killed Maria Flores. Until today. I thought you were a fool for putting that boy on the stand. It's a typical rookie mistake you know – for a defense lawyer to actually believe a client." Marcus smirked. "But, when you put him up there and he started talking about seeing something blue and waving hands and a flash of light, I actually believed him, too."

"He didn't remember that until today. That's why he wanted to testify, to try to get some sort of peace about the whole thing." Sharese sighed. "I shouldn't have told you that. It's protected by attorney-client privilege."

"Don't worry about it. What happens in here stays in here," Marcus said.

"I don't know about that. We're going to have to tell the judge eventually," Sharese said.

"What you need to learn is that the legal community around here is a family – the lawyers, the cops, the judge, the clerk, everybody around the courthouse. We help each other out when we can," Marcus said.

Sharese turned nasty again. "You mean you're all in cahoots."

Oh no, here we go again. "No, Ms. Jackson, I don't think he meant it that way. He just meant that we all have to work together to do what's right here."

Marcus looked at Sara. "What I meant was, we have each other's back."

"You know, I could have your job for this. And Kyle Copeland's law license," Sharese said.

Sara started to cry. "I'm so sorry that I didn't say something sooner, Ms. Jackson. During jury selection, you never actually asked me if I knew Kyle, and I was too embarrassed to volunteer that I did. I was in shock from seeing him again after three years. I thought he'd do something to keep me from being on the jury, but he told me that he ran out of per–perem–some kind of challenge."

"Peremptory challenge. A challenge that doesn't require an explanation by an attorney," Sharese explained. "Wait –you've talked to him about the case? It is highly improper for an attorney to have *ex parte* communication with a juror!"

"I saw him in the stairwell for just a minute or two on the first day." Sara wiped her eyes.

"What does it matter now, anyway?" Marcus said. "If Ms. Anderson hadn't been on the jury and seen Larry Turner up there on the stand, she would never have made the connection that he was at the river at other times during that summer."

God may be putting you on the jury for a reason. Daniel knew before I did. "You're right. I've prayed all week to be let off the jury. I didn't want be part of the deliberation. Not just because of Kyle, but also because my fiancé is in Honduras on a mission trip, and there's been an earthquake there." The tears started again.

Sharese put her hand on Sara's shoulder. "I'm sorry to hear that. Is he okay?"

"We haven't heard from him yet," Sara said through the tears. "But I know God will bring him home to me. Anyway, I've been so upset this week that I haven't heard half of the evidence."

"That's understandable, I suppose," Sharese said. "Did you recognize Larry Turner when he was on the stand?"

"No, but I felt there was something familiar about him."

"That's another time I thought you'd made a fatal mistake during the trial. I thought you should have asked for a mistrial," Marcus said.

"Justin wanted to go forward. He just wanted to get it over with."

"You can't let your client control the case like that, Ms. Jackson," Marcus said. "You're the boss. The client has to understand that, or you'll never get anything accomplished."

Sara could see that Sharese was about to light into Marcus again. "Please don't start arguing again." Sara thought back to Fredonia Miller's suggestion that Sharese and Marcus might be attracted to each other, and the thought made her chuckle. Before she knew it, she was giggling uncontrollably.

"What could possibly be funny at a time like this?" Sharese asked.

Sara tried to get her breath. "I'm sorry, Ms. Jackson. It's just that some of the other jurors thought that you two might be an item someday." Sara doubled over in laughter, tired and spent from the day that she had had. "I'm sorry for laughing, but–"

Marcus started laughing then, and Sharese soon joined him. None of the three could regain control of themselves until they heard a light knock at the door.

"Copeland," Marcus said. "I forgot that I locked the door."

The laughter died down as Marcus unlocked the door and Kyle walked into the small room. He glanced around the room, stopping on Sara's tear-stained face. "I guess the joke's on me, huh?"

"It's been a long night. We're just getting a little punchy." Marcus wiped his hand across his face. "Sit down and let us fill you in."

"Please do."

Marcus slid the photograph towards Kyle. "Sara found this at the cabin."

Kyle froze as a younger, carefree version of himself stared back at him. "The bass. That was the biggest thing I caught all summer."

"Look behind you. The guy in the background," Marcus said. "Look familiar?"

Kyle went pale and dropped the picture onto the table. "That is Larry Turner. But how in the world–"

"He stayed in the cabin between yours and mine that summer. He wasn't around much, but we saw him a few times. Remember?"

Kyle shook his head. "I'm trying, but I just can't."

"The date stamp on the picture says July 18, two days before the accident."

"That was the day before Elizabeth called me and–" His voice trailed off as he looked up at Sara.

"Yes, we've heard all about that," Sharese interrupted. "Can we just talk about Larry Turner, please?"

Sara stood up and turned away from Kyle so that he wouldn't see her face. "I went out to the cabin tonight. I had a small box of things from that summer that I had left there. I wanted to destroy them. Get on with my life."

"You kept this picture all that time," Kyle said. It was more of a statement than a question. Sara nodded.

"Yes. There was a journal, a few letters, and some pictures. I destroyed everything except this picture."

"Letters? I didn't write any letters to you."

"I wrote them. I never mailed them." *Thank God.*

"Oh."

Sara turned to face Kyle. "None of that matters now. All that matters is that Larry Turner lied about just passing through town that summer."

"Why would he do that?"

"I don't know, but I just have a feeling that he had something to do with Maria Flores's death."

"Why would you think that? Maybe he had some reason to be here that summer. Maybe he was just visiting a friend or something."

"No, I don't think so." Sara paused. "Do you know the story of that cabin, Kyle? The one between yours and mine?"

"What story?"

285

"About forty years ago, there was a murder there. A murder-suicide, actually."

"I never heard that. My family has owned that cabin for years, and no one has ever mentioned it."

"It happened before your family built their cabin. There were just the two then – ours and the Turners'."

Kyle wiped his hands through his hair. "How do you know all this, Josie? Why didn't you say something sooner?"

"I just found out tonight. When I saw Larry Turner in this picture, I called my grandmother and asked her about the cabin." Sara chose her words carefully. "She told me that a man named Lawrence Turner had been killed in the cabin. His wife shot him, and then she shot herself."

"Lawrence Turner?"

"Yes. Lawrence and Carmen Turner. They were Larry Turner's parents."

"I thought he was from Texas?"

"Lawrence was from Tennessee, but Carmen was from Mexico. They lived in Nashville. The cabin was a vacation home. After they died, Larry went to live with an aunt in Texas."

"That's quite a story. I can't believe I've never heard it before. I thought everything in Maple Springs was public record."

"Not quite everything," Sharese interjected.

Kyle looked at Sharese as if he had forgotten she was in the room. "Ms. Jackson, I don't know what to say. I really messed up this week. I'm not usually like this."

"I sure hope not."

"Let me finish explaining about the Turners," Sara pleaded. "Grams said that not many people knew about their deaths. Since it happened so far from town and the couple wasn't from Maple Springs, word didn't travel as fast as it normally would have. The sheriff at that time ended up buying the house out of probate for a steal."

"No conflict of interest there," Kyle said sarcastically.

"Seriously?" Sharese said. "You're throwing stones about a sheriff's conflict of interest forty years ago when you've had your girlfriend here on the jury for the last week?"

"Ms. Jackson, please just let me finish," Sara said. Turning back to Kyle, she continued, "Anyway, the sheriff's kids own it now. They live out of state, so they have a real estate agent here in town rent it out."

"Can we cut to the chase, please?" Marcus said. "The judge is going to come looking for us, and we have to decide what to do."

"What do you mean?" Kyle asked.

"After the jury went out, I went back to headquarters. Something about Justin Hargis's testimony got me wondering if there was more to what happened that night than we'd realized."

"Like what?" Kyle asked.

"That kid was out cold that night. He'd taken a hard lick to the head, so I just couldn't believe your theory that he woke up and saw the blue lights from my cruiser when I was trying to wake him up."

"But what else could have it have been, Marcus?"

"You said in your closing argument that my cruiser has blue and white lights, but it doesn't. It only has blue lights, so, even if you were right about the blue being my lights and the hands being my hands, there was still the flash of light."

"This is getting ridiculous. What if the kid just made that up?"

"He didn't make it up," Sharese said. "Can you stop being a prosecutor for a minute and just listen?"

Marcus went on, "So, anyway, I started thinking about what else Justin Hargis could have seen that night that would have looked like a flash of light. I tried to remember the accident scene as best I could. I'd tried to forget it, to tell you the truth. I hate cases where kids die."

"So, did you remember anything?"

"I thought about it long and hard, and something finally came to me. When I got to the scene, Larry Turner was standing in the road by the Hargis boy's car. He had this huge flashlight in his hand. It had steel body but a heavy plastic cover over the light part. Looked almost indestructible. I remember asking him about it because it was much better than my police-issue flashlight."

"Okay, so maybe it was Larry Turner's flashlight that the kid saw," Kyle said.

"Maybe, but that's not what I'm getting at. When I thought back on it, something just wasn't right in my mind."

"Truckers carry flashlights all the time, Marcus. There's nothing unusual about that."

"The first thing he said to me was 'He's killed a girl.' Then, he led me to her body. As we walked along, he told me that the kid had passed him a mile or two back up the road, flying."

"Okay, so?"

"How did he know Hargis hit the girl if he was still a mile behind him when the accident happened?"

"Obviously, he found her body."

"That's the thing. Her body was in a ditch a good fifty feet from Hargis's car, covered in mud and blood. If he hadn't pointed her out to me, I wouldn't have had a clue that she was there."

"So what are you saying?"

"I don't know exactly, but there's something wrong here. There has to be. Why would he lie about just passing through town that night? Why would he act so odd on the witness stand and then skip town as soon as he had a chance?"

"Maybe he recognized you or me," Sara said. "Maybe he was afraid we would make the connection that he was in Maple Springs earlier that summer."

"There's only one way to find out for sure, and that's to talk to Larry Turner," Sharese said.

"We've been looking for him for days," Kyle said. "Marcus even put out an APB on him yesterday."

"Yesterday? He's been missing since Wednesday," Sharese said.

Kyle and Marcus exchanged a guilty look, but neither confessed to their plan to have Sharese ask for a mistrial. Finally, Marcus spoke up. "It doesn't matter now. We've found him. That's why I've been calling you all night. Turns out, he was right under our nose the whole time."

"Where was he?"

"At the cabin."

CHAPTER 36

Kyle couldn't believe what he was hearing. *What if they're right and Larry Turner did have something to do with Maria Flores's death? Sara was at the river this afternoon, too. What if he'd hurt her?* Panic rose up in Kyle as he asked, "Is he still out there?"

"No," Marcus said. "A cleaning lady went to the cabin this afternoon to get it ready for some guests that were coming in for the weekend. When she pulled up in the yard, she saw a man inside. She drove back out to the Winningham Road and called the sheriff's department. When the deputy went to the cabin, Turner surrendered without much fuss. Said he was glad it was finally over."

"Glad what's finally over?"

"Nobody knows. After the deputy put him in the squad car, he refused to say anything else."

"Where is he now?"

"The county jail."

"How much of this does Judge Oaks know?" Kyle asked.

"All he knows at this point is that you're missing in action," Marcus said. "He has the clerk calling around looking for you."

"If she calls the house again, Elizabeth will tell her that I came back here."

"We need to figure out what to do here. Quick," Marcus said.

"Have you talked to your client about it?" Kyle asked Sharese.

"No. Not yet."

Kyle felt as if his head was going to explode. *Think quick, think quick.* "So, what do we know for sure? We know that Larry Turner was lying about only passing through town on the night of the accident."

"Problem is, we only know that because of the picture," Marcus said.

"What if I take a *nolle*?" Kyle asked Sharese.

"A what?" Sara asked. "Is that like a dismissal?"

"No," Sharese said to both Sara and Kyle. "A *nolle prosequi* just means that the State won't prosecute the case further on the current indictment. They could bring the charges up again later."

"Your client could walk out of here tonight," Kyle said. "It's the best deal he could get."

"You don't know that. The jury could have found him not guilty," Sharese retorted.

"But you don't know that either," Kyle said.

Sharese glared at Kyle. "What I do know is that my client will have excellent grounds for appeal. He could even file a complaint against you with the Board of Professional Responsibility."

"You wouldn't do that."

"Why wouldn't I?" Sharese asked. "Why shouldn't I just turn all three of you in for obstruction of justice and jury tampering?"

Kyle sat down, defeated. *She has a point.*

"I'll tell you why," Marcus said, "Because if you don't take the deal and the jury comes back with a guilty verdict, your client will have to go back to prison and wait months or years through an appeal while you try to prove that what happened in here tonight really happened."

At the same instant, Marcus and Sharese both dove for the picture on the table. Marcus had almost reached it when Sharese elbowed him away, grabbed the picture, and sprinted towards the door with it in her hand.

"Wait! I'll drop all the charges" Kyle knew he had no choice but to forfeit the game. "A full dismissal."

Sharese turned around, carefully guarding the picture behind her back. "With prejudice?"

"Yes," Kyle said evenly. "Justin Hargis walks out of here a free man, with no chance of another trial. Just give me the picture. Walk out of here like none of this ever happened."

"What will we tell the judge?" Marcus asked.

Just then, there was a knock at the door. "General, are you in there? I've been looking all over the courthouse for you," the clerk asked.

"Tell the judge we'll be there in about five minutes," Kyle said through the door. "In his chambers."

"But the jury's back," the clerk said. "The judge is having a fit, wanting them to read the verdict so he can dismiss them and get home."

"It'll only take a minute." Kyle grimaced inwardly at the thought of what awaited him when he had to tell the already seething Henry Oaks that the State had wasted a full week of the court's time and had kept the jury out half the night only to have their verdict remain unread.

"All right, I'll tell him. He's not going to be happy, but I'll tell him," the clerk said, her voice fading as she walked away from the door.

"Do we have a deal, Ms. Jackson?" Kyle asked Sharese.

"We have a deal, Mr. Copeland. But the picture belongs to her, not to you." Sharese handed the picture to Sara.

"Are there other copies of it?" Marcus asked Sara.

"No," Sara said. "It was a digital picture. I deleted the file from the camera a few months after Kyle left."

"Give me the picture, Josie." Kyle reached out his hand.

"What about Larry Turner? What if he had something to do with Maria Flores's death? Couldn't the picture be evidence against him?"

"Let me worry about that," Kyle said.

"There's just one thing I have to know, Kyle," Sara said, still holding the picture in her hand.

"What's that?"

"Why didn't you just tell me that Elizabeth was pregnant? It might have made it easier for me to accept losing you."

Kyle sighed and looked at his shoes. "It was complicated, Josie."

"What's so complicated about saying: 'My wife is pregnant?'"

Kyle glanced around at Marcus and Sharese, who suddenly took an unusual interest in the ancient Pinky and Blue Boy paintings on the back wall of the conference room. "I wasn't sure if the baby was mine."

"Well, then," Sara said. "I guess you two deserve each other then, huh?"

"It wasn't like that, Josie. A couple of weeks after Elizabeth left me, she met a guy in a bar, and he slipped something in her drink." Kyle's voice broke as he continued, "I guess you'd call it 'date rape.' She didn't tell me about it until that summer."

"Why not?" Sara was shocked.

Kyle shook his head. "I guess she was in denial. In her mind, if she didn't tell anyone, then it was like it never happened."

"How awful for her."

"When she realized that she was pregnant, she wanted to abort the baby, to get rid of any shred of evidence that the rape had happened."

"I can see why that might be tempting."

"In the end, she decided that I should know about the baby because there was a chance that it was mine and not the guy who attacked her. When she told me, I was angry and confused about so many things. I didn't want to leave you, but – I never told her

294

about you, but my plan was to ask for a blood test after the baby was born. If it wasn't mine, I was going to find you and see if you would take me back."

Sara winced. "I guess it was yours, then."

"Once I saw Evan on the ultrasound, it didn't matter. He was mine regardless of what any test might have said."

"You were right, Kyle. That is a complicated situation."

"I'm sorry that I hurt you, Josie."

"It's okay. You did the right thing under very difficult circumstances," Sara looked down and saw that she was still holding the picture of Kyle and Larry Turner in her hand. She handed it to Kyle. "Now go do it again."

CHAPTER 37

Sara stood on Grams' front porch, uncertain of whether she should knock. Just as she was about to walk away, the porch light flicked on, and Grams opened the door. "Hey Grams."

Despite the late hour, Grams was still fully dressed. "I was hoping you would come by."

Sara wasn't sure what to say. "I only told them what I absolutely had to. Your secret is still safe, so you don't have to worry."

"I wasn't worried."

"How in the world could you not be worried?" Sara asked incredulously.

"I turned all of that over to the Lord many years ago," Grams answered with a quiet resolve. "What's done is done."

"Just tell me one thing, Grams."

"What is it that you want to know, Sara Josephine?"

"How did you tell Grandpa Frank about your affair? How did the two of you get past it?"

Grams drew a deep breath. "I never told him about Lawrence. I didn't see any reason for both of us to suffer."

"Weren't you afraid he'd find out somehow?"

"There was no one left to tell him. After Carmen found out about us, she–" Grams looked away. "After they both died, no one was left except me."

"But didn't it break your heart when Lawrence was killed? Didn't you need to talk to someone about it?"

"I didn't love Lawrence Turner. He was a charming man, yes, but I didn't love him."

"Then why did you sleep with–" Sara struggled to find the right words. "You said that Carmen found the two of you together at his cabin."

"I suppose I was bored, maybe a little lonely. I never meant for it to happen, but it did." Grams sat down at the kitchen table and motioned for Sara to join her. "One weekend, your Grandpa Frank decided he'd take your daddy to the Tennessee Walking Horse Festival over in Shelbyville. I decided I'd go out to the cabin and do some cleaning. That afternoon, Lawrence came over to say hello – neighbors did that back then. Carmen had stayed in Nashville that weekend, for what reason I can't remember now. Lawrence and I... well, we ended up spending the night together."

"That's when the affair started?"

"Yes. It went on for a couple of months before Carmen got suspicious. She was a very high-spirited woman and was very jealous when it came to Lawrence. I don't know what we did to give it away, but she found out somehow. She had to have known before she walked in on us because she already had the gun."

"Did you ever wonder why she didn't kill you, too?"

"She called me some ugly names and then said that she was going to do the only thing she knew to do that would keep Lawrence and her together forever. She pulled the gun out of her purse, fired a bullet into his head, and then turned it on herself. I don't think I stopped screaming for an hour."

"What did you do?"

"When I finally calmed myself down, I got dressed and drove into town. There was no such thing as a cell phone back then, and the cabin has never had a telephone. I went to the sheriff's office and told him that I had gone out to the cabin to get something and had heard gunshots next door."

"And he believed you?"

"He had no reason not to. There's a lot vested in one's reputation, Sara Josephine, and, so far as anyone knew, mine was flawless."

"How did you live with it all these years?"

"I almost went crazy at first. Finally, I confessed to a good friend of mine what had happened. We had grown up in church together, but I strayed away from the Lord over the years. She counseled me and helped me get back on the right path. When I finally talked to the Lord about what had happened, He granted me forgiveness, and I accepted it."

"You must have carried so much guilt all these years."

"Once I knew the Lord had forgiven me, I tried my best to put it behind me. I had a husband who loved me and a son I adored. I owed it to them to concentrate my attention on them, not spend the rest of my life worrying about something that I could never change."

"You make it sound so easy." Sara shook her head. *I don't know if I'll ever get over the guilt of my affair with Kyle.*

"I never said it was easy, Sara Josephine, but through God all things are possible."

Sara nodded. "Yes, I suppose you're right."

"The thing that bothered me the most was Larry and Carmen's little boy. I hoped that he'd grow up without his parents' death affecting him, but I guess that wasn't really possible."

Sara reached out and patted Grams on the arm. "There's something I need to tell you. I wish I didn't have to, but you may hear it around town, anyway."

"It's okay, dear. I already know about you and Kyle Copeland."

Sara gasped. "How did you know about that?"

"Your journal in your father's footlocker at the cabin. I read just enough of it to realize what had happened, and then I put it back into the box with your other things. I didn't look at anything else."

Sara was stunned. *She never said a word.* "I don't know what to say, Grams. I had no idea that you knew about Kyle and me."

"Everyone has a secret, Sara Josephine. Just try to put it behind you and move on with your life."

Sara hung her head. *Secrets are such dangerous things. Why do we torture ourselves with them?* Sara thought about the look on Kyle's face when he had told her about Elizabeth's rape. Three summers before, his carefree manner and contagious spirit had made Sara fall in love with him. Now there was a harshness in his eyes and an edge in his voice that Sara didn't recognize. *How much has it cost him to keep Elizabeth's secret about Evan? To keep the secret of our affair from her?*

Sara looked at her grandmother and saw just how frail she looked. *I wish she didn't have to know this part of the story, but there can be no more secrets around here.* "It wasn't Kyle that I was going to tell you about, Grams."

"What is it then?"

"It's about Larry Turner," Sara said, plunging ahead before she lost her courage. "The police found him at his parents' old cabin this afternoon and took him into custody. After I told Kyle and the defendant's attorney what I knew, Kyle agreed to dismiss the case against the defendant before the jury's verdict was announced. Then, he and the state trooper went over to the jail to question Larry Turner about the death of Maria Flores."

"Did Larry talk to them?"

"Well, it took them some time, but, eventually, yes, he did. At first, he refused to talk, but then had some sort of breakdown and started spilling everything. When it was all over, Kyle and the trooper came back to the courthouse and told us – the defense attorney and me – what Larry had said."

"And what exactly did he say?" Grams face was ashen.

"Turns out, he'd rented his parents' old cabin for that summer three years ago with the intention of recreating his mother's crime. Somehow, in his mind, it would avenge his father's death. He'd been stopping in Maple Springs every time that he had a run through here. He had an old pickup truck that he would drive back and forth from the truck stop where he'd leave his big rig.'

"He was waiting until he found the right girl – one who looked enough like his mother. He was getting ready to head back home for a few days when he saw Maria Flores in the parking lot at Cottons looking for a ride. He knew he'd found the right girl, so he told her that she could ride as far as Texas with him. They headed out Winningham Road about 10 p.m. that night.'

"When they got close to the turn-off to go out to the river, Larry pulled the truck off into a clearing. He knew he couldn't get that big truck down that gravel road without calling attention to himself, so his plan was to gag her and then carry her up to the cabin. Maria figured out that something was wrong and tried to get away from him.'

"She fought him off long enough to get the door of the truck open. She made a run for it, right about the time that Justin Hargis was coming down Winningham Road headed out to the river. Maria ran right out in front of Justin's car, waving for him to stop and help her.'

"Larry had grabbed a big flashlight out of his truck before he tried to chase Maria down. When he got to the road and saw Maria flagging Justin down, Larry threw the flashlight at Justin's windshield and cracked it in right in front of the driver seat. Justin lost control of the car. He swerved and hit Maria, then crashed into a tree.'

"Justin's car was blocking part of the roadway, and Larry knew he couldn't get around him or turn that big rig around. He was also livid that Justin had ruined his plan to take Maria to the

301

cabin and kill her. So, he decided to get revenge by making sure Justin got charged with Maria's death."

"I don't think I can stand to hear anymore." Grams' voice was weak. "To think, it all started with Lawrence and me."

"There's a bit more that you need to know, Grams," Sara said. "Larry also confessed to several other murders. He'd been picking up young girls at truck stops for about ten years, ever since he turned the age that his father was when he died. Maria's murder was going to be the last one. He was going to kill himself that night, too."

Grams went so pale that Sara was afraid she might about to faint. "Grams, are you okay?"

"No, Sara Josephine, of course I'm not okay. I've tried not to think about Lawrence Turner or his son for the last forty years, and now all of this. It's just too much to even think about."

"Can I get you a drink of water or something? You look terrible."

"I'll be okay. I just need to be alone and pray. I'll get this right with God, and everything will be okay again." Sara could see that Grams was trembling.

Sara hugged her, smoothing her white hair. "It's really late, Grams. Why don't you go on to bed? I'll sleep on the couch."

"I think that's probably a good idea."

"It isn't your fault, you know. You didn't cause Larry Turner to be a killer. It must have been in his blood, some sort of insanity or something like his mother. Normal people don't kill their spouse just because they have an affair, you know. And they don't become serial killers to avenge a parent's death."

"I know that in my head, but I'll have to ask God to put in my heart."

"He will, Grams. He will." One last question tugged at Sara's mind. "Grams, if you don't mind me asking, who was the friend that you talked to about what happened with the Turners?"

"Oh, nobody that you would know, honey. Just an old friend of mine from childhood. She's busy with her own family now, and we don't see each other so often anymore." Grams yawned and started down the hallway. "But since you asked, her name was Fredonia Miller."

Sara gasped, but Grams had already gone into her room and didn't hear. Sara wanted to ask whether Fredonia had known the Turners or, at the least, had ever seen a picture of Lawrence. *Maybe I wasn't the only juror who knew something wasn't right in that courtroom.*

Part of Sara wanted to know just how far Fredonia Miller would have gone to keep Grams' secret safe. *Would she have sent Justin Hargis to prison knowing that Larry Turner was lying? Surely not, but if she'd voted not guilty, then maybe I did all of this for nothing. What if she'd hung the jury, and there was a retrial later?*

As Sara lay down on Grams' couch for the night, she resolved to do what Grams had done all those years before, to turn it over to the Lord.

I did what I thought was right, Lord. Please give me peace to accept that there are things I may never know. Let all things be according to Your will, not mine. Amen.

CHAPTER 38

The next morning, Sara was awakened by a knock on Grams' door. When she got up to answer it, she passed her reflection in a mirror in the hallway. She still had on Grams' jeans and shirt from the cabin.

She'd been so exhausted when she'd finally rested on Grams' couch that she hadn't had the energy to change. Her hair was a mess, and her eyes were red and swollen from crying. *Who could be knocking on the door at this hour?*

"Is someone at the door?" Grams called, coming out of her room. Sara was astounded to see that she was already dressed, without so much as a hair out of place.

"Yes. Since you're up, you can get it. I look a mess."

Sara went to the kitchen to start the coffee, but found that Grams had beaten her to it. *She must not have slept at all last night.* As she poured herself a cup, she heard a familiar voice. *Andrew.*

"Is Sara here? I thought I saw her car outside?"

Sara's heart jumped. *Daniel! There must finally be some news.* Without giving another thought to her appearance, Sara ran into the living room. "Yes, I'm here. Have you heard from Daniel? Is he okay?"

There was a big smile on Andrew's face as he stepped aside and Daniel took his place in the doorway. "See for yourself," Daniel said with a mischievous smile.

Sara ran to him and threw her arms around him, nearly knocking him off the porch. She didn't care how she looked or who saw her kissing her fiancé. All she cared about was that he was home safe.

"I've been so worried about you." She finally pulled away from the embrace. "Thank God you're home and that you're safe!"

"I'm sorry I couldn't call you. All the phone lines were down from the earthquake. We stayed and helped the injured as long as we could, but then the government told us that we had to leave. The Red Cross helped us get a flight directly back to Nashville on a private plane. It was the middle of the night when we landed, so we rented a car and drove home."

"I have so much to tell you," Sara said through joyful tears. "You wouldn't believe what all has happened while you were gone."

"Did you jury service go well?"

"That's a really long story," Sara said, glancing around before she answered. Grams' nod gave her the permission she sought. "Maybe I could tell you tonight over dinner? Are you free?" Sara grinned.

"Of course. What's on the menu?" Daniel's eyes twinkled.

"Well, that depends. Do you want pepperoni, veggie, or supreme?"

"Doesn't matter – as long as there's pound cake for dessert."

"Of course – Sara Lee's finest!"

EPILOGUE

August 15

Tennessee Board of Parole
404 James Robertson Pkwy
Nashville, TN 37243

RE: Inmate 38570

I am writing on behalf of my father, Tony Darnell Jackson. He is an inmate at the Morgan County Correctional Complex and will be eligible for parole in a few weeks.

My father committed the crime for which he is incarcerated before my birth, and I met him for the first time only a few days ago. As a child, I was certain that my father should spend the rest of his life behind bars. After all, he was involved in the killing of a police officer, and such a crime warrants swift and harsh punishment.

In recent days, however, I have learned that things are not always as they seem. Sometimes, there is more to a story than meets the eye.

I am now an attorney, and my first case was a new trial for a young man who had been convicted of a crime for which, as it turned out, he was not responsible. He happened to be at the wrong place at the wrong time, and he paid for it with three years of his life. Through the grace of God, that young man has now been given a second chance.

While I cannot ask you for a second chance for my father, I can and do ask that you give him a full and fair hearing on his application for parole. Listen to his story and judge for yourselves whether he has been rehabilitated.

I have listened, and I believe that he could be a productive member of society if given the opportunity. I hope you feel the same.

Sincerely,

Sharese Jackson
Public Defender's Office
302 Main Street
Maple Springs, TN

DISCUSSION GUIDE

1. One of the themes of *The Deliberation* is forgiveness, particularly receptiveness to forgiveness for our transgressions. As long as we place the blame for our mistakes on others, we cannot be at peace with God or with ourselves. At what point does Sara feel she has received full forgiveness for her sin of adultery? How does it transform her?

2. Even after we have been forgiven, we must still face the earthly consequences of our sin, the effects of which can be much farther-reaching than we ever imagined. Viola's infidelity clearly affected Maria and her family, even though Viola's actions happened decades earlier. Do you think this is common or uncommon?

3. The one person who consistently tells the truth, at least as much of it as he knows, is Justin, the accused. Why is Justin telling the truth? Is it because he trusts in God or because he believes that he has nothing to lose?

4. Kyle is a player. He can be wretched at times – dishonest, scheming, opportunistic – and yet he clearly has a tender side – saving Callie, accepting Evan. Did he choose to dismiss the charges against Justin in the end because it was the right thing to do or because he was afraid of the consequences of his affair with Sara becoming public?

5. Sharese badly wanted to win Justin's case, even though a more seasoned attorney would likely have given up hope. Why was Sharese's inexperience a blessing to Justin?

6. There are several important relationships of confidence in *The Deliberation* –Sharese and Justin, Kyle and Marcus, Viola and Fredonia. Why is it particularly important for Christians to have someone in whom they can trust who will also hold them accountable?

7. In light of her father's incarceration before her birth, do you think it was an ironic choice for Sharese to become a public defender? Why or why not?

8. At what point does Sara realize that it is Daniel whom she truly loves? Why did she ever doubt her love for him? Why is so important that she tell him the full truth of what happened while he was away?

9. In the beginning of the story, Daniel tells Sara, "God may be putting you on that jury for a reason." Although it was a difficult journey, Sara's jury service not only helped free Justin but also freed her from the demons of her own past. If Sara had not been seated on the jury, what would likely have happened to her relationship with Daniel? What would have happened to Justin?

10. Although Justin technically killed Maria because he did hit her with his car, he also saved her from a torturous death at the hands of a serial killer. How will he reconcile this in his mind?

WWW.MARTINSISTERSPUBLISHING.COM

ABOUT THE AUTHORS

Donna Brown Wilkerson attended the University of Tennessee College of Law and is a graduate of the Association of Trial Lawyers of America National College of Advocacy. As a former trial lawyer, county bar association president, case law editor, research assistant, law clerk, legal secretary, campaign worker, and jury foreperson, she has a multi-faceted perspective on the legal system. She is also a serious amateur photographer and a former senior adult Sunday school teacher.

She is originally from the Upper Cumberland area of middle Tennessee but now lives in Kentucky with her husband, their four children, and a rescued Australian Shepherd named Tilly.

THE DELIBERATION is her first novel.

Visit Donna's Web site at
www.donnabrownwilkerson.com

Dawn S. Scruggs has been a court reporter in Tennessee and Kentucky for 20 years. Her passion is serving others, and she has served in many ministry positions, including youth director and worship leader and has been a speaker at local Christian women's events.

She has traveled extensively, visiting over 25 countries, including mission trips to Appalachia, Cuba, and the Dominican Republic. She has also traveled to Russia to study the Russian court reporting and legal systems and was amongst the first foreign visitors to visit the Russian Supreme Court. She lives in the hills of Tennessee with her husband and childhood sweetheart, Keith. They have two adult children, Aaron and A'ndrea.

THE DELIBERATION is her first novel.

Visit Dawn's Web site at
www.dawnscruggs.com

Made in the USA
Charleston, SC
20 October 2011